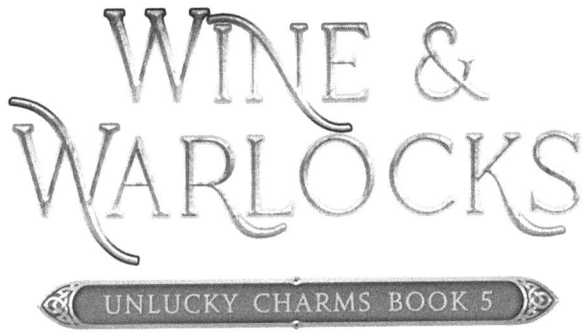

T.M. CROMER

Wine & Warlocks Copyright © 2023 T.M. Cromer

All rights reserved. No part of this publication may be reproduced, distributed, or transmitted in any form or by any means, including photocopying, recording, or other electronic or mechanical methods, without the prior written permission of the publisher, except in the case of brief quotations embodied in critical reviews and certain other noncommercial uses permitted by copyright law.

ISBN: 978-1-956941-06-7 (EPUB)
ISBN: 978-1-956941-17-3 (Paperback)
ISBN: 978-1-956941-18-0 (Hardback)
ISBN: 978-1-956941-19-7 (Large Print)

Cover Design: Deranged Doctor Designs
Editor: Trusted Accomplice

This is a work of fiction. Names, characters, businesses, places, events, and incidents are either the products of the author's imagination or used in a fictitious manner. Any resemblance to actual persons, living or dead, or actual events is purely coincidental.

To my beloved Tink:
The last year without you has been interminable. You were my muse, my fuzzy soulmate, my best friend. Somehow, the words flowed easier with you beside me. I miss your furry face, my darling girl.

CHAPTER 1

The moment Dubheasa O'Malley set foot on the pavement, the wind picked up, the fine hairs at the base of her neck stood at attention, and a chill swept the length of her spine. She stumbled to a halt and cursed her luck when the dark outline of a person separated from the shadowed corner outside her family's pub.

Only one man triggered that response in her—Ronan Fucking O'Connor. Her nemesis. Her family's worst enemy turned champion and the bastard who'd destroyed her career with a few treacherous words from his delectable lips.

She stopped short.

Delectable? Really, Dubheasa?

There was nothing in any way delectable about that mutton-headed man-child. Not the way his silver cat eyes missed nothing when they raked the length of her body, nor the heat they caused, as if it were his large, capable hands caressing her instead of a single, searing glance. Not the thick, wavy hair that refused to be tamed, much like the man himself. Certainly not that well-muscled body without a single extra ounce of fat that moved with a jungle cat's grace and precision.

The one that made her wonder what other deliberate movements he would make should he get her naked and alone.

Again.

Goddess, that night lived in infamy, if only inside her mind. Only her twin, Eoin, knew the truth of her indiscretion.

As she approached, Ronan's arms dropped to his sides and an anticipatory gleam entered his eyes. "Dove."

"Douchebag."

His lips twitched. As did her stomach at the sight of his sexy smirk.

Stupid bloody stomach!

"Nice language ya learned in America, my darlin' Dove."

"I like the American tongue, O'Connor." She said his name with all the derision she could muster. They were, after all, enemies of a sort. Or, at least they *had been*, before he decided to save her family. And didn't she hate that she should feel kinder toward him now? "Yanks have the perfect words for every occasion. Backstabber. Double-dealer. Turncoat."

This time, he didn't even try to hide his grin, damn him. "It could be argued, since our families have been bitter enemies for hundreds of years, I was simply carrying on tradition, at the time."

Hurt made her heart spasm. He'd been deliberate in his actions and cost her a job she enjoyed in a city she loved.

"Right." Dubheasa tried to go around him, only to have him step in her path. "Move out of my way, Ronan."

"Can't do that. We need to talk."

"And yet, I have absolutely nothing to say to you."

He invaded her space, ducking his head to put his lips next to her ear. "Nothing? I remember a time when you had plenty to say. How ya whispered—*oomph!*"

"Whisper that, ya feckin' wanker!" She told herself she wasn't one bit sorry to see him pale, clutch his man parts, and struggle to breathe. Sure, and didn't she warn him the last time that her knee would become closely acquainted with his bollocks if he ever looked her way again?

At the entrance of the pub, she glanced back. Ronan had straightened—somewhat—but he still remained slightly bent over as if struggling against great pain. She wouldn't feel remorse. Not a drop. Liars got what they deserved.

"I don't care for anything you have to say. Stay away from me, O'Connor, or it'll go worse for you next time." Dubheasa whipped open the door and almost slammed into another man. Her hands came up for balance, and she braced herself against his hard chest. His deliciously hard chest.

With the exception of Ronan, he was taller than most men of her acquaintance, perhaps six-two or -three, with shoulders as wide as an American football linebacker. Her eyes traveled the length of his body, admiring the way his form-hugging Henley outlined the muscles underneath. Her breath caught in her throat, and her ovaries sighed at the possibility of this man in her bed.

"Oh, pardon me."

"The fault is all mine," he assured her in a deep, sexy-as-hell voice that would warm her on Ireland's coldest evening. His accent labeled him as American, but perhaps one who traveled a lot. He'd be hard to pin down to one area by his voice alone. "I wasn't watching where I was going."

"'S all right." Her words came out garbled, as if she was already piss-faced—which she intended to be very shortly.

His piercing blue eyes twinkled, and as he leaned forward a bit, a single lock of sandy-brown hair fell across his brow. Dubheasa wanted nothing more than to smooth it back. "Ah, another lovely Irish lass."

She preened under his teasing regard, electing not to inform him "lass" was a Scottish term, and not Irish.

The hair on the back of her neck lifted just before Ronan

placed a proprietary hand on her hip. "We don't say 'lass,' *amadán*. It's *cailín*, for future reference."

Dubheasa shot an elbow behind her and impacted Ronan's midsection. She smiled in satisfaction when his breath rushed past her ear. "You can call me 'lass' if you prefer, friend. I'm not a snob like O'Connor here."

The stranger's wide, delighted grin was her reward. "I'd like to buy you a drink." He glanced between them. No doubt registering her interest and Ronan's scowl. "If you aren't otherwise engaged."

"Nope. No engagement here." *Not now, not ever.* And perhaps it made her a wee bit sad, but she wouldn't think about betrayal at the moment. Especially when a good-looking and exceedingly well-built stranger wanted to keep her company this night. "But the pint is on the house." She pointed up. "My family."

His gaze followed where she indicated. "Ah, O'Malley. Of course. I've had the pleasure of meeting a few of your siblings—"

"Can we move this gabfest inside?" Ronan's surliness wasn't in any doubt. "Some of us want a pint and a warm fire to gather around."

Dubheasa spun back to face him. "You'll not be setting one over-large foot inside, ya lickarse bollix!"

"Now, Dove, I told ya I can explain." Ronan's flush spoke of his anger, and Dubheasa had to give him credit for keeping his cool in the face of her assaults and insults.

"Feck off!" She *intended* to shove his chest. Unfortunately, he caught her wrist at the same time she put her weight behind the push, and she fell into him. When he wrapped one of his steely arms around her waist, she lost the ability to breathe. The second time in less than five minutes!

His slow, wicked smile restarted her lung function—*and* her irritation. What the bloody hell was wrong with her? Had her hormones gone on the blink? Why was she sizing up every male within a kilometer radius for a potential shag? Her response to Ronan should be nothing but revulsion at this juncture.

The stranger behind her cleared his throat, and Dubheasa realized too much time had passed as she stood and ogled Ronan's stunning, albeit duplicitous, face. With a low growl, she struggled free of his embrace and straightened her jumper.

"Eejit," she hissed before turning to smile at the American. "Let's get that pint, yeah?"

Not bothering to see if he followed, Dubheasa strode toward the bar. She was halfway to her destination when she remembered she should walk at a more sedate pace and not stalk forward with her standard no-nonsense stride, the way a man did. Halting and shifting back, she crashed into a granite-like chest. She hadn't expected the contact, and the force of the collision sent her stumbling into the closest table. Curses and mugs went flying.

RONAN CAUGHT DUBHEASA BEFORE SHE HIT THE FLOOR, BUT WAS hard-pressed not to laugh. Her admirer had frozen in horror when she'd upended the table and began to swear like a sailor in Her Majesty's Royal Navy.

"Aye. You should run now, man. This one's got a temper on her, in case ya hadn't noticed." He flared his eyes wide and grimaced. "Save yourself."

Anything the other guy might've said was cut short by the arrival of Ronan's cousin, Ruairí.

"Ronan! You're back in town!"

"More's the pity," Dubheasa muttered as she bent and swept foam off her sweater onto the righted table.

Ronan couldn't resist a smack to her ass. Although it wasn't hard enough to send her into motion, her surprise more than made up for the force of his hand. She let out a squawk as she braced her palms on the slick table to avoid a fall. Unfortunately for her, the spilled beer acted as slip and she landed face-down, arms spread-eagle atop the surface.

The drunken patrons of O'Malley's didn't bother to hide their amusement, and robust laughter rose along with the dark red rage in Dubheasa's fair cheeks.

Ronan was in for it.

He backed up, hands in the air. "Now, Dove—"

She came up swinging.

Luckily for him, he was quick on his feet and had anticipated her reaction. He danced out of her reach, but he couldn't stop his laughter. Of course, her face went from a brilliant scarlet to a dull purple, and Ronan feared her raised blood pressure was at stroke level. He quickly blanked his face of all but a conciliatory smile.

"I didn't know that was going to happen, darlin'. You have to believe that." But the devil in him had come out to play when he saw the way the wet jumper clung to her curves. "Ya must be cold, me darlin' Dove. Come home with me, and I'll warm ya right up."

There was a day when she'd have said yes, but this was not it.

A mug sailed by his ear and shattered on the wall behind him.

"I'll take that as a no."

Ruairí, usually the wisest of his family, showed he wasn't so smart as he stepped in front of Dubheasa. "No murder in the pub, or Bridget will have your arse. Take him out back, where there won't be any witnesses."

"Hey!" Ronan knew familial loyalty only went so far. Sure, and hadn't he cut himself off from those crazy feckers, Moira and Seamus, when they went off the rails? Seamus had died immediately for his sins, but the hateful Moira's death was much more painful, thanks to the Aether. Only his father, Loman, remained at large. But Ronan would see to his da's permanent demise soon enough.

Right now, Ronan was invested in the welfare of his currently irate ex-lover, who he fully intended to win back by any means necessary. Never one to play fair, he'd do whatever it took to make her his again. The O'Malleys could have their magic; he wanted their crown jewel—Dubheasa.

CHAPTER 2

Dubheasa was fit to be tied.

Ronan looked as if butter wouldn't melt in his fine mouth, and yet he'd been the cause of all her woes lately. None of her troubles had started until he arrived in New York, months back, looking like something that stepped out of Men's Fitness magazine. She'd been swayed by his looks and lies, but wised-up soon enough when she discovered his true identity. Then he showed up at Eoin's home a few weeks ago, claiming the lot of them needed to be locked down together—and didn't Dubheasa almost lose her bleeding mind during *that* little party? She'd been less than five minutes from giving in to his carefully crafted charm when the truth saved her.

Now, he'd turned up again, like a bad penny.

"Leave me alone, Ronan O'Connor. I won't be telling ya again."

Something in her tone must've penetrated his thick skull because the amusement died from his face and his eyes turned to gunmetal gray, as if her words caused him distress. Changing irises were a witch's tell, and Ronan's had turned from sparkling to dull in the face of her warning.

"Sure, and if that's what you truly want, Dove, I'll be leaving ya alone." Bravely—or stupidly—he approached her, only stopping when they were mere inches from touching. "I'll grant you anything within my power, love. You've only to say it and mean it."

"What's the catch?"

"Sure, and there's no catch. Whatever you want. You've only to ask, and I'll make it happen."

"What? Like a genie?" she scoffed.

"If you'd like."

Dubheasa paused to consider what he said, and during that time, he kept his steady regard on her. It occurred to her that if Ronan could influence people using his magic, he might help her fix her employment issue.

"I want my job back," she said succinctly.

Through narrowed eyes, he watched her for the span of a few chest-thumping heartbeats. Finally, he nodded. "If that's what you truly want, it shall be done."

"Are ya mad? Of course it's what I want!" Why did it feel like he was tricking her?

"Then it will happen, *if* it's what you truly want."

"Are you fecking codding me? Why do you keep saying it like that?"

He grinned but remained silent.

She squinted her suspicion. Leaning in so only he could hear, she asked, "Are Guardians like genies, then? Do I get three wishes for rubbing your… lamp?"

It shouldn't have, but his bark of laughter thrilled her down to her toes. Trying her best to suppress her own humor in light of his contagious guffaw, she lifted a challenging brow.

"Are ya willin' to rub me lamp, then, Dove?"

"We both know I've already done that. More's the pity. Now you owe me."

His grin brought her back to the night in her apartment.

Right before he'd stripped her of her clothing in the most delicious fashion.

She shivered at the memory. Yes, it was months past, but Dubheasa hadn't forgotten the feel of his hands upon her skin or the loving way he'd worshiped her body throughout the long night. How he'd made her scream his name in the early morning hours—a fake name, it turned out.

She shoved away the warm feeling his grin had created.

Ronan shook his head. "No, love. I don't owe ya a thing."

Scowling up at him, she placed her hands on her hips. "How do you figure?"

"Do you truly wish to do this here?"

Ronan's gaze darted to someone behind her, and Dubheasa turned to see the forgotten American watching them with a mixture of humor and regret.

"Oh!" She stepped toward him, only to be brought up short by Ronan's hand on her arm.

"Beat it, man. Sure, and you can see she's my—"

Dubheasa gasped at his territorial tone. "*She*—meaning *me* —is your nothing, Ronan O'Connor. And you can take that to the grave!"

Jerking her arm from his grasp, she approached the stranger. "As you can see, I need to be off-loading some baggage, but I hope you'll be enjoying a pint on me until I can join you."

The American smiled ruefully. "I suspect that's going to take longer than you realize, but I'm happy to wait."

A wave of indignation rolled off Ronan, and she could feel the heat slam into her back. With a glance over her shoulder, she saw his gaze locked on the American, and if he could've gotten away with it without facing her wrath, Ronan likely would've made short work of the man in an instant.

A small thrill chased through Dubheasa's body at his possessiveness. She wasn't one to care for a man's posturing, but Ronan's interest was genuine—that much she knew to be true. The real problem was that his last name started with O and ended with Connor. Added to the fact he'd lied to her numerous times already, and she had difficulty trusting him in general, not just with her heart.

But, oh, the sex had been grand. And maybe if Ronan simply wanted to shag a time or two, she'd forgive him those few lies and give up the chase. But he'd begun spouting things like "fated mates" and "destiny," which Dubheasa was inclined to shun at all costs. Sure, and she had her own life to live without any help from the Fates.

The American made his way to the bar, leaving her to deal with the problem of Ronan. Dubheasa found herself reluctant to face him. She didn't care to see the disappointment she knew would be on his countenance. Disappointment in her choices. Or rather, her not choosing *him*. But wasn't she a woman grown, without a da to answer to?

"Go have your drink, Dove," Ronan said in resignation. "But if you even think about shagging the man, I'll kill him."

That had her turning.

"You'll be killing no one, Ronan O'Connor," she growled as she drilled a finger into his chest. "I'll fecking shag who I want, when I want, yeah?"

"No, darlin', ya won't." The steely look in his eye made her gulp. Leaning in, he placed his lips next to her ear, causing her to shiver as he said, "You're mine, and don't ya be forgettin' it, Dubheasa O'Malley. I've waited a lifetime for you, and now that I've had ya, I'll not be letting you go."

Sure, and weren't they the words every woman, in her heart of hearts, wanted to hear? But today's women weren't supposed to give in to sexy Neanderthals or their steamy gazes or their… ah, feck. Who was she kidding? Certainly not herself. She wanted to claim Ronan as badly as he seemed to want her.

But she wouldn't.

Not until she had assurances that he'd not be lying to her again, in any way, shape, or form. And certainly not until she could be assured there'd be no coercing her into the job of Guardian before she was ready.

"I hate you." And maybe she did a little because she didn't want to experience the yearning he made her feel with a single look. It was as if he stole her will with every searing glance her way.

A mask fell over his features as he stared down at her. "Fair enough. But remember what I said about the American, yeah?"

"Feck off."

ACROSS THE PUB, DUBHEASA LAUGHED AND FLIRTED WITH THE stranger, and each warm smile, every touch of the man's arm, all the signs she was into the guy, made Ronan's skin feel too tight for his body. His stomach was a mess of bloody knots, and he wanted nothing more than to abduct Dubheasa. To steal her away forever. Away from the desire-filled eyes of the men around her. Away from the loudness of laughter and music. Away so he could slowly undress her as he'd done in her New York apartment when she had no idea who he was and she was open to new thrills with a stranger. But the romantic tower had come tumbling down the second she learned he was Ronan Fucking O'Connor.

He snorted before he took a sip of his pint. Only his Dove, with her fighting spirit, would label him as such.

"You all right there, man?"

He glanced up to see Ruairí wiping down the bar next to him, concern for him in his eyes.

"Sure, and I'm right as rain, I am." And tired to his soul. What was it about him that made women run as fast and as far as they could after bedding him?

"You're not, but I'm not after prying, all the same." His cousin tossed the bar towel over his shoulder and gave Ronan a severe look. "But you're not alone in the world. You know that, yeah?"

"I know." Rising to his feet, Ronan checked his watch and tossed a handful of bills on the counter. "Watch out for her, will ya? Don't let her go home with that plonker out of spite for me."

He didn't have to clarify it was Dubheasa he was referring to. Although they were cousins, Ruairí was like a brother to Ronan, and they overshared when they drank together. His cousin understood his romantic woes, just as Ronan knew his. There were many a time when he had put himself in the line of fire to protect Ruairí from their clan because all his cousin wanted was the woman beside him at the bar. An O'Malley.

Bridget O'Malley.

A firecracker in a compact, curvy body. One his cousin couldn't take his eyes from. The two had gone through hell and back, but a couple more destined to be together than Ruairí and Bridget would be hard to find.

"I'm glad ya went against Shane and Loman to be with her," Ronan said. "You deserve your happiness, Ruairí."

"Why do ya sound like you're sayin' goodbye?" Bridget's tone was sharp, as if she suspected what he hadn't said.

"It's time I found Loman and put a stop to his ways. Permanently this time. The Aether and I have a grand plan."

"Are we to be party to this plan, or is it strictly your secret to keep?" asked a saucy feminine voice from behind Ronan.

Turning, he rested his elbows back on the bar and grinned at Dubheasa, hoping to distract her from the seriousness of what he was about to do. "Sure, and now you're wanting to know what our future holds, love?"

"I'm not your love, Ronan O'Connor, and answer the fecking question."

Goddess, she was a sight, every fierce inch of her, with her hands on her hips and flames practically shooting from her bright emerald-colored eyes. He could get lost in those gorgeous, intelligent peepers of hers. There were many instances since they'd first met when he believed she could see into his soul. At first, it had terrified him, but now, he wanted her to see the affection he held for her.

Yet she refused.

Or if she did recognize what it was, she chose to ignore it.

And didn't that make him sad? These weeks and months wasted because of his necessary deception, though she wouldn't see it that way. To Dubheasa, a lie was a lie, and there was no getting around that.

"It's strictly my secret," he eventually replied, purposefully letting her stew. He couldn't be a complete pushover. If or when they finally mated, she'd rule the household. The thought made him smile, which appeared to irk her even more, if her narrowed eyes were any indication.

"You're good at that. Deception. Secrets." She lifted her chin and sniffed, but Ronan could see the hurt lingering in her eyes. It about broke his damned heart.

"Aye, Dove," he said in all seriousness. "I am. But not with you. Never again, yeah?" Avoiding her accusatory glare, he downed the last of his pint and carefully set the glass on the counter. "I'll not be saying anything aloud in a public place where anyone can listen in, or in special cases, scry. If you want to be privy to the plan, we can meet behind warded walls to discuss it."

Dubheasa shot a glance over her shoulder at the American and sighed.

The regretful sound was a dagger to Ronan's chest, and it hurt for him to take a deep breath. Another indication she wanted no more to do with him, and another rejection in a long line during his lifetime.

"Your American is a warlock, in case you can't tell, Dove," he told her in a low voice in the event any nonmagical mortals were around. "But if he meant ya harm, he wouldn't be able to cross into this pub, since Damian warded the place after it was rebuilt."

She gave him a sharp look. "Are you giving me permission to pursue him?"

"No. But then you don't need my permission, do ya? You'll be doing what you want, and I'll be left in the cold, wishin' I hadn't fucked up our relationship at the beginning and secretly plotting that fecker's demise." With a soft smile, he added, "And, aye, we were on opposing teams when we met, but we're on the same side now, love. If you could find it in your heart to forgive, I won't be fucking it up again."

For a brief moment, she appeared to consider it, but her flash of compassion disappeared just as quickly. After a saucy toss of her long dark hair, she placed her hands on her hips.

Ronan had never wanted her more. His unquenchable desire for her made his bones ache.

"And what about the threat to kill him if we shag?"

"I won't kill him if we shag."

Her growl forced Ronan to bite the inside of his cheek to hold back the laughter.

"Not you and me, ya eejit. Trevor and me!"

Trevor.

Ronan's head shot up, and he looked at the man across the room with a keener eye to detail. "Trevor's the American's name? That wouldn't be Trevor Blane, now, would it?"

"Aye. That's the name he used." Suspicion darkened her expression, and a frown drew her brows together. "And how is it that you know him?"

"He's part of the Aether's plan," Ronan replied grimly. "He's a Death Dealer."

CHAPTER 3

Dubheasa walked with wooden legs back to where Trevor Blane waited for her. Sure, and although the O'Malleys seemed to have regained their magic, their ill luck was still haunting them. What was it, if not bad luck, that the one man who had piqued her interest all these months after Ronan just happened to be the guy they needed to defeat their greatest enemy? Especially when he had to work with her ex-lover to do it?

"Are you a Death Dealer, then?" she asked Trevor when she got to the table.

The admiration left his eyes, and the coldness that took its place felt like a wash of icy water. Yes, this man was as dangerous as they came.

"How do you know what I am?" His tone was as frosty as his gaze.

Needing a minute to catch her breath under his stoney stare, she gestured with her thumb over her shoulder. "Ronan's a Guardian, and he delighted in informing me you were sent by the Aether."

Some of the coolness left him, but he remained detached,

and any friendliness was gone. The man obviously had a job to do and took his responsibilities seriously. Dubheasa could respect that.

"Damian initially told me to meet him here tonight. Only he texted a little bit ago to say he wasn't going to make it due to his wife's unexpected labor." His curious gaze shot to Ronan, who remained at the bar, nursing a second pint. "A Guardian, huh? I sensed his power, but Damian gave nothing away. Said we'd discuss the issue when he got here and he was able to introduce me to all the players."

Dubheasa cocked her head and studied him. "So where did you intend to go after?"

"Thought about seeing if the Black Cat Inn, next door, had a room, or I might head back to my place." He gave her a half smile. "Then you crashed into me, and my plans changed once again."

"Then it's a feckin' grand thing that you can pivot, because we've a serious conversation to be had." After offering one of the two drinks Bridget had poured, she tapped her glass to his. "Drink up, Trevor Blane. You're going to be needing the extra bit o' courage to deal with the O'Connors and O'Malleys, ya are."

He grinned, once again the winsome man she'd first met, and lifted his glass in a toast. "I believe I'm up for the challenge, sweetheart."

"Then you're a better man than most."

His laughter crashed over her, setting her to tingling. Aye, it was a sad sigh she heaved, knowing there wouldn't be anything between them but a mild flirtation.

A Death Dealer was too dangerous to dabble with, according to Ruairí, who'd been party to Ronan's pronouncement not five minutes before. Trevor had the ability to take a life and decimate a soul for eternity. There would be no coming back for anyone unlucky enough to fall prey to the man's special brand of magic.

"I suppose this means there will be no you and me tonight?" he asked as a wry smile curled his lips.

"No, because that big lug back there has threatened to kill you if you and I get any closer than a table between us. I'd have ignored him, but knowing what you are, well, let's just say I'm not keen on witnessing a clash of the Titans in the alley beyond, all the same."

Trevor's deep laugh made her smile. "You're charming to the extreme, Dubheasa O'Malley. Ronan is a fortunate man."

"Ach! Now, why would you be going and ruining a pleasant conversation by saying such a thing!" she demanded with a glare. "I'll not be giving that eejit the time of day."

On the heels of her words, the hair on the back of her neck lifted, and Trevor's amused smirk told her Ronan was directly behind her. She downed half her drink before she faced her nemesis.

"I'm going to put a bell around your bleeding neck. See if I don't!" She shoved his hard chest, irked when he didn't budge an inch.

Ronan placed his large palm over her hand, locking it against his heart. "Ah, Dove, I'll let you put a bell around my neck or a ring on me finger. Ya just have to say the word, love."

She laughed, unable to help herself. Say what you wanted about Ronan O'Connor; the man was a born charmer. "Go on with ya, you fecking tool."

"Sure, and that's a step up from eejit, so I'll be takin' it as a win." With a kiss of her knuckles, he tucked her arm through his. "According to Bridget, I'm to escort you both to the Black Cat, but we need to time it right, so I don't get barbecued by the wards."

"My luck could never be so grand." She gave him an arch look, ruining it with an answering smile when he grinned. As quickly as she could, she suppressed her amusement. It wouldn't do to give Ronan any encouragement. If one gave the man an inch, he'd take a mile and three-quarters, pushing the limit to an entire two. And she needed to stop drinking, or her resistance would be nil by the end of the night.

Leaning in, he murmured just loud enough to be heard over the noise of the pub. "Thanks for not kicking me in the bollocks for holdin' your hand, Dove. If I were to take another shot to the old ball box, I'd be maimed forever."

"I only promised you the one."

"Aye, but you also promised if I looked at you again, you'd do worse. So should I be expecting a knife through my ribs?"

"I don't like to be lied to, Ronan. You should've remembered that the first time." She swallowed down her ire and hurt. "But the second lie as I was wrapping my head around the first? Yeah, I can't forgive that yet."

Ronan halted her at the door and gestured for Trevor, who had been leisurely following behind, to go around them into the alley. When they were alone, he met her probing gaze. "I'm not asking you to, Dove. But 'twas only a trick because I wanted to spend time with you."

"Telling us Anu required a lockdown was not the way to do it."

"We'll have to agree to disagree, all the same. I had a week in your company, and you softened enough for me to sit with you. I'd not gotten that close before."

Dubheasa stomped on the instep of his foot. "You've not learned anything, have you?"

With a dark scowl, he grabbed his injured appendage. "I've learned you got the devil of a temper!"

"You're not the man I want, Ronan O'Connor. The man I thought I met in New York. You can never be *him*, because he doesn't exist." Embarrassed by the thick emotion in her throat and the tears burning her eyes, she turned away. "All I want is a man to be honest with me. And I don't believe you know how."

As Ronan watched Dubheasa sail out the door Trevor Blane had exited through a minute before, he rubbed his aching chest. In his need to muck up his father's life, he'd thoroughly fucked his own. Who knew the pretty *cailín* he'd flirted with to con his way into Lamda Unlimited and whom he'd eventually hooked up with would end up being the one woman he desired above all others? The true love of his life?

A small part of him wondered if his feelings were only an obsession, similar to how he'd been with Rebecca Walsh-Thorne. Aye, he'd loved her once, and sure, he still held affection for her. Bec was *the* major regret that wouldn't go away, but mainly for the way he'd handled the situation. He'd been young and stupid but not entirely to blame, though Bec and her family would claim differently. The coined phrase "it takes two to tango" was an overused cliché for a reason, and she'd been the more experienced adult of the two of them.

Stubborn to a fault, Ronan had pursued Bec with a single-minded purpose, but had she been happy at home, she'd have never fallen for his seduction. Yes, he had the ability to influence her mind had he so desired, but he'd not done it. Never would he claim to be a saint, but he'd not sink *that* low.

"Fucking hell, Ronan," he muttered to himself, rubbing the painful spot in the middle of his forehead, where a tension headache had begun to form. As he observed Dubheasa laugh at something Trevor said, he realized he was in for the fight of his life to earn her trust. "Get your bleeding head out of your arse and smarten up. Make better choices, ya fool."

His desire for her was overwhelming him and scrambling his brains. After one night, Dubheasa had awakened something in him he'd long thought dead. Emotions that trumped his feelings for Bec and everyone else combined. From here on out, he needed to be completely transparent with her if he wanted a snowball's chance in hell of winning her.

"She's hurt, but if you can prove you've changed, she'll forgive ya, Ronan."

He jumped and cursed himself for a lovesick eejit for not hearing Bridget approach. Years of punishment and Loman O'Connor's life lessons had taught him to never let his guard down.

"I thought I had," he replied. "Would Damian let me protect his daughter if he believed I hadn't changed?"

"Your question is valid, but I'm not the one after answerin' it, am I?" Bridget brushed back a lock of her coppery-red hair and sighed as she shook her head. "Sure, and give her a little time. And I'd be laying off the charm if I were you. The more pressure, the more she'll resist. That's her way."

"Are you telling me this to actually help me, then, Bridget O'Malley?" He grinned at the thought of an O'Malley offering to assist an O'Connor in any way. "I'd have thought you'd consign me to the devil and be done with it."

Stretching to the tips of her toes, she patted his cheek. "And there was a time I'd have done just that. But that time has passed. I'm grateful for the help you offered Ruairí and me. And for what you've done for my family when they needed it. Trust is harder won for you, Ronan O'Connor, because of your past, but we're all trying to be fair."

He glanced up and noticed his cousin standing behind her. With a leer and a wink, Ronan said, "I'm certain I heard you say you're in love with me, Bridg. Poor Ruairí will be heartbroken to learn it."

With a gasp, she stomped on his instep—the same fucking place her hellion sister had gotten him not five minutes before. When he bent over to grab his foot, she lightly hit him in the forehead with the heel of her hand. "You're not to be causin' trouble with your flirty ways, ya eejit. Don't think I don't know your cousin's behind me."

"Fecking hell, woman! I was only codding ya both!"

"Well don't. Get your arse in the Black Cat's kitchen before the spell wears off and you short-circuit the wards, why don't ya!"

"You're a shrew." He danced back out of striking distance with a laugh. "But a beautiful one, to be sure." Nodding to Ruairí, he said, "Best of luck to you, man. You're bound to be black and blue for life."

"Go on with ya, you tool." Bridget smiled widely to take the sting from her words.

The two of them had found a common ground of sorts. They both intended to see to Ruairí's happiness.

Ronan looked between the two of them, and thanks to his nifty Guardian abilities, he was able to absorb the sensation of their contentment and love, feeling the rightness in his soul. It only made his self-pity that much stronger, though he'd never let it show.

"It's happy I am that you two found each other again," he said quietly and in all seriousness. "I'm only sorry there were so many years wasted."

Ruairí's smile was understanding as he wrapped his arm around Bridget's shoulders. "Likely we needed those wasted years to appreciate what we have." The love in his cousin's brilliant blue eyes as he looked down at his mate caused Ronan's heart to spasm. Theirs was a love to last many lifetimes. As happy as he was for them, he was jealous and wanted the same for himself.

Without another word, he turned on his heel and entered the alley. Dubheasa looked up, and for the second when her expression was unguarded, she didn't appear to hate him all that much. Ronan's optimism shot up.

CHAPTER 4

"How's Vivian?" Ronan asked Damian after they'd dialed him in for a conference call.

"Well. As is baby Nate." The pride in his friend's voice told Ronan everything he needed to know; Damian Dethridge was as smitten with his newborn son as he was with his wife and young daughter, Sabrina. "I apologize for not attending this meeting in person, but I'm not leaving Vivian when she needs me."

"And if I'm remembering correctly, it's Sabrina's birthday today, too," Ronan said.

"As if Beastie was ever going to let you forget." Damian's dry response was followed by a chuckle. "I'm to take her to pick out two puppies tomorrow, if you can believe it."

"Ah, yeah, she had me escorting her to Baz's place a time or ten to see them. But two? Are ya mad, man? No one in their right mind should be adopting two pups at the same time."

He met Dubheasa's laughing gaze across the table and shook his head. The things the Aether did to spoil his daughter boggled the mind.

Damian's soft snort came through the line. "Yes. I'm

completely insane, or so Viv assures me. A newborn and two puppies? I've completely lost it. Send help."

Everyone, including Trevor Blane, laughed in unison.

A moment later, Damian sighed. "I suppose we should shelve the talk of my family and turn the discussion to yours, Ronan. Does anyone have eyes on Loman?"

"Not yet. He's somehow managed to stay off the deities' radar as well as all of ours."

"It's never a good sign when the Goddess can't unearth his whereabouts," Damian agreed.

Dubheasa leaned forward. "How is that possible? How can one man walk through the portal of the Otherworld, not once but twice, after being stripped of his powers, and *still* escape detection?"

"If I knew, he would be in hell right now." Damian's tone was as grim as Ronan had ever heard it. "That's why I've brought Blane into this. Trevor, are you prepared to do what is necessary?"

"Aren't I always?" Trevor asked with a coolly amused look for the rest of them. "I've spoken to my brother, Simon. He's prepared to accept the abilities you discussed earlier this year. I'm going to pull him in for backup since my father is once again in the wind." For a second, he looked uncomfortable, as if the next part of the discussion was going to be a big ask. "Dethridge, should anything happen to me on this mission, I ask that you please see my brother is trained thoroughly and that his wife, Evelyn, doesn't suffer any of the side effects from his gift as a Death Dealer. Heal her when or if she needs it."

"It will be done."

"Thank you. Who else are we expecting to join our manhunt?" Trevor asked.

"Fintan Sullivan will work with Sabrina to determine the various outcomes of our plans. Alexander Castor has a stake in all of this. He is flitting about space and time as we speak, trying to dig up information or get a lock on Loman's location."

Trevor shot Ronan a questioning look.

"Castor is my uncle, twin to my father. He's likely using his blood as a divining tool," Ronan explained. "He's probably the only one able to find the fecker, other than me."

"You've bled enough last week while searching for him," Dubheasa said, although she looked uncomfortable showing any sign of caring about his welfare.

"Ah, Dove. It warms me puir heart when ya turn all loving, the way you have."

With an arch look that told him to pound salt and die, she turned her attention back to Trevor. "If I'm after understanding this plan, you're going to be the one to stop Loman for good by obliterating his soul and making it so he can't return again."

"That's the goal." Trevor rubbed the back of his neck. "But the trick is going to be finding and containing him long enough for that to happen."

"That's where Alex and Ronan come in," Damian replied. "Alastair Thorne also has his network of spies kicking over stones. We'll find him."

Bridget placed a tea tray on the table and gestured for them all to dig into the biscuits and small sandwiches. "It's our slow season at the inn. If any of your team needs lodging, we'll put them up here. Same goes for you, Trevor Blane."

After shooting a glance Dubheasa's way, Trevor smiled at Bridget. "Thank you, Ms. O'Malley. The offer is appreciated."

"But you'll not be sharing Dove's bed, all the same," Ronan growled.

As one, they turned to stare at him with varying degrees of horror. Trevor's was more like horrified amusement.

"Way to stake your claim, fella."

Ronan leaned forward to emphasize his point. "I've been pretty fecking clear from the moment we met, *fella*."

Dubheasa literally growled. "Ronan O'Connor, I swear—"

"No murdering each other until Loman is a long-forgotten memory, please," Damian said, laughter heavy in his tone. "And on another note, Ronan, have you discovered where your cousin Reggie disappeared to? I want to know if his participation in Loman's death and subsequent escape was intentional."

Meeting and holding Dubheasa's worried gaze, Ronan nodded. "Reggie called Eoin and Brenna when we were all sequestered together. Look, I may be wrong here, but I'd say his move in planting that arrow squarely in my father's chest was impulsive, not thought out."

"Aye. He wasn't about showing remorse, but he wasn't boasting about helping Loman escape, either," Dubheasa added.

"That's one load off my mind." A muffled cry sounded from Damian's side of the call. "I believe Nate is hungry, my friends. We can pick this back up when Alex and the others get there."

"Sure, and who are we to be expecting?" Bridget asked.

"I'll text you the names. They aren't due to arrive until tomorrow afternoon. With that, I'll bid you good nigh—"

A second later, Sabrina Dethridge's sweet young voice came through the line. "Ronan?"

"I'm here, ya wee wild beastie. What will you have of me this time?"

"I just wanted you to know about the puppies. Did Papa tell you we are picking them up tomorrow?"

Ronan grinned. "Aye, he did. And it's excited he is for it."

She giggled, and it was a glorious sound, causing those around their table to smile. "You're so funny, Ronan. But I'm going to have Baz save you one, too. The one with the floppy ears that you said Dove would—"

"That'll be grand," Ronan said, trying to cut her off before she revealed his next step in wooing Dubheasa. Didn't all females love puppies?

"Aye, they do," Dubheasa replied with a twinkle in her eye. When he frowned, so did she. "What?"

"I didn't say it aloud, Dove. But there you went, answering my question without me askin' it."

"But you did ask…" Her eyes widened as their group collectively shook their heads. "I can hear your thoughts?"

"It's because you're going to be his mate, Miss Dove. Guardians can do that," Sabrina informed her proudly, not realizing she'd caused Dubheasa's blood pressure to shoot alarmingly high and her face to turn a worrisome shade of fuchsia.

"I am *not* going to be his mate!"

But Sabrina had already hung up, secure in her prediction.

Sinking her head in her hands, Dubheasa let out a guttural yell.

"Yeah, and it's a good thing the Black Cat is empty," Bridget said with a laugh. "Otherwise, we'd be trying to explain the banshees haunting the place." She rose to her feet and patted Ronan's shoulder. "It's late, and you'll be wanting to rest for what's to come with your da. When you're done with your tea, have Dubheasa show you to room number six. I think it will suit your needs."

"The one I had last time was fine."

"Pfft. Your feet hung off the end of the bed. Sure, and we've got a proper mattress for you now." When Ronan would've opened his mouth to thank her, she waved him off and said, "It was Ruairí's suggestion, so save your thanks for him. I've a pub to run."

"I'll escort you and Mr. O'Connor back through the alley," Trevor said as he rose to his feet and placed his napkin beside his plate. He held up a hand when she would've argued. "Please. Damian assigned me to this mission for a reason. If he didn't believe Loman was lurking in the vicinity, he would never have called me in this soon."

Bridget graced him with a warm smile. "We'll gladly accept your escort, then."

Ronan stared into his full teacup, wondering when he'd poured it.

"My sister did," Dubheasa said absently, then jerked, her eyes flying wide. "I did it again, didn't I?"

With a rueful half smile, Ronan nodded.

"Aw, fecking hell!" Dropping her forehead onto her folded arms, she groaned. "This is going to be torture."

Her words struck him with the weight of a sledgehammer. If she truly wanted nothing more to do with him, it *would* be torturous for her to be on the receiving end of his thoughts. Having been forced into a life he'd not wanted as head of his clan, having to police his mad cousins and try to mitigate the damage they caused at every turn, Ronan knew what it was to suffer through a life not of his own choosing. Dubheasa didn't deserve that, and in the end, he'd free her from it when he could if she hadn't changed her mind.

But there *was* one benefit to their connection.

"It doesn't have to be, love." Risking a severed limb, he reached for her hand. "It could benefit us when my father comes. And we should be testing the distance while we have the chance."

She rolled her head enough to look at their joined hands, seemingly content to let him touch her for the moment. "Did you know this would happen? The telepathy?"

"No. Every day brings a new talent with this job."

She met his steady gaze. "Does it bother you? Caring for the Aether's daughter?"

"Not anymore. But the thought of it terrified the shite right out of me when the Goddess first mentioned it."

"And the process to receive such ultimate magic? I heard tell it was painful."

After a squeeze of her hand, he released her. "Aye, Dove, it was. And it's why your decision isn't a light one. I'll not blame you for rejecting me or the job, yeah?"

Her head came up in her surprise, and she touched his wrist. "Thank you."

The gratitude in her eyes made his stomach flip. He'd thought to change her mind, eventually seduce her, and remind her of their epic chemistry. But it seemed the idea of them as a couple was completely repellent to her, and *that*, he couldn't abide.

"I'll state it plain to you now. I love ya, Dubheasa O'Malley. More than I've ever loved another. But I'll not pressure you anymore, because I see it's not what you're wanting." He downed his tea and stood. "How about we find our rooms, and tomorrow we start fresh?"

Climbing to her feet, she touched his arm a second time, and Ronan tried like hell not to read anything into the gesture.

"Ronan, about Trevor—"

"Aw fuck, Dove! I don't want to hear the man's name right now."

He'd shoved back his chair and had almost reached the door when she said, "All I was going to say was that I'll not be shagging him."

Ronan stopped short, not daring to turn. The other shoe was about to drop. It always did for him. Ronan Fucking O'Connor wasn't allowed things like hope or optimism.

"I'll not be shagging him or thinking about him or any of the things to upset you while we're sharing this link, yeah?"

Her words held an echo, and it surprised him to realize she'd communicated through their new mental connection.

"Thank you," he said gruffly. "That's all I can ask."

Once again, he started to leave, and once again, she called to him.

This time, he turned, and the amusement on her face caused him to suck in a breath at the beauty of it. Like witnessing art in its purest form, was her expressive face.

"Don't ya want to be knowing which room is yours, then?" she asked with a twinkle in her eye.

"Your sister said six. And I just thought I'd open all the bleedin' doors until I found the one with a bed fit for a giant."

CHAPTER 5

"Where's your watchdog?"

Dubheasa glanced up from spreading jam on her scone when Trevor sat at the table. "If by watchdog, you mean Ronan, he's off to his room to make some calls." She carefully set down the knife and studied his expressionless face. "Why did you take so long at the pub?"

"Is this what being married to you would look like? It's fortunate Ronan has claimed you as his in that case." His smile broke through as he sat across from her and stole her scone. "You'd nag me to death every time I was late coming home."

"And would you be coming home late often?" she teased, rubbing her neck to ease the prickle she felt.

"We Americans like our sports and beer. I imagine I'd be a constant trial to a demanding woman such as yourself."

"Then aye, it's a good thing Ronan has claimed me."

Trevor grinned as she spread jam on another scone, following it with clotted cream, then passed it to him. "Are you going to let him get away with being a caveman?"

"Never. It's not in my DNA."

"Good girl. Give him hell every chance you get." Trevor

saluted her with his teacup. "So, tell Uncle Trev why you're fighting so hard against your attraction to him."

She laughed, unable not to. As odd as it seemed, the man was easy to be with. "I didn't at first. When he showed up at my office in New York, I had no idea who he was, and I let him sweep me off my feet."

"What does that mean, 'no idea who he was'? Would it have made a difference?"

"Aye. The O'Malleys and those thievin' O'Connors have been locked in a feud for over two centuries."

"Thieving?" He laughed. "Sounds serious. What did they steal? A cow? Someone's wife?"

"Sure, and you can laugh if you want, but it was an enchanted sword. The Sword of Goibhniu."

"I sense a juicy story there."

Hiding her grin with her teacup, she took a sip and nodded. "The weapon was entrusted to my ancestors, and the god who gave it to them was so enraged they'd lost it, he bound the O'Malley power and gave it to the O'Connors."

The amusement left Trevor's face, and he sat straighter. "So much more serious than a cow or wife."

"Aye. But to be fair, Goibhniu penned a prophesy in the O'Malley grimoire. Somewhere along the way, the O'Connors learned of it and set about blocking it at every turn."

"And that's what Loman is trying to do now?"

"No," Ronan said. The enchantment cloaking him fell away, revealing him where he leaned against the doorjamb. "The prophesy came to pass, as well it should, but Loman O'Connor is a sore fucking loser."

Although Dubheasa jumped at hearing Ronan's voice, Trevor was unaffected by his appearance, as if he'd sensed him all along. As she should've because the prickling sensation at the base of her neck had given her fair warning. She scowled. "How long have ya been there?"

Ronan shrugged in a too-casual manner.

Trevor, on the other hand, reclined and hooked an arm over the chair's back, sending a knowing look Ronan's way. "I'd say it's been as long as I've been sitting here. Isn't that right, Mr. O'Connor?"

"I'll not be trusting Dove's safety with a stranger in our midst, to be sure."

"Answer enough," Trevor murmured, flaring his eyes wide at her before facing Ronan again. "Okay, to recap this little tale... Your family stole the enchanted sword, hers lost their magic, somewhere in there a riddle was solved, and now we have a madman who believes winner takes all despite having already lost. Have I got this correct?"

"Aye." Ronan dropped onto the bench running along the wall, resting his head back and closing his eyes. "And he'll not stop. Two escapes from the Otherworld's holding area can attest to that."

Curious, Dubheasa paused in pouring Ronan a cup of tea. "How did you know it was a riddle to be solved, Trevor?"

"It's the nature of a prophesy to be vague. Interpreting one is pure luck."

Meeting Ronan's tired blue eyes, she shook her head. "The O'Malleys were cursed with bad luck from the second the sword disappeared. I'm beginning to think our fortunes have taken a turn for the better, though." Dropping her gaze, she slid the cup and saucer across the table, then proceeded to smear jam and clotted cream on two scones and shoved them in Ronan's general direction. "Eat something, yeah?"

"How so?" Trevor held a hand over the rim of his drink and shook his head when she silently held up the teapot in question.

"Since Piper Thorne walked through the door to Lucky's, things have turned around for my family. Relationships, finances, the like." And wasn't that grand? Prior to that, the O'Malleys were all struggling to make ends meet.

"It could be argued my family continually caused all those hardships," Ronan said between bites.

Trevor suddenly grinned. "It's like looking at Romeo and Juliet. It's the Montagues and Capulets all over again. Even your last names start with the same letters. Well, minus the O part of it."

"Sure, and the comparison is apt, but more for Bridget and Ruairí than for the two of us," Dubheasa said with a short laugh. "They were the ones who fell in love at seventeen and, just this year, fulfilled the final line of the prophesy."

"Now you have me really curious. How did the riddle go?"

Ronan spoke the first line when he saw her mouth was full from a bite of scone. *"When a mighty Thorne pricks the heart of the Frozen, the end shall start in motion."*

Taking up where he left off, Dubheasa swallowed her food and said, *"When the Golden Son sacrifices for the One, only then can the curse be undone."*

And together, they chorused the last line. *"When the Enemy at the Gate is welcomed by the Keeper of the Sword, all that is lost shall be restored."*

Trevor nodded as if he was processing the words, and he finally said, "Damn, that's pretty crafty."

Ronan's chuckle skated across Dubheasa's skin, and she couldn't help but join in. "Aye. Pretty crafty," she parroted. "Obviously, Piper is the mighty Thorne, and she literally pierced Cian's feckin' heart with a needle to save his life."

"Who were the Golden Son and the One? What was their story?" Trevor asked, leaning forward.

She gestured to Ronan to tell the tale since he'd been in the thick of things.

"The Golden Son is Aeden O'Malley" —he paused for

Dubheasa to insert "my brother Carrick's boy" before continuing— "and the *One* is Sabrina Dethridge."

Trevor suddenly looked sickly. "This is very personal for the Aether, isn't it?"

"Aye, and there's no cocking it up." Ronan's expression turned downright grim. "My father knows the advantage to be gained by killing her and obtaining what power she has. If he were to get that level of magic *and* her visions, he'd be unstoppable."

"And you believe that's who he's after?"

"Eventually. But he has to build up enough other abilities first. He'd be a fool to take on the Aether with nothing to back him up. And my da is no fool. Overly ambitious, aye. Fool, no."

Dubheasa didn't need to think long or hard about what she was about to offer. If it meant stopping Loman, she'd do it by any means. Legal or not. "Ronan, you know I was hired on at Lamda Unlimited as a software developer and I consulted on everyone's program designs, yeah?" At his short nod, she continued. "I've still got a few connections who might help us access your da's old account and any others that would have transferred money in or out. Couldn't we track him that way?"

"It's what I did when I… when…" He sighed and shook his head as if he didn't want to relive the time. "When I deceived you to get access to your laptop's software."

Ignoring the pang she felt, she asked, "How deep were you able to dig, and were you able to access phone records, too?"

"Deep enough to cause him a headache, to be sure. And I have a second set of numbers but never needed to use them. Me dear old da showed his arse first."

The picture of thoughtful, Trevor rubbed his thumb along his chin. "But it stands to reason he may still have access to those numbers or perhaps would've gone into a brick-and-mortar phone store to reactivate one or more of them." He grinned at Dubheasa when she nodded. "Why do I have the feeling you're going to locate him with some hereto-unheard-of technology?"

"Not unheard of, but it's a GPS app I was working on for Nick Lamda's new division. He had a contract with the US government," she told them. Addressing Ronan, she said, "I still have the original prototype software, so if you have Loman's information, I can hack it."

Ronan's smile, full of admiration, was beatific and warmed her from her hairline to her curled toes. "I don't know why I didn't ask for your help from the start, Dove. You've a brilliant mind, you do."

With a toss of her hair over her shoulder and a mock stern look, she said, "I'd not have helped you then, or at least not without good reason. I was after keeping my job."

"You'd have helped had I been wise enough to ask, I think, knowing what you know about the O'Connor clan." His confidence disturbed her. Never did she want anyone to understand her well enough to anticipate her next move. Not that she wanted to appear flighty or rebellious, but staid and predictable was boring.

Eyes locked on hers, he grinned. *"You're anything but staid and predictable, love."*

"I liked it better when I could read your mind, not the other way around. And I'll not be telling you again to stay out of my head, Ronan O'Connor. This is your one and only warning."

His wicked chuckle set her insides on a slow simmer, and not the angry kind of heat. It brought to mind the delicious way he'd laughed with her over a meal and later in bed when he thought her words amusing.

What might they have been, had he been truthful?

Swamped with sadness, she turned away.

Ronan touched his knee to hers under the table, but when she looked at him, he was serious and not flirty in the least. "I'm sorry for what resulted in your termination,

Dove. I'll see what I can do to fix it when this is done, yeah?"

"You mean it?" She didn't dare hope.

"I do."

Stemming the desire to hug him from her deep feelings of gratitude, she turned to see Trevor with his head buried in his phone, and she received the impression he was trying to give them a smidgeon of privacy, in his own way.

"Are you interested in how the last line of the prophesy played out, then?"

With a slight frown and a swipe, he set his phone down and focused on her. "Yes. How did the O'Malleys get their magic back?"

"The third line referred to the Enemy at the Gate—Ruairí O'Connor, though not a true enemy in any sense of the word—and the Keeper of the Sword, my sister Bridget."

"Wouldn't the Keeper of the Sword be the one who possessed it?"

Ronan grinned. "That was my thought, too, but Damian had me considering the riddle from another viewpoint. My cousin Ruairí always was the smartest of us, and he'd already figured it out. So, he brought the feckin' sword here, to the inn, and hid it. He was waiting for Bridget to forgive him for his bone-headed mistakes of the past before turning it over."

"Hm." Trevor's brows shot up, and he gave Dubheasa a pointed stare. "Maybe there's a lesson there for others."

She shot him a sharp look that would wound a lesser man, but both Ronan and Trevor laughed at her bogus indignation. "Sure, and when did you decide to be Ronan's best friend?"

"Who says I'm his friend? Maybe I'm yours."

"You're beginning to grow on me, Blane." Ronan toasted him with his teacup. "And whatever the encouragement, be it for me darlin' Dove or for myself, I thank you." He casually drained his drink and took care in setting the delicate china on its saucer. "But I'll still smite ya if you even think of shaggin' her."

"Jaysus! You thick plonker!" Dubheasa rose to her feet and glared down at him. "You'll stop threatening the man, or you'll be answering to me, yeah?"

She was halfway out the door when Trevor's softly spoken words reached her.

"O'Connor, you fucking lucky bastard."

"Only if she decides she can't live without me." And in her mind, she heard the words he hadn't spoken aloud. *"Like I can't live without her."*

CHAPTER 6

That night's discussion had reminded Dubheasa acutely of her all-too-brief time as Ronan's lover. For the better part of two hours since heading to bed, she tossed and turned, trying desperately to put the memories of making love with him out of her mind. But just like the recent time spent in Ireland at her future sister-in-law's new estate, Dubheasa was having a hard go of it with the man only a few doors away.

Now, as then, his dominating presence tempted her to forget her pique and seek him out. Now, as then, she knew it was a mistake to do it. But the longer she spent in his company, the harder it was to remember why she'd been upset in the first place. Especially after he'd expressed remorse and explained his reasons. Yet she couldn't forget he'd also lied about the forced lockdown. He'd shown up at Eoin and Brenna's place, spouting a tall tale about the Goddess demanding they all sequester in place because Loman was on the loose.

It was only a half truth.

Yes, Loman had escaped. Yes, Ronan had shown up to deliver the news per the Goddess's request. But after that, he'd spontaneously invented the lockdown so he could spend time with Dubheasa. If he hadn't grown a conscience and admitted the truth right before she kissed him, he'd have gotten away with the falsehood.

Shaking her head at his boldness, she recalled that night...

Dinner had been a festive affair, and she'd had one too many glasses of wine in an attempt to wash away the memories of her original date with Ronan. Like that first date, he'd worn a white button-down shirt with a dark-blue suit jacket that contrasted with his mercurial gray eyes and made them more vibrant and silvery by the candlelight. He'd been attentive to her, listening with a smile and refilling her drink whenever she consumed it. The memories had sparked her longing to start over and give him a chance to explain his side of the story, which she'd not let him do until that moment. As the food and alcohol continued to flow, making everyone merry, the cheerful atmosphere ate away at Dubheasa's resolve along with her residual anger. So when Ronan held out a hand and asked her to walk in the garden with him, she readily agreed.

"I'm sorry for deceiving you, Dove. You didn't deserve to be punished for my mischief at Lamda."

She'd simply been too mellow and didn't want to fight, so she had ignored her thirst for answers and allowed him to hold her hand as they walked through the maze. When Ronan guided her to a weathered wooden bench and drew her down beside him, she didn't resist, instead leaning into him as he put an arm around her shoulders to ward off the chilly air.

Maybe it was the romance of the shimmering full moon, or maybe she was tired of running away, but she couldn't find it in her to be hateful.

"Do you think you'll be able to stop your da?" she asked him.

Ronan hesitated before answering. Eventually, he sighed. "I hope so. He's a crafty bastard, he is. And we'll all need to remain alert to his attack."

Lifting her head, she spent an inordinate amount of time memorizing his perfectly chiseled features. The man was truly a work of art. All hard planes and contours, symmetrical in every way. Eyes perfectly shaped, not too far apart, nor too close together. Not too wide, nor too narrow. And his lashes... Dubheasa sighed her envy. Was it fair a man should be so heartbreakingly gorgeous?

Oddly, he didn't seem aware of it and wasn't vain in the least about his looks. And didn't that make him more attractive? Her gaze dropped to his lips, and she longed to have him rain super soft, velvety kisses all over her exposed skin as he waxed poetic about how she made him feel.

Jaysus, had any of it been real? Firmly ensconced within the circle of his arms, she believed it might've been, but unless she dared ask, she'd never know the truth.

Hesitant to go there, she asked instead, "How long before Loman makes his move, do you think?"

Had she not been watching, she'd have missed the flash of guilt on Ronan's face. Why he would experience any guilt for his father's behavior was in question, and for that reason, she firmly gripped his jaw, forcing him to look her in the eye.

"What aren't you telling me, Ronan?"

"Can we shelve this discussion for tonight, Dove? I've a might powerful need to kiss ya, and I don't want to talk about my gobshite da."

There was a desperation in his reply.

"Aye. We can," she agreed. "But we'll talk about it again in the morning, yeah?"

With a resigned expression, he nodded. And again, unease snaked through Dubheasa's wine-soaked mind.

When Ronan lowered his head, it finally clicked what was

wrong. He'd worn that same look the first night in New York when she asked him a few hard questions. That time, like this, he appeared to be fighting an inner battle with himself—and losing.

The instant before his lips touched hers, she shoved her hand between their faces. "You're lying to me. *Again*," she said flatly, somewhat shocked at how calm her voice was, when inside. she was a raging mess.

"Dove—"

"I'll ask you one more time, Ronan O'Connor. What aren't you telling me?"

After a sharp inhale, he hung his head and exhaled slowly, as if perhaps she was trying his patience. Sure, and wasn't that irritating? As if *she* were the one putting *him* out!

"Ronan." Her tone was as diamond-hard as her heart had suddenly become. Why the hell did she keep letting her guard down with him? Why was it that every single time he gave her that special look, the one swearing she put the stars in his sky, all caution dissolved and she found herself taken in?

In a single, rushed statement, he said, "I made up the need for a lockdown. It was a spur o' the moment idea because I wanted to spend more time with you, Dubheasa. I swear I meant no harm to you or yours."

As flattering as it was that he'd desired to explore a relationship with her, she simply couldn't stand a liar. Hadn't her mam lied to her da so many times that he'd had enough and left them all? Was she to follow in the same sorry footsteps as her parents? Destined to have her heart crushed a little more with every lie that poured out of Ronan's beautiful mouth?

"I can't," she whispered brokenly.

"Can't?"

His worried frown caused the ice encasing her heart to fracture around the edges, and she surged to her feet. If she didn't get away, he'd do what her mam had done to her father, and he'd charm her into forgiving him.

"I can't be with a man who spouts lies at every turn. I can't." The near hysteria in her voice made her cringe, and she drew strength from her righteousness, standing tall and staring down at him with cold eyes. "You keep away from me, Ronan. You're not to call me, haunt my dreams, stalk the halls of my apartment, none of it." She poked his chest and ignored the fact her finger didn't make a dent or that it came back a little sorer than when she shoved it his way. "My knee will become closely acquainted with your fecking bollocks if you ever look my way again."

"Dove, you're blowing this out of proportion. Making mountains out of molehills, as the yanks say. It was a *bréag*, sure, but a harmless one, all the same." He rose and lightly cradled her face. "We're Irish, love. If we aren't fabricating a tall tale, we aren't living, yeah?" His attempt at a grin never reached his wary eyes.

"My entire childhood, Mam made a habit of telling Da a harmless *bréag* or two—daily. Until the night he went out for a pack of fags and never came home." Until Ronan used his thumbs to wipe her tears, she hadn't realized she was crying. Shoving his hands aside, she stepped back. "I'll not tolerate dishonesty, Ronan. It's already cost me a job I loved, and I'll not have my heart broken like my da's."

Without a backward glance, she'd fled...

Now, here she was, in the one place she'd always considered home, and Ronan had followed her. Although Dubheasa hadn't for a minute believed he intended to leave her alone for good, she didn't expect to see him so soon. She'd hoped he would take her warning to heart, but that was for her own peace of mind, not from a true desire to never see him for the remainder of her life. Moving forward, she would never *not* see him taking up excess space in the kitchen or delicately handling Granny O'Malley's antique china. Or looking at Dubheasa as if he'd slay dragons for her. Or telling her that he loved her in his soothing, knicker-melting voice that caused her stomach to clench whenever she heard him speak. The fecker had gone and said he'd never lie to her again, and dammit, she wanted to believe him so badly it hurt.

"Oh, Da. Is this what you felt? The constant tug-o-war between hope and despair?" she whispered into the darkness of her room. "Aye, I want Ronan, but is it only desire? How can there be more if he keeps acting the fool?"

As she waited for the answer that would never come, she experienced a strange buzzing in her mind and wondered at the sensation.

Ronan.

It had to be. No one else had the ability to affect her so.

"Are you sleeping?" she asked him telepathically.

The buzzing stopped, and a feeling similar to happiness embraced her.

"No, Dove. I've too many scenarios running through my head." He paused a long second. *"Why are you still awake?"*

"I'm not entirely certain. The oddness of the situation we find ourselves in, I suppose."

"Aye, it's a first for me, too."

She took a moment to mull over the possible reasons why they might be experiencing such a weird phenomenon now, when neither had ever before.

"Do you think this is a temporary connection, Ronan? Like maybe it'll go away after Loman is finally stopped for good?"

"I can't say for certain, love, but it won't hurt my feelings if we were to stay connected this way forever."

"Stop with the honeyed words!"

His chuckle sounded as deep and naughty in her head as it

always did in person. And as quickly as the happiness had washed over her minutes before, a melancholy teased the edges of her mind, making her sad.

"When this is over, I'll ask Anu to give you your heart's desire, Dove. If you wish to go about your life working for the likes of Nick Lamda or sever our new link, or whatever it is you decide you want, I'll see that it happens for you."

An urge to cry caused tears to burn the back of her lids, and she ran her knuckles across her eyes. *"Stop being so bleeding nice to me. I don't know how to feel about it."*

A knock on her door caught her attention, and already guessing who was on the other side, she swung back the comforter and padded across the room to answer.

In the opening, Ronan had his arms spread wide, fingers gripping the wood molding on either side of the frame, and he leaned in just enough to breathe the same air as her. "It hurts my heart when you cry, love." His voice was raspy and raw, testifying to his honesty.

"How did you know I was crying?"

"Same way you knew I was awake." His concerned gaze swept her face, then he met her eyes. "Want to talk about it?"

Did she? Their past should be discussed, and she needed to know what she was in for should she decide to become a Guardian.

"Yes."

Although his brows shot up as if surprised, he didn't comment other than to ask, "Here or downstairs?"

As an answer, she stepped back and swung the door wider.

CHAPTER 7

Ronan paused a few feet inside the entrance and scanned the room, his attention locked on the bed with its rumpled comforter, and Dubheasa literally felt his blood heat and his amorous thoughts crowd her head. It suddenly occurred to her that was why he'd given her the option of downstairs, so perhaps he wouldn't be tempted to seduce her.

And she wouldn't be tempted to give in.

After a small shake of his head, he settled himself on the chaise in the corner of the room farthest from the bed and linked his fingers behind his neck, crossing his ankles. "Let's start with what you want to know about being a Guardian."

She perched at the foot of the chaise, half turned toward him. "Is it a forever commitment? Are we allowed to go about our everyday lives, or is it like being in the military and serving the Goddess whenever she commands?"

"My main commitment is to protect Sabrina until she's an adult, and initially, I was no more happy about the job than you are now, Dove. But I've come around." He paused for a long moment, then said, "It's like being a security guard, but only when Damian isn't around."

"How do you know when that is? Does he call you to come babysit, then?" Why she'd given in to the urge to verbally poke him, she couldn't say. Perhaps with her nerves jumping as they did whenever he was near, she needed an equalizer.

Ronan grinned at her sarcasm, not fazed in the least. "Sometimes. But I've a new built-in alarm that tells me when Sabrina needs me, and I can locate her in an instant." With a shrug, he said, "It must've been something Damian added when he supercharged me to start with. And as for serving Anu or Isis, they reward me for every job I take outside of watching our young Oracle, but the option is always mine."

"Reward in what way?"

"With favors, financial compensation, abilities. It's whatever they feel the mission warrants."

His expression remained neutral as he relayed the facts for each and every one of her follow-up questions. Regarding his thoughts or feelings on the matter, he gave nothing away, allowing Dubheasa to process the information she'd gathered and to make her own informed decision.

"Why are we to be paired, Ronan? Why *me*?"

"Maybe because I was destined to love you, but I don't know." He uncrossed his ankles, straddled the chaise, and leaned forward with an earnest expression on his face. "Dove, you have to make a decision soon. I'll buy you as much time as I can, but the magical world as we know it is shifting. If Loman has created an escape hatch, he's left the door open for others to follow."

"And we need to police all those potential escaped convicts?" The incredulity in her tone caused her voice to rise a few octaves, and they both winced. She cleared her throat and strove for a calmer note. "Ach. Sorry. But I know nothing about hunting down people, and I don't know that I care to."

"I get that, I do. But you wouldn't have been Anu's first choice if you didn't possess cunning and if she didn't see something in you."

"But why do we have to be mated?" Even knowing she sounded like a petulant child, she couldn't help it. Her life had been turned on its ear, and now she was expected to partner with a man she wasn't sure she could trust—for life or beyond.

"You can always say no," he said quietly, his disappointment keen in his darkening gray eyes. A witch's irises were the window to their soul, a barometer for their emotional well-being. Ronan's told her he wasn't happy in the least. "I'll not blame you."

"Won't you?" she asked skeptically.

And why was it that she didn't want him to hate her for not choosing him?

"I could never hate ya, Dove," he replied to her unspoken question. "And you wouldn't be the first to not choose me, all the same. Yeah, and I've had a long lifetime of…" Ronan shook his head, a self-deprecating smile on his face. "It's sorry I am for sounding like a whinging killjoy."

In a fluid movement, he rose from the chaise and towered over her, where she sat on its edge.

Her breath caught in her throat, and she acknowledged to herself that had Ronan been any other man, anything other than a Guardian tasked with righting the wrongs of the world, she might've stopped running and forgiven him his lies. They weren't life-altering; she knew that. But she didn't like that he defaulted to untruths when he wanted to manipulate a situation.

"When you showed up at the New York office, did you once consider telling the truth?" she asked.

"No."

"Why not?"

"Like you told Blane, I was an O'Connor, and you had no

reason to believe me. You have to ask yourself, Dove, *would* you have considered my being there as anything but contrived to bring you grief?"

She thought about it as he stood there, gazing down at her. By his lifted brow and confident look, she suspected he already knew the answer.

"But why the dinner and… after? I liked you. Or the man I thought you were."

"I liked you, too, love. And that's the honest truth of it." He knelt in front of her, which made their faces level, and ran his knuckles lightly down her cheek in a caress reminiscent of the night they shared. "I didn't expect things to go so far, and leaving you the next day was a cleaver to my heart." Dropping his arm, he fell back, resting his butt on his heels. "But I had to do what I could to stop Loman, and I'd do it again."

"Why can't you be honest?"

"I promised you I would from now on, didn't I? And so I will. That's what I'm after telling you. I'll do whatever is necessary to take him down for good."

"For Sabrina?"

"And your family. And for those in my own family who are deserving: Ruairí, Alex, maybe even Reggie."

"And you, Ronan. You're deserving," she reminded him softly.

"I've done terrible things in the past, Dove. I don't know that I *am* deserving. Not of your forgiveness, not of you, not of the trust the deities or Damian and Sabrina have put in me."

The fear and uncertainty in his eyes slayed Dubheasa, and her desire to reassure him was entirely overwhelming her logical side that warned her away from him. She fell to her knees in front of him and placed her palms flat against his chest. Absently, she noted the rapid hammering of his heart. "You *are* deserving, Ronan O'Connor. If you weren't, we'd all likely be dead and your father would be using the O'Malley magic to do more harm."

Without warning, he wrapped his arms around her, hauling her close and burying his head in her hair. He held her like a desperate man would a lifeline. And perhaps she was his. Maybe she'd been looking at his past behaviors all wrong, and like a small, wounded child who didn't know up from down or how to get attention from adults in a nondestructive way, Ronan did the only thing he knew how. He deceived to achieve his goals.

"Yes, Dove. That's exactly right."

For a while, she'd forgotten he possessed the ability to read her mind. And although she wasn't particularly comfortable with the fact, she didn't mind that he could see her reasoning.

"I can't be your lifeline, Ronan. That much responsibility scares the feck out of me."

Slowly and with great care, he released her and climbed to his feet, offering her a hand to help her up. "I know, Dove. And I'd not put so heavy a burden on ya."

As she looked into his hauntingly beautiful face with those tragic eyes, she realized she wanted to say yes to all he was offering. It was enough to make her backpedal.

"I'll not fight with you anymore, Ronan. We'll work together to stop your da. But I can't make any decisions regarding my future until the present is secured."

"Like I said, I'll try to buy you time. But you can't run much longer. If it isn't you, I'll need another partner to work with."

Anger clouded her mind, and she pinched his nipple through his shirt. "You claim to love me in one breath and tell me you'll choose another in the next? Are ya mad?"

He surprised her when he laughed and wrapped a hand around the nape of her neck, drawing her forward until their bodies were touching. "I'll love you until the day I die, Dove, and no other. But I'll need a partner to accomplish what the

Goddess requires. It will need to be a female to balance the scales—what Isis and Anu are calling the Yin-Yang effect—and my partner will share in the mental connection with me, like you do now. But I'll not be shaggin' her or taking her as a mate." He lowered his head until his lips were but a breath away. "I desire no other but *you*, my love."

"Aw feck!" Closing the distance, Dubheasa sealed her lips over his.

He tasted of minty toothpaste and dark, steamy nights filled with passion. Of unbroken promises and an exciting future. Lost to the sensations his talented tongue created, she moaned. He shifted to wrap his arms around her, just below her arse, then lifted her until she was slightly above him and forced to grip his shoulders to hang on.

Giving into her desires, she wrapped her legs around his waist and gazed down into his laughing eyes. "Mind you don't make me hit my head, you fecking giant."

"In case you didn't notice, love, your sister created more headroom when she rebuilt the inn."

Scowling because she'd been too distracted by Ronan to notice the changes, Dubheasa glanced around, then looked back at him and grunted. "Shut up and kiss me again, Ronan O'Connor."

"Gladly. But then you're off to bed, *by yourself*, to get sleep. Tomorrow we'll both need to be alert for what's to come."

"Sure, and that's fair enough." Digging her fingers through his thick, platinum-blond hair, she tilted his head back even more and cast him a wicked grin. "Unless I can convince ya otherwise."

"You don't play nice, Dove."

"Aye, and I never will."

CHAPTER 8

Ten minutes later, Ronan was back in his room, suffering from a raging hard-on. Dubheasa had kissed him to within an inch of his life—multiple times—and touched him in all the ways his body was eager to remember from their single night together in New York.

He could've given in to her resistance-melting overtures and made love with her, but he wanted more than to scratch an itch, hers or his. He wanted her to submit to him completely. Accept what was meant to be and the position of his forever mate. But chances were she wouldn't.

He caught his reflection in the mirror over the dresser. "You're a fecking fool, Ronan Fucking O'Connor!"

"I doubt anyone would argue—"

Ronan instinctively struck out with a roundhouse kick and connected with Trevor Blane's jaw before he could register the man wasn't a threat. The impact sent Trevor crashing through the armoire door.

Ronan winced. Not on the guy's behalf, no. But on his own! Bridget O'Malley was going to have Ronan's arse for breaking an antique if he didn't get it repaired before she saw it again.

"Fucking hell, O'Connor!"

Reaching out a hand, he hauled Trevor out of the cupboard and onto his feet. "Sorry, man. Damian should've warned ya to never sneak up on me."

"He did." Trevor's irritated expression shifted to sheepish. "I forgot and got within range of those freakishly long legs of yours."

With a laugh, Ronan gestured to a nearby chair. "Why don't ya have a seat, and I'll conjure ice for your jaw. Then you can tell me the reason for this impromptu visit."

Trevor touched the ice pack to his cheek an instant before Dubheasa rushed through the door, a flaming ball balanced in the palm of her hand. Her troubled eyes were wide as she summed up the situation, and with a heavy expulsion of breath, she shook her hand to disperse the flame.

"Were you going to save me, then, Dove?" Ronan asked with a proud grin. Over the week they were at the Sullivan estate, he'd made her practice creating flame after flame until she was thoroughly irate and promised to fry his arse. That it had become second nature to her was promising for any future conflict she encountered.

"Saving you would've been a side effect." Hands firmly on her hips and brows raised in challenge, she gave him a back-the-hell-off look. "My main goal was to maim anyone who was out to cause trouble."

Taking his life in his hands, he approached her and ran his knuckles along her jawline. "Admit it, love. You were here to play the hero. *For me.*"

"Feck off, O'Connor. I was not." But like a cat, she leaned into his hand, belying her words. Seeming to catch herself, she stepped back and bounced a glare between him and Trevor. "Are you fighting, then?"

"Not in the least," Trevor said with a warm smile.

Irritation prickled Ronan's skin. He hated the man his easy charm.

"Then why are you here at this hour?" she asked, suspicion heavy in her voice.

"Merely to tell Ronan I was deliberating over the problem of his father and I think you should sit this one out."

She drew back in shock. "And why would I be doing that?"

"Because you're a novice, Dubheasa, and I don't think Ronan will be able to concentrate if you're in the middle of the fray."

"Do you believe this eejit?"

Her outraged question echoed in Ronan's head and made him wince. "Ouch, love. You'll need to dial it down a bit if you're going to be calling Blane names, yeah?"

After an elbow to the ribs, which prompted Ronan's chuckle, Dubheasa faced Trevor. "Look, and he wasn't supposed to rat me out that way. And I only said you were an eejit, truth be told. That's practically an endearment in *Éire*."

Ronan laughed harder and dodged Dubheasa's foot when she tried to donkey kick him.

"I swear, Ronan O'Connor, if you don't hold your *whist*, I'm going to—"

Dropping a hard kiss on her lips, he followed it with a light smack on her arse. "Don't be threatening me with a grand ol' time, Dubheasa O'Malley. We've got company."

"I feel like I should leave the two of you to your violent foreplay," Trevor said dryly.

"We'll have our entire lives and then some to hash all this out." Ronan stared down at Dubheasa's flaming face and smiled without humor. "Or we will if me darlin' Dove accepts the role of mate and Guardian, but in response to your suggestion, Blane" —Ronan's gaze bore into hers to make his point— "I'll not be going behind Dubheasa's back or excludin' her from the planning process, all the same. She'll fight by my side if she's of a mind to."

The softening of her expression and the gratitude in her eyes made Ronan feel like he'd finally done something correct where she was concerned. But she wouldn't like his next words.

"Dove, you'll not want to be hearing this, to be sure, but our friend here made a valid point. You're still a novice when it comes to your abilities. And for sure, you'll put yourself at risk if you join this war against Loman."

"I thought you wanted my help to locate him?" She looked adorably confused.

"Aye. But I'd be happier if you did it behind the scenes, I would."

As she took the time to think it over, her focus shifted between him and Trevor. Finally, she nodded. "I promise I won't purposely put myself in harm's way. But you both need to train my family as best you can in the interim. Should Loman come after them again, I want my siblings and nephew to be safe."

"Sure, and you need to know I'll lay my worthless life down for all of you, Dove. I'll be after training you as time allows, and Ruairí will help."

"Thank you."

"You're welcome." Ronan yawned, kicked off his boots, and flopped back on the bed, tucking an arm under his head. "Tell us the other reason you're here, man."

Trevor waited until Dubheasa perched on the edge of the mattress, then took the chair in the corner. "I think we need backup for whatever plan Damian Dethridge has knocking around that devious mind of his."

"You don't trust him?" His words came out harsh, but one thing Ronan didn't care for was someone questioning his friend's integrity.

"What? *No!* Of course, I do. I meant for your father, should he outsmart us. We need a fail-safe."

"Oh, aye. And we'll have that, to be sure."

"Do tell," Trevor said.

Dubheasa glanced over her shoulder, a questioning expression on her face.

With a tired sigh, Ronan rolled to a sitting position. "As Damian said before, we'll have Fintan Sullivan and my uncle. With Castor comes other key players like his son Quentin, Alastair Thorne, and Knox Carlyle. Those three men are the most powerful of our kind, excluding you, Damian, and me."

"I've met a few of them. And yes, while I agree they are formidable, they can be defeated. We need the undefeatable."

"Then who and what are you suggesting?" Dubheasa asked quietly.

Ronan recognized it as her thoughtful voice. Only when her mind was going at a mile per minute did she grow silent.

"There are others. Another Guardian, like Ronan," Trevor told her.

Surprised to hear of another, when he'd been told only a single Guardian couple existed at a time, Ronan demanded details, and Trevor was happy to respond.

"There is a group called the Authority, higher than the Witches' Council. They are the ultimate overseers of humans, both magical and mortal alike. The table is comprised of the Fates and a handful of gods and goddesses, along with a few retired Sentinels. They rule with an iron fist."

Ronan shared a disbelieving look with Dubheasa, then asked Trevor, "How is it we've never heard of them before?"

"They like to remain mysterious." He muffled a yawn and rubbed the back of his neck before he continued. "I work for the Authority. Have for quite a few years, as has my father and his father before me. They're after Damian, in that they want him to answer to them."

"And so far, he's been reticent," Ronan concluded with a nod. "Is that why you're here now, then? As a gift from the Authority to tempt him?"

"Yes and no. I'm on loan, it's true, but they know I'm not temptation enough to draw him into the fold. However, they also know he'll do anything to keep his daughter safe, and someday they'll exploit that fact. If they haven't already."

"So I'm assuming this Authority has the best and brightest working for them, yeah?" Dubheasa asked.

Trevor nodded. "Something like that. The other Guardian's name is Draven Masters. Last I heard, he was somewhere down in New Orleans, in the States, dodging his responsibilities and picking fights over card tables."

As he mulled over the idea of seeking out Draven, Ronan gave in to the temptation to curl one of Dubheasa's dark locks around his finger, taking pleasure in the silky feel of her hair on his skin. If she noticed or minded, she didn't care enough to say.

"If he's in hiding, how do we find him?" she asked.

"His best friend," Trevor replied with a grin.

"And that would be?"

"Me."

Ronan chuckled when Dubheasa blew out an exasperated breath. "Ya had to know that's what he was about when he mentioned the man to begin with, love."

"He dances around a subject same as you." Her pert reply made them laugh. In a move that surprised Ronan, she gave him a quick kiss on the mouth before turning back toward Trevor. "Who else did you have in mind for this little party, then?"

Meeting Trevor's amused gaze, Ronan grinned. "Is it any wonder why she's stolen my heart?"

"None at all, friend. I'm just sorry you saw her first."

"Quit with your male bonding, and let's get back to business," she scolded. But a smile teased her tempting lips, and Ronan wanted nothing more than to tell Trevor to feck off so he could take Dubheasa to bed.

As if he knew exactly where Ronan's thoughts had wandered, Trevor snorted and shook his head, then answered Dubheasa's question. "There are a few. I could approach them on the down-low and hope like hell the Authority doesn't get wind of it. Begging forgiveness is easier than getting their permission."

"They wouldn't approve additional help?" Ronan asked, more than a little concerned about angering the ultimate judge and jury of all mankind. "And why not, if Loman's second escape from the Otherworld's holding area is creating a hole in the veil between dimensions? Sure, and it's in their best interests too, yeah?"

"One would think." Trevor shook his head. "But they are a mercurial bunch."

"That's just feckin' grand," Ronan muttered as he released Dubheasa's hair and climbed to his feet. "Let's get started."

Rising, Trevor stretched his back and gave them a tight smile. "You two get some sleep, and I'll send a few texts. We'll meet back here in the morning. Say" —he glanced at his watch— "six hours from now?"

"Aye." Ronan gestured to the door. "You leaving that way or teleporting as ya did before?"

Trevor strode out of the room, then turned, purposefully shoving the door wider and flaring his eyes. "To clarify, sleep isn't code for sex."

"Feck off," Ronan said with a hand gesture to back up his comment.

The other man's low laugh made him smile in response. Now that Trevor understood Dubheasa was hands-off, Ronan liked him a lot better.

"I don't think we should pull in anyone else, Ronan."

He faced Dubheasa and lifted a brow in question.

Her frown deepened as she shook her head. "You heard what he said. The Authority is 'a mercurial bunch.' That worries me."

"We'll not do a thing without their permission, love. I promise. Now, come to bed and be my cuddle toy. I need a few hours sleep." He punctuated his statement with a yawn.

"If I climb under those covers, the last thing we'll be doing is cuddlin'." She stood and approached him, rising on her tiptoes to give him a light, lingering kiss. "If tomorrow wasn't so important, I'd join ya in that oversized bed of yours."

Ronan rested his forehead against hers and sighed. "I really hate me da."

She snorted and patted his chest. "He's a right proper gobshite, he is. When the time comes, you'll kick his arse for the both of us, yeah?"

"Count on it."

"Grand. Now let's fix Bridget's wardrobe, or it's likely *she'll* kick *your* arse."

CHAPTER 9

An obnoxious ringing bell woke Dubheasa from dreams of making love with Ronan. And it annoyed her to feel so unfulfilled over a meaningless fantasy. After swiping the alarm app off her screen, she sat up and stretched, frowning as she noticed a tray on the dresser that hadn't been there when she went to bed. She threw back the covers and went to investigate.

On a white bread plate was a warm croissant, with a small ramekin of jam and another with butter. In a shallow bowl next to the plate, her favorite fruits were sectioned by color. There was a carafe of strong coffee and an oversized twenty-ounce mug to pour it into. And finally, a single, short-stemmed daisy, bright and cheerful, sat in a tiny glass jar filled with water.

Ronan.

The morning after their one-night stand, this exact meal was sitting on her dresser, organized the same way. She'd adored him for his thoughtfulness. That was until he never called or contacted her again and she was fired from a job she loved.

However, if she had it to do all over again, knowing what she did, she probably would've made the same choice. Ronan had burrowed under her skin and into her mind so deeply that she feared she'd never get him out. It had gotten to the point she wasn't sure she wanted to.

With startling clarity, she could recall how he'd first appeared at Lamda. He'd strolled into her office with cool confidence and the claim that he was a consultant hired by her boss, Nick, to find a leak. The lie was smooth and convincing, and Dubheasa had readily agreed to help him delve into the possible breach, not bothering to check his credentials. She'd only learned after the fact that he had the ability to influence another's mind, and after a long talk with her sister-in-law Roisin, Dubheasa was certain he'd manipulated her along with everyone else he came into contact with at her office.

"Oh, Ronan," she whispered with a shake of her head as she poured herself a cup of coffee. "You were such a beguiling devil that day."

Taking a sip and savoring the rich flavor, she smiled and dove back into the memory.

After hours of working on their respective sides of her desk and sneaking glances at each other, they'd finally called it a day. When Ronan had asked her if she knew a good place to grab a meal, she offered to show him since it was on the way to her apartment. He'd used his roguish charm and her longing for a taste of home to convince her to dine with him, and from the moment she'd sat down across that table, she was a goner. He'd made his desire obvious, and she'd been unable to drum up any objection.

Of course at that time, she'd believed he was Connor O'Rourke—the name he gave when he conned his way into Lamda.

With a grimace, Dubheasa took another sip of her coffee,

then broke off a piece of the croissant to pop into her mouth. Feck all if it wasn't the best tasting pastry she'd ever tasted.

"You smooth bastard," she murmured. "You conned me then, and you're about to con me again. The damned crux of it is that I know what you're up to this time. I'm watching the fecking high-speed train come at me, and I'm doing nothing to get off the tracks."

Did he truly love her? She suspected he did. No one could fake interest to the degree he had, right? His every look, softly spoken word, tender touch, they all counted for something, didn't they?

Closing her eyes, she concentrated on the low buzzing at the back of her mind.

"Are you there, Ronan?"

"Aye."

"Thank you for breakfast. Now, as then."

It should've been impossible, and yet she felt his smile through their connection.

"You're welcome, love."

"Have the others arrived?"

"A few of them. You have about ten more minutes to get your lovely arse down here before the talk turns serious."

She debated having him meet her for a quick shag, but rejected it as swiftly. A rushed joining was the farthest thing from what she wanted.

"Aye, Dove. When I make love to ya again, we'll be taking our time." His tone sounded growly and promising in her mind, and she shivered from the anticipation.

"Yeah," she replied. *"I'll be down in ten."*

"Do you need more coffee?"

She laughed, loving that he remembered her addiction. *"I'm grand, Ronan. Thank you."*

Would he be this thoughtful always? She could definitely get used to it.

Finishing what was in her mug, she poured another, then headed for the shower, silently toasting Ronan for providing her with what she needed when she needed it most.

Exactly nine minutes later, Dubheasa strolled into the kitchen, and the tension in Ronan's shoulders released. Her smile encompassed everyone, and yet when her bright eyes met his and it widened, he felt like they shared something intimate.

Could be it was all his imagination, but he'd liked to think she was softening toward him. Surely that's what her recent affection was all about, right? She'd been less antagonistic and openly laughed with him, touching him at every opportunity. All similar to when they'd first met, and then again on their last night in Ireland before he'd royally fucked up and revealed the lockdown was a sham.

After taking the empty seat beside him, she absently rested a hand on his knee, and any remaining worry left him. A woman didn't touch a man she didn't feel connected to in some small way.

"What have I missed?" she asked.

"Not a bleedin' thing. We're waiting for Damian to arrive, and Trevor seems to have forgotten the appointed meeting time."

"Do you want me to check his room?"

"Feck no!"

All eyes turned to him, and he found his cheeks heating. He hadn't meant to shout, but the idea of Dubheasa possibly finding Trevor Blane in the altogether had Ronan seeing red.

More subdued, he said, "What I meant to say was that if he isn't down shortly, we'll start without him."

"Is that what you meant to say, then? Hmm. Sure, and it's

not jealousy?" Her mouth twitched, and her eyes danced with humor.

Ronan tucked her curtain of hair behind her ear and leaned forward until his mouth brushed its delicate shell. "You know well that I'm jealous of anyone who looks your way, Dove, and I'll be so until my dying day."

Her shiver pleased him, and he grinned when she rubbed her neck as if the hairs at her nape were live wires. He always experienced the same sensation when she was near.

"Good," she whispered.

He couldn't hold back his bark of laughter, and those present turned toward them once again. This time, it was Dubheasa's turn to be embarrassed, but she had no qualms about putting the others in their place.

"Mind your own bleedin' business and not mine," she snapped at her two oldest brothers.

"Sure, and were either of us sayin' anything, then?" Cian asked with an incredulous laugh.

"No, but you were damned well thinking it, now, weren't ya?" she retorted.

Her brother shook his head with a scowl. "Aye, and you've a worse temper than Bridg, ya do."

"And don't you be forgetting it, Cian O'Malley." When Dubheasa turned her flashing eyes Ronan's way, he held up his hands in submission. With a low growl, she dragged him forward by his shirt front and kissed him like he'd been off to war and had just returned. When her tongue brushed his, he lost all sense of up or down. Lost all but his need for her.

Their kiss was interrupted by her brothers as they sputtered their indignation. Someone—probably Cian—pounded on the table to get their attention.

"None of that. You're our sister, and we don't want to be fighting the giant, yeah?" Carrick said with a fierce scowl.

Ronan suspected it was for Cian's sake because the second his brother's back was turned, Carrick grinned and winked.

Any retort Dubheasa had planned was aborted by the arrival of Trevor, followed closely by Damian. He wanted to curse them all to perdition and steal Dubheasa away, but he held his tongue. It wasn't as if he could form full sentences yet, anyway. His brain and body hadn't recovered from their bone-melting kiss.

Ronan shot her a quick side glance and saw she appeared as addled as he was, and he felt marginally better that it wasn't all one-sided.

Trevor took the chair next to him. With a knowing look and a thoroughly irritating smirk, he said, "I thought I told you two to get some actual sleep last night."

"Feck off, Blane," he replied good-naturedly.

The other man laughed heartily.

Other than a curious glance his way, Damian seemed eager to get down to business. "Has Castor contacted you, Ronan? I haven't heard from him or Quentin yet today."

"Time difference, maybe," Trevor inserted with a glance at his watch. "The friend I contacted hasn't messaged me back, either."

"We'll give them a little longer to respond." Damian took the seat at the head of the table, forcing Cian and Carrick to sit to his right. "Where are Bridget and Eoin? This concerns them, too."

"Eoin messaged me about five minutes ago to say he'll be here soon with Fintan and Brenna," Dubheasa told him. She glanced at her brothers. "But I don't know about Bridg, Ruairí, or Roisin. That's for you to answer, yeah?"

Cian nodded. "Piper was feeling off this morning and asked for Bridget and Roisin to attend her. Ruairí is keeping an eye on Aeden, and we're to fill him in after."

"If you need to step out, Cian, we'll understand," Damian

said as he poured himself a cup of tea. "I know all too well how stressful the birth of your first child can be."

"Fecking hell!" Perhaps it hadn't occurred to Cian to ask his wife if she was in early labor, but he paled and jumped to his feet the instant the Aether finished speaking, and ran for the door.

"Should we delay this, then?" Dubheasa asked with a concerned glance at Cian's retreating back. "Surely one day won't matter."

Ronan was set to tell her differently. His father wasn't likely to wait for babies to be born or the sun to be shining on a beautiful day. The man would strike when everyone least expected it, and they needed to be prepared.

Damian beat him to the punch. "It will, I'm afraid," he replied grimly. "Members of the magical community have gone missing, according to the Witches' Council. Trevor has consulted with the Authority, and they believe Loman is responsible. They won't officially intervene. However, the Council has stated that *they* will and would prefer this mess to be cleaned up, like, yesterday. We can use whatever resources we need to accomplish it."

Anything else he would've said was lost in the commotion of newcomers. Alexander Castor, Quentin Buchanan, and Alastair Thorne all arrived together. Since Loman's first attack on their home, the wards had been altered earlier to allow those members of the magical community who were friends of the O'Malleys to come and go at will. Anyone they didn't know would need to request permission to enter.

Trevor's phone buzzed. After a quick glance at the screen, he said, "Can you lower the wards enough for Draven to enter?"

Two minutes later, the other Guardian entered the room, and the fecker was as powerful as any Ronan had ever seen.

Light practically pulsated off the man, making him a walking light bulb to anyone able to see magic.

"Good Christ, tone it down, Draven," Castor ordered, holding up a hand to shield his eyes. "You'll blind us all."

When the man masked his magic, Ronan got his first glimpse of him.

Draven Masters wasn't attractive in the way a standard witch or warlock was, but instead was more rugged. Almost saddle-worn in appearance. The look was set off by the aged black leather duster he wore over his torso-hugging white t-shirt and ripped-at-the-knees jeans. His shoes, however, were in direct contrast with his worn clothing. New and pricey, they didn't fit his overall vibe.

Draven's left hand was in constant motion, and a poker chip traveled across his knuckles, only to disappear at his pinky, then reappear at his thumb to start the routine all over again. The gesture seemed more absent-minded and habitual than deliberate. His eyes were flat, as if he'd seen too much in life and it had left him cold. Oddly, there were deep laugh lines at the corner of his eyes, as if once upon a time, he'd laughed often. The man was an interesting individual for all his seriousness. His age was impossible to discern.

After Ronan and Draven sized each other up, the man shrugged, turning his attention to Dubheasa. His casual catalog and dismissal of her person set Ronan's teeth on edge, and had Draven not treated the others to the same measuring look and subsequent shrug, he might've challenged him. But the man was systematically weighing the magical worth of everyone there. He was in for a surprise, to be sure. Although, most members of their team didn't possess close to the power of a Guardian, they had more heart and determination than any Ronan had ever seen.

"You'd be wise to place your bet on any person here,

Masters." Ronan gestured to their group as a whole. "They've been up against Loman and came out winners every time."

"It's not a win if the man is still runnin' free, friend." Draven had a raspy Cajun accent that spoke of the old South, and Ronan was left to wonder how old the man truly was.

Trevor held out a hand to Draven. "Thank's for coming. We could use the help."

With a wary glance at the Aether, Draven returned Trevor's greeting. "Not to put too fine a point on it, but it was Fintan who convinced me I should hear y'all out. His message was cryptic as always, though, so why don't you fill me in, *cher*?"

Damian didn't offer to shake hands, merely nodding to an empty place setting. "Please, have a seat, Masters, and we'll tell you what we know."

CHAPTER 10

As cryptic and no-nonsense as Draven Masters was, Dubheasa liked him. He portrayed an I-don't-give-a-fuck attitude, but if one were to look deeper into his whiskey-colored eyes, they would see wariness and glimpse the pain he kept in check. Whether it was physical or emotional, she couldn't say, but the man had experienced the worst life had to offer and came out on top.

It didn't take long for Damian to get him up to speed, and the Guardian showed no reaction, content to keep his thoughts on the situation to himself. Only when Fintan Sullivan appeared with Brenna and Eoin did Draven show emotion. One side of his mouth curled upward, and warmth lit his eyes. A clear indication the two men were good friends.

The expression was so fleeting, Dubheasa thought she'd imagined it until Draven slapped Fintan on the back. "It's about time you showed up, *cher*. We were holdin' up the party, waitin' for your arrival."

"Doubtful," Fintan growled in what Dubheasa had come to realize was his preferred way of speech. It turned out that Fintan was Brenna's first cousin once removed, with his mother being sister to Brenna's grandmother. They bore a striking resemblance to one another, with multicolored hair and sharp features, but where Brenna's eyes were more aquamarine, Fintan's were a light sea-foam green. Those pale eyes lent to the eeriness of his gift as a Seer, and whenever he turned them on Dubheasa, she felt a shiver, as if the man could see down to her soul—and likely he could.

As the first male born to the Sullivan line in over a century, Fintan had become the caretaker of the Sullivans' Irish estate, also known as their main stronghold, and he had taken up the mantle when the Seer before him passed away. In his desire to remain hidden and only interfere should he be directed to by his deceased ancestors, he'd refused contact with any of the living Sullivan family. Brenna had shown up on his doorstep over a month ago and changed all that. Or rather, technically, *her* doorstep, since Brenna's grandmother had willed her the estate upon her death.

Fintan spared Dubheasa a look, then turned his attention to Ronan. Pure delight danced in his eyes as his gaze bounced between them. "Ronan Fucking O'Connor has made progress, he has."

Heat crept into her cheeks. "Not in the way you would think."

With a shrug and a wide grin, he said, "So you're still running from your fate, then. Good for you, girl. Pave your own way, I say."

She couldn't help but smile in return. Fintan always wore a fierce scowl—until he didn't. And when his humor shone through, it was impossible not to join in.

"But don't you already know the outcome?" she said saucily. "Couldn't you just give me a hint?"

"And have you do the complete opposite of what I've seen for ya?" He shook his head, a smile playing about his mouth. "I think I'd rather sit back and watch you decide your future for yourself."

"That's not nice, and you fecking know it."

"Aye." The humor dropped from his face, and he turned back toward the others. "We'd best be waitin' for Cian. His wife won't be havin' her babe early."

"To have his gift would be grand," Ronan murmured in Dubheasa's ear.

She nodded, having thought much the same since meeting Fintan. "But maybe it would be a burden, too. Always knowing what the Fates have in store for everyone and yet unable to help or save those you care about. I think it would be sad and perhaps a little lonely, all the same."

"Likely you're right, love."

Dubheasa glanced up to see Ronan watching Fintan with considering eyes. Before yesterday, she might not have credited Ronan with thoughtfulness, but looking back over their moments together and recalling the times he'd been kind or sacrificed for the others in her family when he didn't need to get involved, allowed her to see him differently. The realization made her heart flutter.

Calling to him with her mind, she said, *"I'm sorry for being a right proper bitch and not giving you a chance to explain."*

His head whipped toward her, and his mouth fell open before he had the presence of mind to snap it shut. The expression he wore bordered comical, such was his disbelief.

"You don't think a woman can have a change of heart?" she teased softly, with no little humor.

"I'm not exactly certain what you're tellin' me here, Dove. But if it's what I think it is, it's grateful I am that you've had that change of heart, to be sure."

"I still don't know that I want the responsibility of a Guardian, but you and I, we'll be talking soon, yeah?"

"Soon," he promised, and relief flashed across his handsome face.

That, too, affected her. She hadn't grasped the fact he'd been on pins and needles, waiting for her to come around, and with the understanding came shame. He'd done what he could to stop Loman the best way he knew how. Having been brought up by that monster, his tactics could've been far worse. Yet, he'd merely seduced her and stolen her software. The first, because he wanted to, according to him, and the second, because he had to, believing she'd never betray her boss—especially to an O'Connor.

Dubheasa laced her fingers with his and smiled when his tightened over hers in a gentle acknowledgment of his gratitude. Odd, how she could suddenly experience what he felt. But maybe not so strange since she was already sharing thoughts with him. She'd have to ask her siblings if they had similar experiences with their lovers. With a glance at Eoin and Brenna, she assumed they could. The constant cow eyes and secretive smiles without words led her to believe they had a silent language all their own.

"Brenna once told me they have the same ability, like the one you and I share," Ronan said in a low voice. "Don't quote me, but I believe it comes with the next level of magic, Siren or Guardian."

"That would make sense since the Aether can read minds. And I'm thinking it would come in handy if we find ourselves in a situation not of our choosing."

"Aye."

RONAN DIDN'T KNOW WHAT TO ATTRIBUTE DUBHEASA'S CHANGE of heart to, but he was thrilled it had happened. Perhaps now, he might achieve his greatest desire: her by his side for eternity. To another, it might be strange that he fell so hard, so fast, but he hadn't been able to stop thinking about her from the moment they met. After a single night in her arms, he was determined to get there again.

Returning flustered, Cian headed straight for a cabinet above the stove. He pulled down a bottle of liquor and poured himself a shot, then downed it. After a second, he capped the bottle, added the glass to the sink, and faced them all with a scowl.

"Let's get to it."

Dubheasa rose and crossed to her brother. After a few long seconds spent studying him, she wrapped her arms around his middle and hugged him. Apparently, it was just what Cian needed since his scowl dropped and he hugged her tightly in return.

It didn't surprise Ronan to learn Dubheasa had a natural ability to see beneath a person's outer shell and understand the root cause of their problem. She'd done it to him a time or two, and as one who'd experienced her comfort, Ronan realized he wanted to always be the recipient of her extraordinary gift.

"Is she an empath like you, then?" he asked Alastair, who watched the brother and sister curiously.

"Maybe not on my level, but yes, I believe she is. It'll come in handy, should she decide to accept her role as a Guardian, I think."

Alastair was the patriarch of the Thorne family, one of the original Six families to be graced with magical abilities by the gods and goddesses. His line was descended directly from the Goddess Isis, and she had always favored Alastair in particular. Where anyone else might've been punished or lost their powers for the rebellious acts he pulled, he'd gotten away with crossing the line time and again. It wasn't a well-known fact outside the man's inner circle that he possessed keen empathic abilities and used them to ferret out those who would do him or his family harm.

None were as crafty as Alastair. One had only to look into his cool sapphire eyes to know they'd not outsmart the man, though many had tried. Those keen eyes turned on Ronan.

"I haven't had the chance to tell you this, but I'm glad you're the opposite of Loman. Many would heap the sins of the father on the son. I'm not one of them. Every man should be judged on his or her own actions."

"And it's thanking you, I am. It's always been a—and pardon the expression here—thorn in my side that he's my da at all."

An appreciative grin curled Alastair's mouth, and he gave Ronan a respectful nod. "I'll offer you one piece of advice for free, and you can do with it what you will."

Ronan lifted his brows in question as Alastair tugged the cuffs of his dress shirt from under his suit jacket. Finally, after Ronan had given up the hope the other man would get to the point, he spoke.

"Your future mate is as spirited as they come, O'Connor. Much like my beloved Rorie. If you haven't already guessed, Dubheasa will chafe under what she perceives to be authority. Yours included. Never try to dominate her, and always respect her wishes." His blue eyes twinkled when he added, "And for the love of the Goddess, never lie to your woman if you don't want your balls served to you on a silver platter."

"Aye, and she's tried to serve them up to me a time or two already," Ronan replied with a glance over his shoulder at the woman in question. "But I'll take your advice and be glad for it."

"Good man." Alastair clapped him on the back. "Let's get down to business. I don't have all day." As he walked away, he straightened his tie and smoothed his hands down the material of his navy jacket.

Ronan was hard-pressed not to laugh.

CHAPTER 11

As Damian laid out the past events leading up to the meeting for Draven and Fintan, Dubheasa listened intently. She'd only received secondhand accounts from her siblings and hadn't been in the thick of things as they happened, like the rest of the O'Malleys were. A large part of her was upset that her sister and brothers had held back the bulk of the information from her. Despite being the same age as Eoin, she was still considered the baby of their family, and as such, the rest of the O'Malleys tended to protect her from hardships or strife. She wished they knew her a little better and gave her more credit as an adult.

"Sounds like Loman O'Connor is a real fine piece of work," Draven said with a sharp look toward Ronan. "Why didn't you stab the bastard in his sleep before now?"

"He warded his room each night," Ronan replied with a grimace. "But don't be thinkin' I didn't want to."

How awful must it have been to hate a parent so much one wished them dead? And for that reason to be because they broke their child's trust and abused them unmercifully? Dubheasa's anger toward Loman was building with each transgression she heard. If the man were standing in front of her, she'd gladly shove a blade through his unfeeling heart.

Across the table, Damian locked eyes with her. His narrowed in consideration as if he was weighing her thoughts and feelings, but he never stopped detailing the rest of the situation. When he concluded his speech and opened the floor for a question-and-answer session, Dubheasa held up her hand.

"How do we get Loman's attention and provoke the man into action? From what I've heard here, he's always been the aggressor and steps ahead of everyone in our group." She glanced at her brothers. "You know we can't let him strike first this time. The collateral damage is always too great when he does. We take the fight to him, yeah?"

Eoin looked on board with her plan while Carrick appeared more thoughtful and cautious. Cian, on the other hand, was already shaking his head. "You and Bridget will be sitting this one out, to be sure."

"You seem to have me confused with someone you can be ordering about, brother," she replied tartly.

"Dubh—"

"No, Cian. This concerns Ronan, and by default, me." Reluctantly, afraid of what she'd see, she turned her head to meet Ronan's steady gaze. Pride, or something like it, shone in those silvery depths, and she released the breath she'd been holding. "He's not seen my face, and I'm the one who stands the best chance of getting close to him."

Adamantly, he shook his head. "That's not our most brilliant move, Dove. He's not after caring who you are and will steal your magic, given the chance."

She grinned. "Then that's our plan to lure him out. What better way to trap a mouse than offer up a slice of cheese?"

He opened his mouth as if to argue, but closed it again with a resigned sigh.

"You know me better than my own brothers," she told him through their link.

"I know you're after giving me heart failure. But the idea has merit."

"No!" Cian came around to their side of the table and crouched next to her chair. "Dubheasa, you've not met the man, and you've no clue how dangerous he can be. It's a fool's errand for you to put yourself in his sights, it is. I'm askin' ya not to do it."

"If you come up with a better plan to get to him, I'll listen, but we'll do it my way before we sit here like ducks and wait for him to use us for target practice."

"I agree with your sister," Damian said. "With each attack, your family has had to be on the defense. It's time to be on the offense."

"He'll not take kindly to being hunted," Castor warned. "I know my brother, and if you corner him, he'll turn rabid. Ronan, back me up here."

"Aye. He's deadly either way, sure, but you've got the right of it. The man's cunning on a good day. On a bad one? He's Machiavellian and pure evil."

Trevor leaned forward. "It's not as if Dubheasa will be left alone. We'll all have eyes and ears on her. And I feel we should plant an electronic device somewhere on her person, should Loman anticipate a magical tracker."

"That's all well and good, but we need to find him prior to delivering her up as bait," Alastair inserted. "My understanding is that the man isn't on anyone's radar, the deities' included, so this entire conversation is a moot point."

In the corner of the room, Draven straightened from where he'd been leaning against the wall. "What if we offer two for the price of one?" He looked right at Ronan. "You and your girl, in a location he's sure to hear about through the grapevine?"

"Please explain, Masters," the Aether said, an intrigued expression on his face.

A crafty smile curled Draven's mouth, and a wicked gleam entered his eyes. "Ask yourself, friend, will Loman O'Connor be able to resist attendin' his own son's weddin'? I think not."

Dubheasa's heart jumped up into her throat, and she sputtered an automatic denial. A faux marriage didn't sit well with her, not for herself and certainly not for any other woman pretending to join Ronan in holy matrimony. But it was the latter that had her the saltiest.

"Draven Masters, you devious delight!" Castor laughed and turned sparkling eyes their way. "There's no way he doesn't show to ruin your life, nephew o' mine. The fucking vain peacock."

Stomach churning, Dubheasa glanced at the faces around the table as Draven's plan formed. Anyone not related to her looked like they thought his idea a fecking grand one. Her siblings were going to be harder to convince.

Ronan's terse "no" caused her to whip her head back toward him.

"Sure, and what's wrong with it, then?" The question poured out of her mouth before she could prevent it. It wasn't as if she was enthusiastic about the suggestion, but if he was rejecting her involvement in either the marriage or the trap, he'd be telling her why and soon.

"I'll not have you be a sitting target, Dove," he said in a gentle tone. If it weren't for his troubled eyes, she might've chafed under his comment, regardless of how sweetly he said it.

"And I'm not chuffed to be bait, either. But what is the alternative, then? How are we to draw him out?" Damn her own logical hide! Why was she suddenly okay with something she'd planned to object to a minute before?

"What if we use an alternate bride?" Quentin suggested, speaking for the first time since arriving.

Dubheasa glanced in his direction and was taken aback when she registered his resemblance to Ronan. Not in coloring. No, he was quite the opposite, with his twinkling milk-chocolate eyes and his dark mocha hair. But his strong, perfect features were pure Ronan: chiseled jaw, high cheekbones, and full mouth that looked as if he smiled frequently. To say nothing of his large build and shoulders that took up a great deal of real estate in the room.

Quentin appeared happier and more laid back than Ronan, who never quite relaxed, but perhaps Quentin's peace came from having people who cared about him. Healthy relationships made a world of difference.

As his words sunk in, Dubheasa scowled. "If anyone will be standing up at the altar with Ronan, you can be sure it will be me, yeah?"

Eoin laughed heartily at the same time Cian choked on a biscuit. Bridget remained quiet for the first time in her life, but she didn't appear surprised by Dubheasa's emphatic response. Only Carrick remained unaffected, as if he didn't care if she wanted Ronan for her own.

And she did.

Want him.

A forever kind of want that hadn't struck her until she heard the word "bride" bandied about.

Standing abruptly, she croaked, "I need air."

RONAN FOLLOWED DUBHEASA AS SHE DARTED TOWARD THE ALLEY between the inn and the pub. He hung back to give her a minute to herself, but it was dangerous for her to be out of his sight. Of course, he hadn't mentioned it before, but if Loman took one look at her, he'd see those brilliant green eyes of hers and instantly know she was an O'Malley. But Ronan was proud of her fierceness and her willingness to stop his da no matter the cost.

As Dubheasa paced along the cobblestones, muttering to herself, Ronan turned off their mental connection and lounged in the doorway of the Black Cat, allowing her the privacy she needed to work through her thoughts.

Draven's plan was clever and likely to work, but Ronan's reticence to involve Dubheasa came from the desire to keep her safe. His father possessed a cunning mind, and the others seemed to forget he wasn't a dumb animal to fall so easily into a trap. Loman was a strategist and weighed every move before he made it. Yes, the man could be reactive, but he actually listened when others spoke and took things into account.

Until now, Ronan had forgotten exactly how great his da was at these types of war games. And it *was* war. One evil O'Connor remained and was willing to destroy an entire family to get what he wanted. Loman had no conscience and cared not who he hurt to gain the power he craved.

"You're awfully quiet."

Dubheasa had stopped in front of him, calmer than when she'd left the kitchen. The cool mid-morning air colored her skin, making her cheeks and nose a berry red. Ronan smiled at the sight.

"You forgot a coat, love." He straightened and opened his arms. "Come, and I'll warm ya."

She grinned. "The first magic I learned from GiGi was to warm myself."

"Sure, and it was worth a try." Her laughter made his soul lighter, and Ronan wished he could make her happy every day of their lives. The chances were nil that he could, but he'd give it his best go if he might hold onto this feeling forever.

Dubheasa surprised him when she wrapped her arms

around his waist and pressed her cheek to his chest. "Why didn't you attempt to calm me when you entered the alley?"

Taking a moment to shift through his thoughts on the matter and formulate a response, he said, "You didn't need me to placate ya, Dove. You were after workin' the problem around, and I was after lettin' ya." He drew back and tipped her chin up. "From the moment Anu and Isis told me I was to be a Guardian and you were to be my mate, I wasn't given a choice. If I wanted my magic back, that was the way it had to be. But you already have abilities, and you deserve to make the decision on your own, yeah?"

"You didn't want me for a mate?"

Her confused, somewhat-hurt frown tugged at his heartstrings.

"When I left you that morning in New York, I felt a crushing guilt for my trick. But I also experienced sadness and a longing to stay." Lightly brushing her bangs back from her forehead, he said, "When the word 'mate' came up, the very first image to come to mind was you. I remembered you sleeping on your stomach with your lovely legs on display as they played peek-a-boo with the sheet. The graceful curve of your lower back was exposed, and I desperately wanted to place my lips there to tease a response from you. To spend one more day in your bed. Forget who and what I was."

Ronan wove his fingers in the hair at the nape of her neck and tugged her head back so she was focused on him and could see he was one hundred percent serious. "Do I want you for a mate? Aye. But only if you want me in return. Only if you don't feel pressured into it. Sure, and only if you love me as madly as I love you, Dove." Releasing her, he set her away from him. "I've chased and annoyed ya long enough, and now it's time for you to figure out what it is you want. You know what's at stake, but don't use it to decide. Dig deep and analyze your feelings, decide what you want from life, and then, if it aligns with what the Fates have laid out for us, grand. If it doesn't, you'll have your answer, love."

"You told me I had to make a decision soon." Her uncertainty was reflected in her voice and troubled eyes.

"Aye. I also told you I'd try to buy you some time with the deities."

"But we don't have time, do we?"

"No."

"Then why were you willing to lose me as a mate forever?"

He grinned at her clever deduction. "Because I love you, and love isn't selfish. It's meant to be freely given. Sure, I could've badgered you into making a decision, but you'd always wonder if it was the right one, no?"

"Ronan O'Connor, you are much more clever than anyone gives you credit for." Once again, she hugged him around the middle and rested her ear over the area of his heart. If she listened closely, she'd hear it drumming like mad, ready to fly out of his chest.

"Don't be spreadin' the fact, love. It's lazy, I am, and I don't want others lighting a fire under me arse or attempting to make me better myself."

Dubheasa's laughter was light and airy, the very thing his soul needed.

"I choose you, Ronan." Her words were so low, he almost didn't hear them. And when he didn't immediately react, she tilted her head back and repeated them louder. "I choose you because you're the only man who's ever thought about my needs. About giving me a choice for my own future. The only one who's accepted me for who I am."

He waited her out, hoping to hear her say she loved him, but the words didn't cross her lips, and he had to ask himself if he could live with only desire on her part.

When her mouth fell open, as if she were waiting with

bated breath for him to kiss her, he suspected he could. "Is that all, love?"

"I don't know what else I can give you at the moment. Do I desire you? Yes. More than anyone I've ever met. The night with you has haunted me for months—in the best of ways. Do I love you? Look, and I don't know." Inching back, she shook her head. "I care deeply, to be sure. And I can't seem to get your smile out of my mind. When I close my eyes, it's the first thing I see. And I don't want another woman to have you, all the same. Can that be enough for you for now?"

"Aye, it can." He touched his mouth to hers in the most tender of kisses. She might not love him yet, but he'd never give up hope that she one day might. "And I choose you, Dubheasa O'Malley. For now. For always."

Lightning flashed overhead, and the ensuing boom was thunderous, causing them both to jump.

"What do you suppose that means?" she asked shakily.

"Perhaps it was Anu shouting, *'It's about fecking time!'*"

CHAPTER 12

As Loman strolled through the derelict prison wing, he sneered at the miserable faces peering out through the bars. Male or female, it didn't matter. He housed them all in the same area to make them easily accessible for his magic-syphoning needs.

Fortune had smiled down upon him when he discovered this place the first time he returned from the Otherworld. The disappearing island housing the prison was just off the coast of Scotland and fairly easy to get to if one knew where to look. And having worked with the former owners of the hellhole, Loman did.

Previously, the place had been used by an anti-witch group known as the Désorcelers Society to house their victims. Carved over the opening of each cell was an ancient Celtic symbol to suppress abilities. By using the blood of the prisoner and a spell—ironically created by a powerful witch for the express purpose of stealing another's power—the room could not only contain the victim, but their magic as well. Drawing from their body, it gifted their abilities to the witch who had performed the spell. Or in Loman's case, warlock.

Next to him, someone moaned and held out a hand beseechingly.

"Feck off!" Loman snarled at the man, delighting when the guy cringed from the venom in his voice. Satisfaction filled him. He was close to achieving his goals. Incredibly close.

After escaping the holding area of the Otherworld and landing in England, he'd begun walking down the lane, and the first person to offer him a ride was a young, fresh-faced witch who had no idea who he was or what he was capable of. Halfway to his destination, he'd slit her throat and used her blood to perform a ceremony he'd long since committed to memory. As he absorbed what remained of her fading magic, his cells had felt alive once more. So he'd done it again and again, until he had enough power to confront the Succubus, Odessa Sullivan.

"Crafty minger," he muttered.

He'd mistaken her age for weakness, of which, she had little. But he wouldn't be making that mistake again, all the same. His plan had backfired on his niece Moira, and she'd been burned alive by the Aether.

Loman shuddered. Sure, and for all the times he'd used fire as a weapon, the idea of burning to death was the only thing that gave him nightmares. If Damian Dethridge got ahold of him, he'd not only die in the most excruciating manner possible, his soul would be obliterated to boot.

"And the key is to avoid the Aether until I've drained his girl dry," he murmured. "Then, I'll be as formidable as that arrogant fecker, I will."

At the end of the corridor, he stopped in front of Reginald's cell. Unlike the others, his nephew was sitting on his bed, seemingly uncaring of his surroundings, with a book of poetry in his hands.

"Are you ready to do your part, boyo?"

Reggie glanced up as if he was surprised to see Loman.

"Part?" He placed his index finger between the pages as a bookmark. "Oh, you mean in luring Ronan here?" Pretending to think it over, he finally shook his head. "So sorry, but that's going to be a hard pass from me." He opened his book and glanced up one last time to say, "Go bugger yourself, old man."

Rage exploded in Loman's brain, but he didn't strike as he once would've. Firstly, Reggie was out of reach for a fist to the face. Secondly, the enchantment encasing the cell would boomerang a bolt or fireball right back at Loman, should he shoot one his nephew's way.

"Sure, and you should be takin' care not to rile me, Reginald, me boy. Once I get Ronan's abilities and that of the girl Aether, I'll have nothing but time on me hands and a fierce plan to enact revenge on ya."

"*If* you get their abilities, you mean." Reggie flipped a page and shrugged. "It's highly doubtful you will, despite all the magic you've stolen from these unfortunate souls. I can't see Damian Dethridge allowing you within one hundred feet of his precious daughter." Another page turned. "Oh, and you may want to check the cell diagonal to mine. That poor bitch has breathed her last breath, I'm afraid."

Loman spun around, and sure enough, the old witch he'd housed there was on the floor, arms spread wide and eyes staring unseeingly at the ceiling.

"*Fuck!*"

He absolutely hated disposing of bodies, and it was risky to use any of his prisoners to do it.

"You do realize, with as much power as you're generating here, you won't be able to keep this place hidden for long, don't you?" Reggie's cold-eyed stare caused Loman's skin to prickle. His nephew had graced him with that same look just before shooting an arrow into his heart a few weeks before.

If only the boy had been more malleable, Loman would've gladly involved Reggie in his plan. But he was a wild card.

Unpredictable on his best day. Once, the O'Connors had feared Loman, but as time passed and his family witnessed Ronan's defection, they'd become bolder. Most had struck out on their own, spoiling all his grand plans to destroy the O'Malley clan and retain the power gifted to them by the God Goibhniu.

With a narrow-eyed glare for his nephew, Loman asked, "What are ya yammerin' on about, boy? Of course, I'll be keepin' this place hidden."

"Do you honestly believe the Aether doesn't have every possible resource scrying for you? You can cloak this facility, but magic like you're amassing creates a unique signature, Uncle. Eventually, you'll be found."

"For all you know, ya eejit! Sure, and didn't I build this place months ago when I first walked through the bleedin' portal?" Loman waved his arms to encompass the entire prison wing. "There will be no signature, because I've been buildin' this place at a steady pace, I have. And I know enough to not be greedy with the getting of magic, all the same."

Reggie laughed. "Your arrogance will be your downfall. See if it isn't."

Loman turned on his heel and stalked away. Partially in anger and partially because Reginald's words sounded too fecking prophetic for his tastes.

Anu sauntered into the clearing where her contemporary Isis was gazing into a lake. As she approached, Isis slammed her staff into the earth with a disgruntled huff, causing the ground to quake.

"Are you still unable to find Loman O'Connor, then?"

"I feel like there are others helping to hide him. Demigods perhaps," Isis replied, disgust and frustration heavy in her tone.

The wind picked up, and the acidic feel in the air prickled

along Anu's bare skin. The fine hairs on her arms danced like live wires. Had she been mortal, it would've stung, but those within the Otherworld would only experience a heaviness in the atmosphere.

"The Fates better have a good reason for their mischief in allowing him to escape a second time." Isis's amber eyes flashed with her ire. "I've half a mind to go over their heads to Ra."

"Do you think he would intervene on the O'Malleys' behalf? Or for that of the Aether's daughter?" Anu cast a troubled glance at the murky water. "It's troublesome that we are unable to see the final outcome."

"Indeed." Isis faced her and sighed heavily. "My father has been in seclusion for centuries, but Set is his second-in-command, and I shall put forth an inquiry through him."

"If I didn't know better, I'd believe it was a trickster god. But the *why* of it all eludes me."

"Yes, this does have an air of mischief. But whoever is playing with the lives of our witches will face my wrath. The hole in the veil needs to be repaired, and soon, or we will have others escaping the holding area just as Loman did."

"Tell me what we need to do to repair the rift, and I shall see it done," Anu promised.

"I don't know yet. And *that* is the odious part of this. If the souls I'm tasked with watching are able to return to the earthly plane at will, it creates a problem on a greater scale. Timelines will shift and fates will alter."

"Yet if the Fates are responsible for Loman's return, they must have an idea of the consequences, no?"

"One would believe so." Isis gave her a frustrated look. "They are playing a dangerous game, whatever their final design."

"Aye. They are. Loman O'Connor should never have been allowed to return to the world at large. He's a bad apple, bound to spoil the entire barrel."

"Agreed." Isis gave her a tight smile. "Let us hope Ronan is up to the task of finding his father."

"Without it costing him more than he's willing to give," Anu replied grimly.

CHAPTER 13

Dubheasa refuses to give in to superstition. Ronan, on the other hand, insisted we skip chapter thirteen. He feels they need all the luck they can get to neutralize Loman. So, in keeping with the chapter thirteen omissions, you are encouraged to take a break, hydrate, then dig back into the story. :)

CHAPTER 14

"How do we move forward with a faux wedding if you don't want me to be the bride?" Dubheasa asked Ronan once they returned to the kitchen. Yes, it chapped her arse to think of another woman standing up with him, but she was trying to take his objection into consideration.

Alastair weighed in first. "If you'll allow me. I propose we find someone skilled with magic, who can hold a glamour under fire. She can take on your appearance, Ms. O'Malley, and you'll take on another."

"You believe I'll be a prime target, then?" The thought made her stomach queasy, but she refused to show it.

"Aye," Ronan said grimly. "If my da can steal your magic and destroy my happiness in the process, he'll do it. And he will be after the grandest prize of them all. You."

When she pictured the engaging young boy Ronan might have been, then imagined what his childhood must've been like with a father like Loman, her heart ached.

"Okay. We'll do it your way."

Tension eased from Ronan's frame, and the tightness around his eyes lessened. "Thank you, love."

"Don't be thanking me just yet. The important thing is to catch this gobshite and end his reign of terror." Glancing at the others, she considered the problem. "It was mentioned that members of the magical community have disappeared. Can I get a list of names, last known locations, and dates they went missing? If we can't track him by magical means, I might be able to find him the old-fashioned way, by tracing his movements or uncovering a pattern."

Ronan's appreciative grin went a long way toward boosting her confidence. Perhaps there was something she could bring to the table, after all.

"I'll have them for you within the hour, Ms. O'Malley," Alastair assured her with a warm smile. "You're a very resourceful young woman, and I'm delighted you're on our team."

"Thank you, sir." A weight of wistful emotion settled in Dubheasa's chest as she watched him pull out his phone and exit the room. Would her own father have been so encouraging and kind, had he remained in her life? She couldn't say she'd taken his loss the hardest of her siblings, but she certainly thought of him frequently in one capacity or another. Not a day went by when she didn't miss his amused half smile and those dancing green eyes filled with love for her.

Ronan's large hand engulfed hers, and when she looked up, it was to see his genuine concern for her well-being. Her earlier decision to accept him as her mate was cemented. "When do I get the Guardian infusion of magic?"

"That'll be up to Anu and the Aether. But the sooner, the better. I won't be sleepin' well at night until you're fully charged and my da's dark soul is destroyed permanently."

"We should make that our first order of business," Damian stated. "The more firepower we have, the better our chances."

Dubheasa met Fintan's thoughtful gaze across the room. "And you? What do you know that can help us?"

Fintan's eyes lost focus for a moment, but finally he said,

"Your power should be bound and not added to, Dubheasa O'Malley. It's the only way to protect against Loman's theft."

A chill chased along her spine, and her lungs refused to draw breath. It wasn't until Ronan's grip became painful that she got control of her anxiety.

"What do you know, Fintan Sullivan?" Ronan's voice was as hard as raw granite and twice as rough.

"She'll not survive a confrontation with Loman, should he get to her first. And if she has an ounce of magic in her veins, he'll take it for his own." The Seer appeared less thrilled to be imparting his dire prediction than Dubheasa was at hearing it.

"What the fuck is this, then?" Cian demanded with a fierce glare at Ronan. "You've been pushing for Dubheasa to amplify her abilities since the day you became a Guardian, ya have! Is this a trick to hurt our family again?"

Ronan's hand grew clammy, and Dubheasa desperately wanted to tear hers away, but his fingers tightened in a stranglehold. A simple tug had her facing him.

"I've not lied about the magic, Dove. I swear on me soul, and if I'm lyin', may the Goddess strike me dead."

Through their mental connection, a wave of sincerity washed over her, assuring her that he was telling the truth.

"I believe you," she said softly. "I trust you, Ronan O'Connor. Probably more than I should, considering our families' history."

"Thank you, love." His relief was palpable, and he drew her into a tight hug. Biceps like small tree trunks crushed her to him, but he loosened his grip as soon as she shoved his chest.

She placed her hands on her hips and scowled. "If you're after suffocating me instead, I'll not be happy."

His grin didn't happen often but was a thing of beauty when it did, and Dubheasa caught her breath at the sight of it. The world fell away as their gazes locked, and in her heart of hearts, she knew he didn't have it in him to betray her.

"I'll never hurt you, Dove. You know I don't make war on women and children. But even if I did, I'd never be able to double-cross you to such a degree. You're the other half of my soul, you are." He cupped her cheek. "And without you, I'm naught but a broken husk."

"Feck, O'Connor. You're making us weep, you are." Eoin winked at Dubheasa. "If you don't marry him, I will."

The devilish sparkle in Eoin's eyes tickled her funny bone, and she shouted a laugh. Her twin had been her staunch supporter in all things, and he'd die to protect her, as she'd die to protect him. But Eoin could read people's true intentions. Perhaps it was the watchful artist, or maybe he had a deeper ability to separate the wheat from the chaff, but Dubheasa trusted his instincts. And if he was encouraging her to claim Ronan for her own, then she'd listen and be happier for it.

"That's a fantastic idea!" Brenna said. Her enthusiasm caught the group's attention, and more than half looked at her as if she'd lost her fecking mind. With a laugh, she shook her head. "Not in the way you think, but as Dubheasa's stand-in for the fake wedding. If Eoin is in danger, my Siren will come out and annihilate the threat. It's doubtful Loman would stand a chance against her."

"The plan has merit." Castor studied Brenna an extra moment, then faced those at the table. "And I'll be there. So will my son. If anything goes sideways, it's possible the two of us could reset time."

"Wait! What?" Quentin pushed off the wall he'd been holding up. "What do you mean by reset time? As in, create a new timeline? Because that doesn't always work so well."

"No. I mean reset the *current* timeline."

A deep frown drew Quentin's brows together. "We can do that?"

"We're Travelers. Our talents are many."

"How did this never come up before now?"

Castor shrugged. "We never needed to utilize that type of power before. And I didn't necessarily say we *could* do it. Simply that it's *possible* we could do it."

Quentin scowled. "So you're making shit up now?"

"No," Damian said, coming to his friend's defense. "A pair of previous Travelers were able to reset time a little over a century ago. They, too, were related. Alexander is merely suggesting since it was done once before, you might be able to do it as well should the need arise."

"That's all well and good for the Travelers of the past, but since neither of them is still around and we don't have the spell to pull it off, it's a moot point, isn't it?" Quentin reached for a finger sandwich from the tray Bridget held out. After thanking her, he shrugged at the Aether and popped the entire thing in his mouth.

"It's eerie how much he resembles you," Dubheasa told Ronan through their connection.

"I like him better for it."

"Who said we don't have a spell?" Castor cast his son a smug smirk, to which Quentin rolled his eyes and picked up another sandwich.

"Do you or don't you?"

"Actually, *you* do, Quentin," Damian responded for Castor with a hint of a smile. "In the ancient grimoire you possess."

"And you know this how?"

"I was the one who encouraged the previous Travelers to reset the world's timeline." Damian's reply was succinct.

With a sharp look at him, Bridget sat down. "Sure, and why would the world need resetting?"

"It's too long a story, but like Loman O'Connor, another became too big for their britches and wreaked havoc upon the magical world. The Authority was forced to step in."

"But they aren't now?" Dubheasa shook her head. "How is

this so different if Loman is possibly killing other witches to amass power?"

"I don't know that it is, Ms. O'Malley. But if we use the time-reset option moving forward, we'll need to keep it amongst ourselves. Without permission from the Authority or the Fates, we all face dire consequences for our actions," Damian said.

He didn't look thrilled by the prospect.

"You included?" she asked.

"Me included."

Alastair strolled back into the room, looking for all the world like a man on a mission. In his hand, he held a flash drive to Dubheasa. "Here you are, my dear. Everything you requested."

"I don't know where it is you get your information, Mr. Thorne, but I'm after meeting the source, I am."

He chuckled. "I'll introduce you to Alfred someday soon."

AFTER DUBHEASA EXCUSED HERSELF TO WORK HER PARTICULAR brand of modern magic with her laptop, Ronan and the others got down to the business of setting the faux-wedding trap. Damian, Alastair, and Castor brainstormed locations as Bridget, Brenna, and Eoin discussed everything from flower arrangements to dress designs.

"We could use Reggie for his fashion sense," Eoin muttered with a shake of his head. "If only the scut would call me back!"

Ronan's cousin cared for few people, but he had a soft spot for Eoin, and it didn't sit well that Eoin hadn't received a return call from Reggie. "When did you last speak to him?"

"It's been a good four days, I'm thinkin'."

Brenna glanced up from the Pinterest board she'd started

on her phone. "It's odd, isn't it? Reggie touches base with Eoin every other day, at least."

"He's been known to go silent when he meets a new friend, though." Eoin shrugged but frowned just as quickly. "But usually, he'll tell me he's going dark for a bit, he does."

"Sounds like we should be worried about our cousin Reggie," Quentin said in a contemplative tone. "Where does he live? I'll go check it out."

Castor, who had previously appeared lost in discussion with the Aether, faced his son. "Not alone, you won't."

"I've been on my own my entire life. I don't answer to you." Quentin's response was clipped and his expression unyielding.

To prevent a war of wills, Ronan stood. "Yeah, and I'll go with him. I know a few of Reggie's old haunts. Eoin can give me a list of the new ones." He glanced at Fintan. "Care to be our early warning system, Seer?"

Fintan gave them a sharp nod, but nothing in his expression indicated he was worried about their journey, and Ronan breathed easier.

They arrived outside Reggie's flat in London twenty minutes later with a list of places he liked to frequent tucked firmly in Ronan's back pocket. Doubtful any of them would be able to enter his cousin's warded place, he prepared to counter the enchantment with a charm from the Aether.

Quentin's hand on Ronan's arm stopped him before he got started. "Let's get the attendant to let us in. If he's a nonmagical human, he should be able to enter without difficulty."

"No building manager will be lettin' a group of strangers into the flat of one of their owners, to be sure," Fintan said.

"Probably not, but they'll let Reggie in." Quentin's grin was pure mischief, and not for the first time, Ronan wondered what it might have been like to grow up normal, with a sense of self, like his new cousin had.

"I'm guessing I'm to play the part of Reg?"

Quentin gave a one-shoulder shrug. "Well, you could probably emulate him best."

After a quick search of the area to ascertain if there were onlookers or cameras to catch his transformation, Ronan glamoured into Reggie's slighter, shorter frame. After two or three tries, he perfected his cousin's posh English speech and arrogant expression.

"Let's hope I can pass through the wards without getting my arse electrocuted."

"It's uncanny," Quentin said with a shake of his head.

Five minutes later, the attendant was using a master key to grant them access to the flat. "Did your uncle find you, sir?"

"My uncle?" Sick dread settled in Ronan's gut.

"Yes, sir. Your uncle. He came by about three or four days ago, now. Said he had a grand surprise for you."

"I'll just bet he did," Quentin muttered as he shared a grim look with Ronan.

"You have Reg—er, my contact number, correct?" Hoping the guy missed his slip, Ronan sighed when he nodded. "My uncle and I have had a bit of a falling out in recent years. Should you see him again, text me or my cousin Ronan." He rattled off his own number as the attendant put it in his personal cellphone.

"Yes, the man is bad news," Quentin added. "Stole the family jewels and all that. I'm also a cousin of Reggie's and Ronan's. From America, but I'll be hanging around, so if you can't reach them, call me."

After all the numbers were entered into his phone, the attendant left the three of them in the entryway of Reggie's flat.

Fintan remained quiet as he followed them through the door to the marbled foyer.

"Why doesn't he have this warded against strangers?" Quentin murmured as he cautiously moved forward. "I can't help feeling like I'm about to step into a trap."

Ronan morphed back into his true form and paid special attention to the details of the entry, looking for anything that might be a deterrent or weapon to hurt them should they progress into the flat. "Aye, and I can't shake the feeling something's not altogether right here. Fintan?"

"The ancestors aren't speaking to me, but I feel we're relatively safe."

Quentin gave the Seer a disgusted glance. "That doesn't sound reassuring in the least." Of Ronan, he asked, "Reggie wouldn't *not* ward the place against strangers, would he?"

"Maybe he wasn't after viewing us as a threat," Ronan replied with a thoughtful frown. With a deep, stabilizing breath, he walked into the living room. "Reg?" he called. "Are ya here, man?"

The space felt void of life, as if no soul had been there recently.

"Reg?"

A book fell off the shelf to Ronan's right.

"What the fuck?" Quentin whispered. "Is this place haunted?"

"By Reggie?" Fintan shook his head, but in a blink, his eyes lost focus and turned opaque.

"Jaysus!" Ronan lurched toward him at the same time Quentin surged forward, and they caught Fintan before he could hit the ground.

Quentin wasn't as quiet with his second *what the fuck*.

CHAPTER 15

"*R*onan. I was hoping you'd come looking for me."

Ronan stared at Fintan in alarm as his cousin's voice spilled out of the Seer's mouth. Never had he seen a possession, and witnessing one now made his bollocks shrivel. "Reg?" His voice cracked, so he cleared his throat and tried again. "Reggie?"

"I've limited time, so listen closely. I enchanted my flat so you could enter and we could have this little chat. Pick up the fallen book."

Quentin left him holding Fintan to retrieve it, then handed it off and exchanged places with Ronan.

"Keep it at all times. Whenever you need to contact me, give it to the Seer and have him turn to page thirty-seven. It's a blank page for him to write his questions. I…"

The pause was so long that Ronan worried the connection was severed. "Reg?"

After half a minute, Fintan spoke again in Reggie's hushed tones. "Loman is walking the cellblock where I'm being held. Write your questions on page thirty-seven and look for the responses on page forty-one. If there are none, I've been caught out."

"Where are ya being held?"

"An island off the coast of Scotland. I don't know the exact location. But it was a stronghold used by the Dés—fuck! Page thirty-seven," Reggie reiterated.

Fintan's body arched up, and his opaque eyes snapped shut.

"I think he's gone," Quentin said slowly with a glance toward the tome in Ronan's hands. "The dude is brilliant."

"Aye, he's a crafty one, to be sure." With a nod to Fintan, Ronan said, "Let's get him back to the Aether. Maybe—"

The next instant, Fintan came up swinging. Ronan, unprepared for the attack, caught a fist to the jaw, which snapped his head back on his shoulders. Before Fintan had a chance to strike a second time, Quentin froze the man in place, allowing Ronan to scramble out of reach.

"Jaysus!"

"I was about to say the same thing," Quentin replied dryly. "Okay, I'm going to release him. Be prepared."

A resounding pop sounded in Ronan's ears, and he startled at the loudness.

Snarling and ready to continue his fight, Fintan jumped to his feet and looked around wildly. "What did ya do to me, then?"

"Not a damned thing," Quentin told him. "Seriously, man. Your eyes rolled back in your head, and you began channeling Reggie. It was freaky as fuck."

The sincerity must've gotten through because the fight left the Seer and he gave Quentin a cautious nod. "Aye. Freaky as feck for me, too."

Ronan took a tentative step forward. "You've never had that happen, then?"

"No. And I can't say as I liked it, to be sure." Fintan gave a full-body shiver and shook his hands out. "What was said?"

"You're to communicate with Reggie through the book there." Ronan nodded to the discarded tome. "Page thirty-seven for your questions, with the answers comin' back to ya on page forty-one."

"Me? Ach, and why not you?" Fintan's dark, put-upon scowl almost made Ronan laugh.

"Sure, and we'll not be knowin' that until you write to my cousin, now will we?"

"I feckin' despise the bleedin' cloak-and-dagger shite, I do." The Seer snatched the thick book from the ground and promptly dropped it again with a yelp followed by a savage curse. His palms were a deep scarlet. "The fucking thing burned me!"

"May I?" Ronan nodded to Fintan's blistering hands. "I can heal ya if you're of a mind."

In his mind's eye, Ronan visualized the bubbled skin smoothing and returning to a standard flesh color as he pulled the heat and pushed a cooling breeze across the angry marks. With each minute that passed, Fintan's palms returned to normal.

"Thank you, O'Connor," Fintan said gruffly. "I've not much call to ask for the assistance of others, but I'm appreciative, all the same."

"You can be prepared to return the favor, yeah?"

Tentatively, Ronan reached out a hand to lift the book from the ground. Though warm to the touch, it didn't sear his skin as it had Fintan's. With a sharp look at Quentin, he asked, "Did you feel anythin' when ya picked it up?"

"It got warm, but it didn't burn me."

"Will ya touch it now?"

Cautiously, Quentin did as he asked, shrugging when he had the tome firmly in his grasp. "Warm still, but no searing heat."

"It's feckin' blood magic, it is." Fintan strode to the shelf the book had originally fallen from. "Ronan, pick up the athame and prick your finger. I'll need three nice-sized drops in a glass."

After he'd done as the Seer commanded, Ronan faced him. "What's next?"

"Do the same to your cousin."

Quentin didn't appear thrilled. "I don't participate in blood magic."

"You'll be participatin' in this one if ya want me fecking help," Fintan snapped. His pale eyes turned the churning shades of the angry sea during a hurricane. "I'm not fond of the bleedin' process either, but your schemin' cousin has given us no choice."

"Tell me what you're attempting, and *perhaps* I'll participate."

Ronan noted the steely tone and Quentin's equally hardened expression. With all his standard teasing aside, Quentin Buchanan looked like a vengeful god. An immovable, stubborn-as-hell deity who would rather smite the lot of them than give a single drop of his life's blood. Knowing how precious it could be and exactly how easily one's own blood could be used against them, Ronan was sympathetic to his cousin's plight. But they also had a job to do.

"Look, and can we take all this back to the inn and have Castor contribute to your spell instead?" Ronan asked Fintan.

"There's danger in delayin' and in the moving of tools we intend to use. It's best to complete the spell here, where the original was cast." After a deep sigh, Fintan faced Quentin. "Sure, and I understand your reticence, I do. But the only way I'll be able to access that book is to use blood magic from two of Reggie's relatives. You and Ronan."

"The process," Quentin barked.

The man wasn't budging when it came to knowing what he was getting into, and Ronan couldn't blame him. If he wasn't fearful that Reg might not make it out of his prison alive and of not stopping Loman, he wouldn't so readily have offered up his own blood.

"'Tis simple, really. After Ronan pricks your finger and your blood combines, I'll consume it, so it will be minglin' with mine." Fintan never broke eye contact with Quentin. "It should trick the feckin' book into allowing me to handle it, short term, until your blood is out of my system."

"You'll drink it? That's it?"

"Aye."

"Goddammit, I hate this." Quentin ran a hand through his shoulder-length hair and laced his hands behind his head as he began to pace.

Both Ronan and Fintan allowed him the time he needed to come to the right decision.

Finally, Quentin stopped in front of Ronan and held out his hand, shooting a warning look at Fintan. "If this backfires and affects my family in any way, I'll crucify the lot of you. Understand?"

For the first time, Ronan saw Fintan's expression soften. "Your children will never have anything to fear from me, Quentin Buchanan."

"Children? I only have a daughter—ah." Quentin smiled wryly. "Well, at least you told me I'll make it out of this particular battle in one piece."

With a half smile as acknowledgment, Fintan turned and met Ronan's watchful gaze. "Begin."

FIFTEEN MINUTES AFTER THEY'D FINISHED THE QUICK BLOOD-letting ritual and confirmed Fintan could handle the enchanted book, Quentin washed the athame clean, salted it, and returned it to Ronan to hide on Reggie's shelf. Ronan was careful to tuck it behind a collection of Shakespeare's works, knowing if Loman or his minions ever managed to break in, it might be the last place he'd think to look for any ceremonial tools. One could never be too cautious with his da.

They arrived at the Black Cat Inn just as Dubheasa was joining Trevor and her siblings.

Her voice was breathy and sweet when she said, "Hi."

Jaysus! How the hell could she take him out at the knees with one sexy-sounding word? How did one warm smile make him want to grovel at her feet and promise her the moon and stars if she'd smile like that at him for the rest of their lives? Crossing to her, he tenderly traced the line of her mouth with his fingertips.

"Hello, Dove," he replied huskily.

Dubheasa licked her lips and shivered, assuring him he wasn't the only one so greatly affected. Her response reminded him of their dinner date and how she'd readily agreed to become his lover. Wanting nothing more than to steal her away for a repeat performance of their first time, Ronan barely held himself in check. With her, he could forget about warring families and monstrous parents. And if he could, he'd spend the next year in bed with her, only leaving it for necessities. He'd explore every square inch of her porcelain skin... taste her...

Someone cleared their throat, but Ronan continued to drown in Dubheasa's incredible eyes.

"What did you find out about Reggie, O'Connor?" Eoin asked.

Ignoring Eoin, Ronan brushed his lips across Dubheasa's, capturing her soundless moan.

"O'Connor!"

Dubheasa blinked, releasing Ronan from under her spell. Scowling, he faced Cian. "Ya can't wait a bleedin' second for me to greet me mate with a simple kiss?"

Cian's lips twitched as the rest of their group chuckled. "I was afraid you were after shagging her where you stood."

"Feck off."

But her brother had read Ronan's intent correctly. His restraint had frayed, and he'd been one second from teleporting her to his room.

Eoin shared an amused look with Cian. "Sure, and I'll ask again. What did you find out about Reggie?"

"He's being held by Loman on an island somewhere in Scotland," Quentin answered for Ronan, not bothering to lift his head from whatever held his attention on the screen of his phone. "Fintan has the means to communicate with him."

"What island?" Alastair nearly came out of his seat, but Damian placed a restraining hand on his arm.

The sharp bite of Alastair's question caught Quentin's attention as quickly as it had Ronan's. "He didn't say. Only that he was being held in a prison that was once a stronghold for someone other than Loman. It sounded like Reggie intended to say the Désorceler Society, but I can't be sure." He held up his smartphone. "I've been searching Google Earth, looking for any sign of a private island."

"What's the Désorceler Society?" Brenna asked.

"It was a group dedicated to eradicating witches, Thorne witches specifically," Alastair replied, and his tone was decidedly grim.

Ronan hadn't made the connection earlier when Reggie contacted them, but now that Quentin had mentioned the name of the disbanded organization, it somehow seemed to fit. "My da told me the tale of working with them. I'm not certain it was voluntarily, but it might've been, all the same. Never a day passed when he didn't curse the name of their leaders. He had a powerful fierce hatred for them all."

Alastair and Damian shared a worried look, but it was Castor who spoke. "If it's the island the three of us believe it is, the place is a fortress. No one comes or goes without being seen."

"The cells are a primary concern," Alastair added. "They were designed to rip away a witch's gifts and power a central magical grid to feed into another source. Usually someone without abilities."

"If Loman has working knowledge of that prison, we're fucked." Castor scrubbed his face with the heels of his hands. "Christ, what a mess!" Addressing Ronan directly, he said, "If your cousin is there, the chances of him getting out alive are slim to none."

Though they'd never been close, Ronan's chest tightened at the thought of Reggie meeting such a fate at Loman's hands. Dubheasa clasped Ronan's fingers and squeezed, and the gesture eased the constriction and allowed him a steadying breath.

"We have to at least try."

Castor addressed Alastair, his expression bordering on worried. "Are you up to revisiting the place, Al?"

"I thought I'd seen the last of it, but I don't see where we have a choice, do we? Still, we need a location before we attempt any heroic acts."

CHAPTER 16

"I believe I've narrowed it down." Dubheasa opened her laptop and gave everyone gathered a cursory glance. "I've taken the list Alastair gave me, and I've worked out a pattern based on dates and locations where the known witches went missing."

"And does the path of abducted witches lead to Scotland, *cher*?" Draven asked as he pulled a flask from beneath his leather duster.

"Aye, it does. In a roundabout way." She turned the laptop to face their group. "I've placed pins along the route. But there's a discrepancy a few weeks back, in America and again in Ireland, close to the Sullivan estate."

"No. Those timelines actually match," Eoin replied. He glanced at Brenna. "That should be about the time Loman thought to take on your Aunt Odessa, yeah?"

She leaned closer to see the first of the two pins. "Yes. That's close to Odessa's house. She said Moira and Loman paid her a visit. I imagine those dates would match." Looking reluctant, she offered to call her aunt.

"No need," Damian told her. "It's too much of a coincidence for it to be anything else."

"Would any of those poor bastards on the island still be alive?" Trevor asked. "Weeks of having their magic drained in any fashion would weaken them to the extreme."

Alastair's expression was so grim it turned Dubheasa's stomach. She could already guess what he intended to say. When he spoke, he confirmed her thoughts. "Some will have perished in the process. It's torturous."

"Is that what happened to you, then? Was your magic drained?" Not quite certain where she found the courage to ask Alastair Thorne so personal a question, Dubheasa waited nervously for his answer. If he had come through such an experience, there could be hope for others.

"Not quite. The men who ran the place had other plans for me. I was moved frequently, so no one could get a bead on my location and form a rescue. The idea was to make everyone assume I'd died." When he continued, the bleakness in his eyes chilled Dubheasa. "I was held for a number of years, but only six months of my incarceration were spent on the island. A huge portion of my time as a prisoner was at a monastery in the Himalayas."

"I'm sorry you had to go through that, Mr. Thorne." Her heart ached for him. Though his eyes were frosty in the retelling, the brief look of desolation that crossed his face spoke of his helplessness.

"Thank you, child. But it was a long time ago. The biggest concern is rescuing anyone still alive."

Tapping the last pin on the onscreen map, Dubheasa cleared her throat and got back to the point she wanted to make. "And this is our best clue as to the location of the island. That person was reported missing two days ago. Do any of you notice the pattern here?"

"Aye. It forms a wide arch around the coastline. Starting

there and ending here." Ronan pointed. "Sure, and if I had to guess, the island is close to the middle of the C."

Beaming at him for his clever mind, she nodded. "It's as if he tried to avoid abducting anyone too close by, not wanting to give himself away, yeah?"

"Yeah." Ronan's smile was savage. "But he didn't count on your skills, love."

"We haven't found the place yet, but look." She typed in a code, and the weather patterns for the last few months overlaid the map. "Notice the fog? It's not typical for Scotland during that season. Yet every time it rolls in, it's within hours of an abduction, and only in the area of the coast."

Castor laughed. "To hide his comings and goings. Looks like my brother isn't as brilliant as he'd like to think. Is he?"

"Oh, I don't know. To my knowledge, Loman O'Connor doesn't make fatal mistakes," Damian said slowly as he narrowed his eyes and studied the screen. "Will you do me a favor, Ms. O'Malley? Reveal the weather patterns for this area on the opposite coastline, between Ireland and Scotland. I'd like to see if they match what you've come up with."

"What are you thinking, Dethridge?" Alastair asked.

"That perhaps Loman is smarter than we've given him credit for." Damian lifted his tea and drained the cup, then set it down with deliberate care as if the group wasn't waiting with bated breath for him to reveal his thought process. Finally, he said, "If it were me, I'd throw a red herring into the mix. It's possible his fortress is on the other side of Scotland, well away from any notable activity."

It hadn't occurred to Dubheasa to check disturbances on the opposite side of the country. Once she found the original pattern, she'd reached the same conclusion as Ronan. Now, she was kicking herself for not putting more effort into the project.

Turning the laptop around, she began the process of discovery. First, she checked for private or hidden islands rumored to be in the area the Aether had indicated. Then she overlaid the weather as she'd done for the first map. The timing of the rain and fog was suspect in that each occurrence was always within minutes of the weather pattern in her first compilation.

"Here." She shifted the screen so Damian could see it.

"Only in that particular spot, and so fleeting you'd not notice it if you weren't specifically looking." He gave her an approving smile. "Well done, Ms. O'Malley."

To the others, he said, "In the morning, we'll split into two groups. One will check out the original area Ms. O'Malley mapped out, and one will investigate the other location." Damian met Ronan's eyes. "I believe you, Quentin, and the Seer should attempt to contact Reggie, in the meantime."

After their group had agreed on a time for their late-morning mission and disbanded, Ronan, along with Fintan, Dubheasa, Castor, and Quentin, adjourned to the sitting room.

"What's our best course of action here?" Quentin asked his father. "Do we use the O'Malley ceremony room, or should we just try to dial into Reggie from here?"

Castor sent a speculative glance in Fintan's direction. "I think the person we should ask is the Seer."

As Fintan opened Reggie's book and reviewed each page preceding the one they'd been instructed to use, Ronan watched him carefully, searching for any sign that creating a communication line was a bad idea.

Fintan spoke without bothering to look up. "Here is grand. I don't think a protection spell is necessary, but if it would please the lot of ya, we can do it all the same."

"I'd rather we not have everyone traipsing about where they don't need to," Dubheasa said. "But I'll concede to a majority vote."

Ronan understood her reticence when it came to allowing others to dabble in her family's sacred space. He'd been mighty protective of his own in the past. Not that he truly had anywhere to call his home anymore. Since Loman first returned to Ireland looking for the Sword of Goibhniu, Ronan had been hopscotching around the country and the United Kingdom in an effort to outrun his father. When he was afforded the gifts of a Guardian, he'd been able to stop running. Most recently, he'd resided in the guesthouse on the Dethridge estate to be available to protect Sabrina. And still, he preferred his privacy when he could get it.

Castor rose and crossed to the sideboard. Having previously stayed at the Black Cat Inn, he knew exactly where to go for fortification. After he helped himself to a drink, he said, "Let's get started, shall we?"

"You should check page forty-one to see if Reggie sent you a message first," Quentin suggested.

Fintan flipped a few pages and shook his head. "Not yet, and here goes nothing, yeah?" With a healthy sigh, he held his hand flat above the page, and words began to form.

Ronan read over his shoulder. "Be sure to ask how many mercenaries my da has workin' for him."

"And how many witches are being held," Dubheasa added. "We'll need to have a healer when we stage a rescue."

Castor frowned and opened his mouth, but Ronan cut him off with a minuscule shake of his head.

"I don't know that there'll be anyone left to rescue, Dove," he said gently. "If my da hasn't drained them dry by now, they may be casualties in the longer game."

She stared at him as if uncomprehending his meaning.

"He means we may have to bomb the island," Quentin said.

"But all those innocent people!"

Her horrified expression cut Ronan to the quick, but they had a job to do—stop Loman O'Connor. Permanently.

Castor squatted in front of her where she sat, his stare solemn. "We'll save who we can, but you have to be prepared, Ms. O'Malley. Not everyone is getting out of this alive. Part of our own team might not make it."

Her wide-eyed gaze snapped to Ronan. "Fintan said the only way to save my life was to bind my power, not add to it. What if we hired nonmagicial mercenaries?"

"My da would wipe out the lot of them," Ronan said flatly.

"Then what about a temporary binding of all our powers? He can't steal what we don't have."

"And have *us* be powerless against him? Are ya mad, woman?"

Surging to her feet, she nearly knocked Castor on his arse to get to Ronan. In three long-legged strides, she was in front of him, ready to do battle. And damned if she wasn't a fierce sight! Passions high and green eyes snapping, she seemed prepared to tear his head from his shoulders.

Ronan fought a grin as he held up his hands in surrender. "Now, Dove, I didn't mean it the way it sounded."

"And what way was it supposed to be soundin'? Because from my side of the conversation, it sounded like you were after being an eejit!"

There was a laughing snort behind him, and while normally Ronan would've given the snorter what for, he ignored Quentin to placate Dubheasa. "Sure, and I'll be admittin' you're right, love. I was definitely an eejit." As some of her anger dissipated, Ronan wrapped an arm around her waist and drew her flush against him. "It's after apologizing, I am."

"P-whipped," Quentin coughed into his hand.

Again, Ronan disregarded his cousin. "Please say you forgive me, Dove."

For one delicious moment, she softened against him, but in the next instant, she leaned back, her palms planted firmly against his chest. "What's this, then? Are you using your special brand of influence to sway me?"

"If that's code for the two of you making out, I'm going to need eye bleach," Quentin quipped.

With a warning glare over his shoulder, Ronan addressed him. "If you don't shut the feck up, I'll be littering the field down the lane with what's left of your remains."

"Can't. You need my ability to stop time."

"Anythin' you can do, I'm wagering your da can do better."

Castor grinned. "It does my heart good to see you boys getting along so well, but we need to return to the main issue." To Dubheasa, he said, "Your boyfriend's balls might shrivel up at the idea of angering you, but he wasn't wrong to say you're nuts if you think to go up against my brother without any magical backup."

She stiffened within the circle of Ronan's arms. "So I can't face him with magic, according to Fintan, but you're telling me I can't face him without it. What's it to be, then?"

"You don't confront him at all." Castor was deadly serious, and Ronan silently but wholeheartedly agreed with his uncle's declaration. He didn't want her anywhere near his father.

"We still haven't found Loman's lair, Dubheasa," Quentin added. "So all this is a moot point."

She spun back around in Ronan's arms and gazed up into his face, searching for what, Ronan didn't know. He hated how unsettled she appeared, and he desperately wanted to soothe her mind.

"He's right, love. There's no sense worrying until we have our sights on the island."

"Ronan—"

He placed a fingertip over her parted lips. "Please, Dove. I'm not interested in fighting with you when we don't know what our next move is." He replaced his finger with his mouth, giving her a light, lingering kiss. Lowering his voice for her ears alone, he said, "And I'll never use my influence on you. Your thoughts are your own. Always."

Before she could respond, Fintan spoke up. "Look, and Loman's prisoner count could be higher than Dubheasa has marked on that map of hers."

CHAPTER 17

"Higher?" Dubheasa's stomach dropped. How could one man be so evil? She'd met some shady characters in her life, but Loman was the worst of the worst. His relentless quest for more power put him firmly at the top of the arsehole list and made him a lethal adversary. Despite her seemingly naive response of sending nonmagical humans to fight him, she wasn't completely ignorant. Paying soldiers to do a job seemed wiser than sending novices like her siblings or herself into the mix.

"My guess is that he's been targeting witches who are easier to abduct than most." Castor cut her a sharp look. "You've never had any real ability of your own due to Goibhniu's curse, but the O'Malleys are one of the original Six families who descend from the gods and goddesses. Your family's magic makes all of you a part of the upper echelon of witches and warlocks, and while they possessed it, it made the O'Connors stronger than you could imagine."

"And Loman would've become addicted to that power," she concluded. "He'd feel weak without it and strive to compile as much as he could to confront us and get back what he lost."

Castor nodded approvingly. "Now you're catching on."

"Are we going to be forced to fight him? My brothers, sister, and me?" The churning sensation the dread created inside her stomach made her want to vomit. Her worry wasn't for herself. She simply couldn't bear to have someone she loved die.

Whether Ronan was privy to her thoughts or simply sensed her distress, he was quick to comfort her, drawing her against him and encasing her tightly within his strong arms. A weak part of her wanted him to never let her go. His answering squeeze told her he had indeed read her mind.

"It won't get that far, Dove. I'm after stopping him before he gets close enough to hurt you or anyone you love."

Tilting her head, she met Ronan's potent silver eyes, and her heart stuttered in her chest. In that instant, she realized he fell firmly into the category of those she loved. "I don't want you to fight him, either." Her voice broke, and she cleared her throat in preparation of her confession. "I love you, Ronan O'Connor. I think it may be that I always have, and I'll be mighty salty should anything happen to you at Loman's hands."

Ronan opened his mouth, but closed it just as quickly. His audible swallow caused his Adam's apple to bob between the muscled columns of his throat. And when his lips tightened, Dubheasa understood his reaction. She'd felt a similar response the first time the L-word tumbled from his lips. The knowledge of holding another's heart in your hands was humbling, and sometimes that emotion was too great in the moment to reply.

She squeezed the forearm banded across her upper chest, acknowledging his feelings. They didn't need words, the two of them. Everything he wished to say was expressed in his eyes, and his told her exactly how much he loved her in return.

Stretching on the tips of her toes, she gave him a lingering kiss. As she drew away, he halted her with a hand at the back of her neck. Bringing his other hand up, he cradled her head and gazed down at her with such longing and heat that she thought her soul would be branded throughout eternity.

"And I love you, Dove. If I live a thousand lifetimes, I'll be after holdin' that love close and looking for you first in every one hereafter."

"Aye, and you'd better." But she couldn't prevent her happy smile, effectively ruining the sass behind her reply.

His answering grin stole the air from her lungs and curled her toes.

When she could breathe normally once again, she drew away from Ronan and crossed to where Fintan was sitting. "Did Reggie reply?"

Just as he shook his head, a neat scrawl appeared on the page.

Old Désorceler Society stronghold.
Loman and a handful of mercenaries.
Reference prisoners, number unknown. My cellblock houses twenty rooms. All full.

"Fecking grand." Dubheasa dropped onto the sofa and gnawed her lower lip in consternation. "If Loman's already gained the abilities of those prisoners, we're in for a fierce fight."

Loman wants Ronan's and Sabrina's abilities.
Intends to kill both.

Dubheasa sucked in her breath so hard, she coughed long and loud, causing tears to stream from her eyes.

"Jaysus!" Ronan's complexion paled as he stared at the written words.

"Get details," Castor barked, all humor gone. The normally jovial man had become a vengeful warrior.

Quentin was already on the move. It seemed he'd barely cleared the door before he returned with Damian and Alastair in tow. Trevor was hot on their heels.

Silently, the Aether read the message Reggie had sent. Any

father would be out of their fecking mind at this point, and Damian Dethridge was likely no different, yet his expression remained guarded, giving nothing away. But Dubheasa sensed his turmoil underneath the stoic façade. Loman O'Connor had signed his own death warrant by stating his desire to kill Damian's daughter. In no scenario that Dubheasa could think of would the man be kept alive to carry out his dastardly plans.

"I need to return to my family." Damian finally tore his gaze away from the book. "Blane, you'll do what you do best and obliterate that bastard's soul when you see him, yes?"

"Consider it done."

With a short nod to acknowledge Trevor's comment, Damian then faced Ronan. "You're to stay away from my daughter."

Hurt flashed in Ronan's eyes before he purposely blanked his expression. "Aye, if that's what ya wish."

"It's not what I wish, my friend. It's what's necessary." Strain tightened the skin around the Aether's dark, almond-shaped eyes, and his lips thinned in a grimace.

"I don't understand what—ah." With a shake of his head, Ronan gave him a self-deprecating smile. "Your aim is to separate the targets and make it harder for Dear Ol' Da to get us both in one place. You think he'll come for my power first."

"Yes."

"Then you should be refortifying your wards to exclude me." There was a sorrow in Ronan's words, as if the last of his allies were lost to him.

Dubheasa's heart hurt for him. Standing, she entwined her fingers in his. He didn't look her way, but his hand tightened over hers.

"I'm not ready to do that quite yet, Ronan, but you'll be alerted if the need arises. I have complete faith you'll win this round." Oddly, Damian appeared more tired than frightened. "I'll wish you luck."

With that, the Aether was gone.

As many times as she'd witnessed a teleport in recent months, Dubheasa found it difficult to wrap her mind around an immediate disappearance.

"Would the stolen abilities revert back to the original witch if Loman's power source was shut down?" she asked.

"No. He'd only lose the means to amp up more than he already was," Trevor replied. "His new abilities wouldn't necessarily go away."

"A spell would revert those abilities if someone present was to cast it," Alastair said, giving her a thoughtful look. "What do you have in mind, child?"

"The fake wedding we discussed this morning. If it was made known Sabrina would be there as our flower girl, Loman might risk an attack. He'd have to know he couldn't reach her any other way, yeah?"

"Probably."

"I propose we stage a rescue while he's distracted."

Alastair nodded slowly. "It's worth a shot."

Castor sent him a measuring look. "Should we talk to Isis about pulling the Six from both sides of the veil, Al? Like in the battle with the Enchantress?"

"Yes. I believe we should." Alastair straightened his cuffs and strode from the room to presumably contact the Goddess.

Dubheasa hated that she constantly felt like the uneducated outsider of their group. "What does that mean?"

Ronan sat and drew her down beside him. "Two hundred years or more ago, Isolde de Thorne, Damian's mother, was the Aether. Only she was possessed by a mysterious evil destined to consume all magic and drive her mad in the process. Isis gathered the most fierce from Earth and the Otherworld to battle the woman, knowin' they had to stop her."

Enthralled by his story, Dubheasa remained silent, eagerly anticipating what came next.

"Sure, and some died, their souls destroyed by the Darkness, but stop her, the Six finally did. Isolde couldn't be killed, but she could be entombed in a magic coffin. And that's exactly what Isis achieved with the help of those families from both sides of the veil."

"Who are the Six families?"

"The Thornes, Dethridges, Champeaus, O'Malleys, Carlyles, and the Drakes," Castor answered.

She frowned. "Not the O'Connors?"

Ronan sighed. "No, love. My family are a right bunch of thieving bastards, they are. And they gained their magic through stealing it or marrying into it."

His response didn't surprise her. "So is the Enchantress still entombed two hundred years later, then?" What must it be like to lie in a tomb year in and year out, never able to escape and slowly being driven mad?

"Ach, no. She found a way out by possessing Mackenzie Thorne. By then, Damian had taken on the mantle of Aether. And his evil mother went after his young daughter."

Castor's smile was hard as he finished Ronan's story. "Damian fried her ass. When it comes to his daughter, he doesn't play around."

"Yeah, and I heard the story of Moira just last week," Dubheasa replied. "How he burned her alive for attempting to hurt Sabrina."

"He's ruthless when crossed, and rightfully so."

"Heavy is the Aether's crown, to be sure," Ronan added. "I wouldn't want to be makin' the decisions he has to."

"What type of decisions is he after making?" she asked.

Castor was quick to answer. "Life. Death. Everything in between."

"Damian has that kind of power?"

"Aye," Ronan replied.

Dubheasa found it hard to fathom. Life and death were for

the gods and goddesses to decide, not mortals. Although the Aether was the highest order of mortal and harder to kill than other magical beings, he could still die and he retained human emotions. The weight of his choices had to be heavy indeed.

"And it's why neither the Authority nor the Goddess stepped in to stop him from barbecuing Moira. They understood it was up to him to exact retribution and remove a dangerous player from the game." With a gesture toward Ronan, Castor continued, "To protect his daughter, he'd do anything, and they know it. Case in point, transferring a Guardian's power to an O'Connor."

"Yeah, and what better way to balance mine than with an O'Malley Guardian?" Ronan grinned at her.

"It's a grand way to end a centuries-old feud," she agreed. "But speaking of Sabrina, as the Oracle, wouldn't it be possible for her to tell us the outcome of our plan?"

Castor's visage became thoughtful, but then he seemed ready to reject the suggestion.

Quentin cast him a sharp look. "With someone as dangerous as Loman, this may be the time to see what the human Magic 8 Ball has to say."

CHAPTER 18

When Damian's phone dinged, he could've cheerfully thrown it into the nearest river. Nate's feeding time was one of his small pleasures. To see his wife's expression, soft and loving—even if it wasn't directed at him but at their son—reminded Damian of better times.

His phone dinged again, causing him to glare at the text on the screen.

WE NEED TO TALK.

Castor wouldn't be denied.

From his place beside Vivian on their bed, he grimaced and turned the ringer to the off position. Pausing long enough to caress his son's downy head, he met Viv's gaze and smiled half-heartedly. "Sorry, my love. I've got to answer this."

She stopped him from leaving with a hand on his arm. "How dangerous is it for you to go after Loman O'Connor, Damian?"

"For me? Not at all. For the others… well, that's quite another story."

"Can you see the future, or is your ability still on the blink?"

"The Authority is holding it hostage until I agree to their terms," he replied grimly. "I'm of the mind to tell them to go bugger themselves."

"What are the consequences of doing that?"

He met her worried ice-blue eyes and smiled. "Few. They need me, or so they are leading me to believe."

"And when they don't need you anymore?"

"Why the twenty questions, Viv? I'll see you, Nate, and Sabrina are cared for should anything happen to me."

Her irritation was obvious in the speed with which she removed her hand from his person. "I'm not a gold digger, Damian, and I resent when you make me feel like I am."

"That was never my intent." No, he was well aware that she was only with him for the children's sake. Although his wealth far exceeded hers, Vivian came from old money and probably couldn't blow through her entire inheritance in her lifetime, should she choose to. Upon her parents' early demise, the bulk of the Stephens' assets were transferred to Vivian and her three sisters—Josie, Soleil, and Taryn—with a portion held in trust for future generations.

"Regardless of what you believe, I don't want anything to happen to you." Her glacial tone belied her words, but with Vivian, Damian could rarely tell what truly went on in her mind.

Prior to their separation, she had appealed to the Goddess to sever their psychic link. She'd done it so she could hide her escape plan from him. And one day when he left the estate to assist a friend, she'd taken Sabrina and run. Damian couldn't bear to hear what she truly thought of him, and so their previous connection had never been restored. Not the one of the heart and certainly not their mental link.

He had been unable to bridge the ever-widening gap between them, and perhaps a huge part of him didn't care to. If he convinced himself she was nothing more than the mother of his children, he would never again be devastated by her defection.

Weary down to his soul, he turned away and climbed from the bed. "My apologies, my dear. What else would you like to know?"

Her full mouth tightened into a thin line. "Nothing."

"Very well."

As he started to leave, she called his name. Had he imagined the catch in her voice?

He paused and turned.

Her pained expression arrested his heart.

"I do care, Damian. Maybe not in the way you believe I should, but I do."

"I'm just thrilled you care at all, Viv. There was a time it seemed like you didn't." He didn't mean to sound as gruff as he did, but his disaster of a marriage hurt like hell. Vivian was the only woman he'd ever thought to marry. The only one he'd ever wanted to share a piece of himself with, but it had all turned to shit after Sabrina was born, and they couldn't seem to find their way back to each other.

She lifted her chin. "You know why I feared you."

"Yes. You believed another over me, the man you professed to love. But I gave you no reason back then, nor now, to fear me, Viv. Remember that, won't you?"

"Your very existence is reason to fear you, Damian. The choices you've had to make, the people you've had to eliminate," she argued.

After all these years, her words shouldn't have the power to cut so deeply, and yet they did. "So in your eyes, I'm still a monster?"

"I didn't say that."

"You didn't have to," he said dully. His gaze dropped to Nate, nursing at her breast. "We've done two things right. I suppose that has to be enough. Good night."

Not waiting to hear any more of her excuses or reasons why she couldn't love him, Damian strode from the room and headed straight for his study. Once there, he poured himself a tall drink and took a hearty sip. The burn of the alcohol was in no way satisfying, so he guzzled the rest and prayed something would numb his mind and heart.

He slammed the tumbler on the sideboard table and reached for the crystal decanter that held his favorite scotch. Twisting the stopper from the bottle, he experienced a wave of concern not his own, and he carefully set the bottle down before recapping it.

"Hello, Beastie."

"Hello, Papa."

Hiding something behind her, she inched into the room.

He had to forcefully hide his amusement at her stealthy side shuffle. "What do you have there, my love?"

"Don't be mad, okay?"

"I can't promise anything. Why don't you tell me what I shouldn't be angry about, and we can go from there?"

"Willie ate your slipper."

"Willie? Oh, Hellhound number one. Right." Pursing his lips to avoid laughing, he nodded sagely. "And how did Wee Wicked Willie get my slipper, Beastie?"

"She's really a good dog, Papa." Sabrina infused earnestness into her voice. "She just likes your stuff so much, and she can't help herself."

"Mine? Why not yours or your mother's?"

"I don't know."

"That's a first," he replied dryly. "The Aether's Oracle daughter, who knows literally everything, doesn't know how her wretched puppy keeps getting into her father's closet. I'm stunned."

Eyes wide, Sabrina shrugged. "It's a mystery."

Giving into laughter, he knelt and hugged her. "Here's

something you may not know. You, my darling girl, have been the greatest gift a father could hope for. There isn't a day that goes by I don't thank my lucky stars you decided to be born to us."

Beaming, she sandwiched his face with her palms. "Really, Papa?"

"Really."

"And you're not mad that Wee Wicked Willie ate your slippers?"

"Slippers? I thought it was one."

"It might have been two."

"Ah." He grinned. "I'm not mad, but how about you keep the hellhounds out of my wardrobe from here on out?"

"I can't make any promises." She frowned down at the mutilated slipper. "They *do* like to do naughty things."

"Can I tell you a secret?"

Her eyes lit with excitement. His daughter loved nothing more than to be in the know.

With a soft chuckle, he kissed her button nose. "All puppies like to do naughty things. Just like their owner. That's *you*, in case you were wondering."

"I'm not naughty!"

Squinting one eye, he tilted his head and crinkled his nose. "Really?"

With a giggle, she kissed his chin. "Okay, maybe a little naughty. But you love me anyway, Papa."

"Yes, I do." He released her and rose to his feet. "Now run along and restore all my abused footwear to their original state—or no pancakes for dinner."

Her happy smile as she skipped from the room was his reward for not scolding her.

The vibration of his phone chased away the last of his good humor. Checking the caller ID, he sighed and swiped to answer.

"Dethridge."

"It's unlike you to not reply to a message. Everything okay?" Castor asked, concern heavy in his voice.

"Right as rain," Damian lied. "What's the problem?"

"Ronan, Alastair, and I would like to run something by you."

He checked his watch and silently debated the merits of allowing Ronan so close to Sabrina when Loman intended to target them both. "How soon can you be here?"

"Two minutes."

"See you then." As Damian stared out at the setting sun on the horizon, he sighed. Would there ever be a time of peace in the witch community? Only his daughter could say, but he couldn't quite bring himself to ask her.

TO REMAIN ALERT TO EXTERNAL DANGERS, RONAN KEPT HIS attention locked on the landscape beyond the Aether's darkening garden. He also kept his ear tuned to the conversation between the three friends gathered in the sitting area behind him.

Damian Dethridge, Alastair Thorne, and Alexander Castor—a perfect trifecta. Three crafty men with unique powers, all destined to walk the line dividing good and evil for the ones they loved. Rumor had it, they'd crossed that line plenty of times in recent years. It made one raise a brow at the frequency with which it happened, but Ronan had been privy to enough of their secrets to understand the why of it.

Case in point, Good Ol' Uncle Alex had the brilliant idea to question the baby Aether about the future outcome of their plan to trap and destroy Loman. But based on their heated conversation, Damian was adamantly opposed to details being revealed for *any* reason.

"It would limit the loss of life," Alastair argued, backing

Castor's request. "People we all care about are putting themselves at risk, Dethridge. It's only natural to want assurances."

"We don't know what kind of repercussions it might have, Al," Damian replied with what sounded like fatigue heavy in his voice. "We've been over this numerous times."

Satisfied there was no immediate threat outside, Ronan watched the three friends in the reflection of the glass.

"Quentin and I can find a way to summon our future selves, but it would only give us one or two possible outcomes at most." Castor shrugged. "Option three would be to secure the Traveler's sphere Athena gifted to Francesca."

"My understanding is that it was only meant for Quentin's daughter when she came of age," Damian warned. "It's not wise for either of you to use what belongs to another."

"Could you or I use it?" Ronan asked Damian as he joined the others. "As individuals with uniquely universal abilities, would either of us have the power to turn it on?"

Damian shook his head. "Me, perhaps. You? It's doubtful. You would need to possess the knowledge to not only activate it, but to control it as well. If one isn't careful, they could get lost in time with no way to return."

"That would suck, sure." Sitting on the sofa, he rested his head along the back and stared at the ornate ceiling of the Dethridge study. "But we can't go into this blind, Damian. My da is always steps ahead of us on a good day, and I don't fancy anyone else's blood on my conscience."

"It's quite possible the Fates designed it so some would perish."

"Do you know that for certain?" Ronan asked him. "You're the Aether and a law unto your own self, man. There isn't another who can take your place or offer up your distinctive perspective. The Fates, and by extension the Authority, would be fecking eejits if they punished you for doing what is necessary."

The Aether's reaction was wry amusement. "You're young by comparison to the rest of us, O'Connor, so you don't know. But my advice to you would be to not throw out statements of that nature. Tempting any of the Fates will cause instant Karma. They don't like to have their choices questioned."

Unease skidded along Ronan's spine, and he suppressed the urge to shiver. Again with ghosts walking over his grave!

Damian frowned as their gazes locked. "Premonitions?"

"Why do you ask?"

"Your visceral reaction to my comment."

Ronan shrugged. "Look, and I don't know. The closer it comes to taking action, the edgier I become. If I had my way, we'd be done with this right now."

"Trust your instincts, my friend. They may save your life one day," Damian warned.

"What's it going to be, Dethridge? Should I check with Mackenzie to see if she's had any visions?" Alastair asked.

"No need. We'll consult the Oracle."

CHAPTER 19

As Damian left to retrieve Sabrina, Ronan studied Alastair Thorne. The flaxen-haired warlock was always impeccably dressed and seemingly in complete control. Although the man appeared cool and collected, Ronan sensed a whirlpool of emotions underneath the calm surface.

"Are you worried, then?" he asked quietly.

Sapphire-blue eyes rose from where they contemplated the scotch in the tumbler he held to meet Ronan's. What Alastair saw when he looked at him, Ronan couldn't discern. Was it the image of Loman? Or was he inclined to view Ronan as he did Castor? As a friend.

"I am." Raising his glass, Alastair sipped his drink, then shut his lids as he seemed to savor the flavor. Finally, he returned to the present. "Sorry. I refuse to taint the enjoyment of a hundred-year-old scotch with unpleasantness."

Castor snorted and sat beside Ronan. "We all know you love a good scotch. Tell us what you're thinking, Al."

"When I popped off to speak with Isis, she didn't feel it was necessary to invoke the Six families from either side of the veil, but she wanted to keep the option open." He sighed tiredly.

"That tells me she's uncertain of the outcome. The only time the Goddess isn't forthcoming is when she can't see the future. It's rare, but the Fates can and do block the gods and goddesses for reasons of their own."

"Why do you believe they've blocked her?" Ronan sat forward and rested his elbows on his knees.

"Her investment in all of us, her descendants, would be my guess. She's been known to protect us, thus incurring the wrath of the other deities." Alastair set his glass down, straightened his tie, and avoided looking toward Castor. "It's possible one of those close to us could perish as a result of Loman's mischief."

Drink halted halfway to his mouth, Castor swore. "You think it's Quentin, don't you?"

"I don't know, Alex, and I'm not going to speculate. It's why we're here to ask Sabrina."

"What did Isis say to you?" he demanded, and the hard edge in Castor's tone left no doubt he expected the truth.

"She said the Fates have allowed us to alter the course of things once too often. Death is meant to follow a timeline. To be permanent and not subject to a mortal's will," Alastair replied grimly.

"Sure, and that could mean anything," Ronan reasoned. "They might've been referring to my da and the lives he's taken."

"True."

"But something feels off to you?"

"It does."

Another wave of unease crashed over Ronan. For too many years to count, he'd had to survive by his instincts, and right now, they were screaming at him. He suspected Alastair and Castor had lived much the same way. If they were feeling trepidation, like him, then all was not as it should be.

"Let's just hope Sabrina has insight for us," Alastair said with an attempt at a smile. It never reached his eyes.

They drank in companionable silence until Damian returned with his daughter in tow.

Ronan stood with the expectation that she'd run to him for a hug, but her expression was downcast as she avoided him. His heart began to hammer painfully in his chest. Nothing deterred Sabrina Dethridge.

"No hug for me, then, wee wicked beastie?" he asked gently, praying to Anu he'd misread the situation.

She shook her head and used the back of her hand to wipe her eyes.

The sight of her distress caused Ronan's stomach to knot, and he sent Damian a questioning look.

The Aether appeared as confused as Ronan felt.

Gathering his courage, he approached her, dropped to one knee, and tilted her chin up. "Whatever you're worried about, it can't be so bad, yeah?"

She brushed the tip of her bedazzled pink running shoe back and forth across the carpet, disrupting the direction of the pile with each sweep of her foot.

"You can talk to me, wee wild beastie. I'll not get upset, and I'll still be your friend."

Lifting her head, she stared at him. "I'm not allowed to tell. Papa says."

Ronan glanced up to see Damian's quicksilver frown.

"I brought you here to reveal what you know, my love. It's okay to tell Ronan whatever it is."

"No!" Sabrina jerked her hand from her father's. "You told me it's bad to tell."

The shock on the Aether's face was priceless, and Ronan intended to bust his bollocks at a later date—when the situation wasn't so fecking dire.

With remarkable speed, Damian recovered. Kneeling in front of her, he unfolded her crossed arms and held her hands within his. The picture of a comforting father. "You're correct,

Beastie. In the past, I've told you to refrain from blurting out things that might alter another's future timeline. However, I'm asking you now to please reveal what you know."

"No!"

One second she was there, and the next, she was gone. Only the fading pink light was any indication she'd been present at all.

"What the hell was that all about?" Castor asked from behind them.

Ronan and Damian rose as one.

"She's troubled by what she's seen," Alastair said, joining their small group. "It doesn't take an empath to sense her turmoil."

And Ronan couldn't help but feel that turmoil was directly related to him. "What do we do now?"

"We seek her out and try again," Damian replied grimly. "It's obvious she's had a vision and is bothered by what she knows."

"I don't want to traumatize the girl."

"She's the Oracle, and with that title comes a responsibility to the witch community. Sabrina cannot throw a temper tantrum whenever it suits her to do so. If called upon, she needs to understand what is required of her."

Alastair shook his head. "She's a child, Dethridge. You can't expect her to be fine with everything she sees. Especially if it has to do with someone she cares about."

"I know exactly how difficult it is, Thorne," Damian stated coldly. So coldly, in fact, that the air contracted with his anger and a thin layer of frost covered the window panes. "Have you forgotten I was made the Aether at only eight years old? Did the deities show *me* mercy when I was called upon to do my duty? The removal of another's magic is excruciating for them and not a joy to be a part of."

"He didn't mean anything by it, Damian," Castor said, attempting to placate him. "And we get that you're worried about her. But you need to pull back your anger before you encase the house in ice."

As if the central heating had kicked on, a warm breeze flooded the room, removing the last traces of the bitter cold. "My apologies, gentlemen. If you'll excuse me, I need to find my daughter."

"We'll help you look," Ronan offered.

After a sharp nod, Damian strode from the room.

"I'll take the kitchens," Alastair said.

"All you ever think about is your bottomless pit of a stomach, Al," Castor complained.

Alastair grinned. "You're just irritated you didn't think to call it first."

For the first time in what felt like hours, Ronan laughed. "He has you there, Uncle. I imagine Damian has gone to check the wee beastie's room, but I think I know where she went, all the same. If there's not any chocolate gelato left for me when I get back, I'll be knowin' the why of it," he warned them.

RONAN FOUND SABRINA HIDING IN BAZ'S BARN WITH A BLACKand-tan Rottweiler puppy curled in her lap.

"Are you angry with me, then, love?"

She shook her head and swiped a tear from her cheek.

"Do you want to talk about what has ya so upset?"

Again, she moved her head in a negative fashion.

"And it's something you can't be telling your da?"

Sabrina gave a half-hearted shrug.

Crouching down, Ronan scratched the sleeping pup behind the ear. "I think I recognize this one, I do."

"It's the one you picked out for Dubheasa."

"I picked, or the one you picked for me?"

A fleeting smile flashed across her face, but she sobered again just as quickly. "I don't want to tell you."

"You think I'll be upset by what you reveal, yeah?"

She nodded.

His stomach dropped. Her prediction had to be dire, to be sure. "And there's no chance you could be wrong?"

"No," she whispered.

Ronan sat beside her. "Do ya want to know what I think, wee wild beastie?"

Lifting her head, she stared up at him. The agony of indecision was written on her dirty, tear-streaked face. "What?"

"I think you don't have to tell me anything that brings tears to your grand eyes. But if ya think there might be something that helps others, it's okay to let your da in on the secret." Ronan gently bumped her shoulder with his. "He's been around a lot longer than the two of us, and he might have a few tricks up his sleeve. I'm after betting he can help."

"But it always ends bad, Ronan." With a choked sob, she set the puppy aside. "I d-don't want it t-to end b-bad," she croaked and flung herself into his arms.

Holding her close, he rested his cheek on the top of her head and rubbed her back as she continued to cry. "It's gonna be alright, love. Nothing is worth such grief." When she sobbed harder, Ronan's emotion got the better of him, and tears stung his eyes. Her pain gutted him. "Hush now, darlin' girl."

A sixth sense told him Damian was close, and Ronan visually searched the darkened corners of the barn for his friend. Chances were, if Sabrina was in distress, the Aether wouldn't be far. Movement in the shadows to his left caught Ronan's attention an instant before Damian stepped into the dimly lit room.

"Has she told you?" her father asked quietly.

"Nah. It breaks her puir heart to say. I'll not push for details."

Damian squatted beside them and placed a hand on the crown of his daughter's head. "If you don't mind, I'd like to sit with her for a while."

"And I'd be going, but she's clinging to me like an ivy, she is." Ronan put his mouth by her ear and, in a conversational tone, said, "There are those who aren't aware of it, but ivy is a tough, tenacious plant, to be sure. It grows wild, climbing trellises and trees alike. Not so different from a wee beastie I'm acquainted with."

Her head came up, and curiosity lit her red-rimmed eyes. "Poison ivy?"

"Well, sure, if you want to be aggravatin' others, you could be the poisoned variety, but I'm guessing you want to be the pretty English ivy whose flowers provide nectar for bees and that produces berries for birds come winter, yeah?"

She grinned, and his heart ceased to ache on her behalf. Like English ivy, she was resilient.

"Tell your da what ya know, wee wild beastie. Trust him to help you."

"I love you, Ronan."

"Sure, and why wouldn't ya?" he asked, infusing his tone with surprise that she might not.

With a giggle, she released him and reached for her father.

Over her head, Damian's grateful gaze met his. "Thank you," he mouthed.

With a half smile, Ronan left. Part of him was tempted to eavesdrop, but they'd sense his presence, and it was a given that those who listened at keyholes never heard any good about themselves. The Aether would tell him what he found out in good time, and while he waited, Ronan intended to enjoy the chocolate gelato the Dethridges kept on hand.

CHAPTER 20

"Would you like to tell me what that was all about, Beastie?" Damian gently asked his daughter.

As she drew back, she sniffled, and the tragic expression she turned his way damned near broke his heart. When she remained quiet, he made an educated guess, based on her behavior.

"It's about Ronan, isn't it?"

Tears welled in her eyes, making them large pools of distress.

Damian brushed the wild black curls away from her beloved face. "Does he die in your vision?"

Her lower lip trembled before she pressed her mouth into a firm line.

"I would like for you to try something for me. Are you ready?" When she nodded gamely, he smiled his approval. "Excellent. Now, I want you to go to the point where Ronan dies in your vision, and—"

The small distressed sound she made tore at his conscience.

"It's all right, Beastie. I'm going to teach you how to set aside the pain and explore other possibilities."

"But you already taught me that, Papa."

"Well, yes, but not the part that mattered." He kissed her forehead. "I suspect you've only looked at a handful of options before what you saw became too much for you to continue. Am I correct?"

She nodded.

"Right. So I'm going to link with you, and we'll explore the future together."

"I don't want him or Uncle Alex to die," she cried.

Inhaling sharply, he got his own worry under control and tried again. "Sabrina, I want you to listen very carefully and try to understand. We may not want to see the truth, and it may hurt our hearts, but our friends need our help. What we are requires us to provide that assistance when we can."

"Okay, Papa."

"Good. There is a spell in our grimoire that will allow you to numb your feelings for a short time. Then, you and I can explore all the varied scenarios to see which option is best for everyone without it upsetting you. Would you like to use that spell?"

"Y-yes." Her lip trembled, and her eyes brimmed with tears again.

"Then let's return this sweet girl to her mother and go see what we can discover."

"We have to take this one home too, Papa."

"No way in hel—uh, no. We are *not* taking another dog home. The hellhounds we have are quite enough, thank you."

"But it's for Dubheasa."

"I don't care if it's for Isis herself. The puppy stays here until we are ready to hand it over. Got it?"

With both hands, she gripped his and tugged. "Please, Papa? It will make me not sad anymore."

"Emotional blackmail is beneath you, my love." He picked

up the pup and set it in Sabrina's arms. "Now, please return the dog to where you found her."

Feet dragging with every step, as if she were going to her execution, his daughter walked to a whelping box in the corner. A large female Rottweiler lifted her head, and across the distance, her concerned eyes met his.

"We're sorry to disturb your rest, lovely lady," he murmured as he joined Sabrina by the box. Only the one puppy remained from a litter of five. "Who did Baz foist the other two little gremlins off on?"

"The Thornes," the man in question said from behind them. "Mack convinced two of her cousins they each needed a guard dog."

"Did we get the worst of the lot?"

Baz laughed and shook his head. "No, that honor went to Alastair's son, Nash."

Damian grinned. "Excellent."

"You have a bloody mean streak, Dethridge." Baz crouched beside his beloved Rottie and rubbed her chest. If the blissful expression on the dog's face was an accurate indicator, she adored the attention.

"We must be going," Damian said. "Give our love to Mack and your beautiful baby girl."

"Bye, Baz!" Sabrina waved over Damian's shoulder as he lifted her.

Visualizing his private ceremony room, he teleported. When they arrived, Damian set her in the center of the pentagram etched in the wood floor. "Let's get to work, Beastie. We have interlopers eating us out of house and home."

He thumbed through the grimoire until he found the spell he was searching for. One penned in blood by the first Aether at the dawn of magic.

"Build a ring of protection like I showed you."

After depositing salt along the outer rim of the pentagram,

Sabrina placed white pillar candles on all five points. A simple touch of her finger lit the wicks.

With a proud-as-punch smile, Damian joined her at the center of the circle, book in hand. "Well done, my love." He knelt, making himself level with her, and turned the grimoire to face her. "Can you read this for me?"

In a soft, clear voice, she repeated the spell on the time-worn page.

> "Goddess, hear my plea,
> Assist me in this time of need,
> Allow the sight to come to me
> Without pain for the vision I see."

The atmosphere in the room grew thick, and Damian shut the tome in his hand, setting it on the topmost point of the star. Shifting, he sat cross-legged and drew Sabrina down to the floor so she could copy his position, then he linked hands with her.

"Allow the visions to come, but pay special attention to my voice throughout the process. I'm going to help you sift through them until we find the best-case scenario for Ronan and Castor, okay?"

"Yes, Papa."

The room grew dark as their consciousnesses merged. Only the candles provided any illumination. As the future events began to roll through Sabrina's mind, Damian was privy to every one, and he gained a better understanding of why she was upset and why she refused to tell what she'd witnessed.

This was the part of his gift he hated the most. The knowing. To anyone else, the idea of seeing the future unfold would be appealing—until they actually had to live with what they had learned without altering the course of history as it was to play out.

Exactly four hours after they started the process, Damian and Sabrina closed the circle and had a deep discussion about what needed to be done to limit the damage.

ALEXANDER CASTOR GLANCED UP FROM WHERE HE WAS SPRAWLED on the sofa in the Dethridge study to see a grim-faced Damian enter the room.

"Where are the others?" his friend asked.

"I sent them home and told them one of us would contact them as soon as you had something concrete." Alex shifted to a sitting position and set the book he'd been reading on the coffee table.

With an absent nod, Damian read the cover of the hardback. "Military strategies, Alex?"

"It can't hurt."

"Indeed."

Castor's stomach clenched at the lack of emotion in his friend's voice. Damian tended to become stoic and difficult to read when he was worried. "It's dire, then?"

"It isn't great. Sabrina and I explored every potential outcome."

"How many were there?"

"I lost count. But we feel we've come up with one to cause the least casualties."

Watching Damian carefully, Alex asked, "How many are we to lose?"

"Just one."

"Is the resetting of time an option?"

"No."

"Fuck." He scrubbed his hands up and down his face, knowing he wasn't going to like the answer to his next question. "Who?"

"I cannot tell you that, Alex, as you well know." Damian's grave tone grated.

Stomach like a lead weight, Castor stood and crossed to the sideboard to pour two drinks. After handing one to Damian, he took a fortifying gulp of his scotch. "I'm going to insist you tell me it's not my son, or I'm cutting him out of this altogether."

Complete honesty shone in Damian's eyes as he said, "It's not Quentin."

The relief Alex felt was profound, and his knees threatened to buckle. "Okay." Hands shaking, he set his glass on the table, next to the book, and sat down. "Okay."

Another thought occurred to him, and he looked up sharply. "Not you."

The Aether opened his mouth to reply, paused, and shook his head with a pained grimace. "Alex."

"Fuck this. Just tell me."

"You know I can't." Damian downed his drink in one swallow. "Please stop asking."

"What about the fucking Authority? Why can't they do their goddamned job and eliminate Loman?"

"We are their tools, my friend. We always have been, and we always will be."

"Not you."

"Especially me, and *especially* now."

Alex tried to get a bead on Damian's thoughts, but he'd shut down. The Aether was in full command, with a purposeful blank expression designed to give nothing away. So Alex vented his frustration. "I fucking hate this BS."

"I know." Damian released the tight control he held on himself enough to plop down in the closest armchair and drop his head to rest on the seat back. "I do, too."

"Is Sabrina all right?"

"She is. I taught her a spell to remove all emotion from her vision so she could clearly divine what was meant to happen without being influenced by her feelings."

"But you didn't do that for yourself, did you?" Alex guessed.

"No. I've witnessed a lot in the two-plus centuries I've been alive. I'm numb to most of what I see, but for those closest to me, I feel it would be a disservice to desensitize myself."

"I'm sorry."

Damian glanced up and met Castor's concerned gaze. "Don't be. I form relationships because I want to experience what normal mortals do. The cycle of life is unrelenting."

"We've never talked about this type of thing before."

"No." A smile tugged at Damian's mouth. "I'm getting maudlin in my old age."

Alex snorted. "Old is relative for you, isn't it? You aren't even middle-aged for an Aether."

"True." Damian sighed. "I suppose I should lay out the plan for you to tell the others in the morning. But first, text them and tell them to enjoy a night off. Nothing more needs to be done or decided tonight."

CHAPTER 21

Those who stuck around to await the outcome of the Aether's vision quest had decided to adjourn and relax for a bit at Lucky O'Malley's Pub at Ronan's suggestion. The tension from a day of planning had reached an all-time high, and nothing more was getting done.

Somewhere around Ronan's third pint, his phone buzzed with an incoming text from Castor.

After reading it, he showed the others gathered around the table. "Sure, and it appears we have the rest of the night off. Everyone is free to make merry until tomorrow mornin', when we'll be forced to save the day."

"I'm pretty sure that's what we were all doing anyway," Brenna said dryly as she tapped her glass with Eoin's.

"Yep, and Castor decided a group text was the way to go." Trevor sputtered a laugh as Draven replied with a middle-finger emoji. "I guess I don't have to tell you how much Draven hates group texts."

"Almost as much as the scut hates mornings," Fintan replied before taking a long pull of his pint to finish it off. "Can't say as I blame him."

Sleep had always been scarce for Ronan, and being neither a morning person nor a night owl, he had no particular opinion either way. His thoughts turned to other pleasurable activities associated with a mattress, and his attention was drawn to the woman he desired to be active with.

Across the pub, Dubheasa loaded a tray to serve up the locals. Ronan's first instinct was to help her by relieving her of the weight and passing out the drinks himself, but he held back. If she wanted his assistance, she'd let him know in no uncertain terms.

"I'm going to do you a solid, O'Connor," Trevor said as he rose to his feet. "I'm going to curtail my own fun for the evening and take Dubheasa's shift. Go steal your woman away and enjoy yourselves while you can."

Surprised by the kind gesture, Ronan stood and shook his hand. "You have my thanks, Blane."

"Yeah, get out of here before I change my mind."

Not needing to be told twice, Ronan crossed to Dubheasa and removed the empty tray from her grasp. After handing it off to Trevor, he pulled her against him and kissed her like he'd been dying to all night. As the passion clouded his brain and swiftly consumed other parts of his anatomy, he drew back and inhaled deep lungsful of air.

When passing out from lack of oxygen was no longer a concern, he tangled his hands in her hair and dove back in. A few of the drunker patrons catcalled and added their encouragement, but Ronan happily ignored them to taste his fill.

Dubheasa was the first to pull away, and her happy, flushed face made him feel ten feet tall.

"Your American is willin' to assume your shift for the night, Dove. Are ya interested in having dinner with me, then?"

"Dinner? After all that snogging?" The disbelief in Bridget's tone was laughable. "Sure, and I'm after thinking you'll be doing more than having a bite to eat."

Ruairí snorted and passed a fresh-drawn Guinness across the bar to Bridget. "More like a bite of each other. Let me know if you're after takin' a page from their book, *mo ghrá*, yeah? I'll snog ya proper and make me cousin look like an amateur."

Bridget grinned as he leered. "You're a proper eejit, Ruairí O'Connor, but I love ya just the same."

The dopey, lovesick look he gave her in return was a joy to witness.

"They're feckin' adorable," Dubheasa said loudly, earning a scowl from her sister and a wink from Ruairí.

"Get out of me pub." Bridget shooed them toward the door. "You're useless as tits on a bull when ya only have eyes for your man."

After bussing her sister's cheek, Dubheasa grabbed Ronan's hand and led him through the alley, pausing along the way to kiss him again and again. By the time they entered the Black Cat, they were laughing like small children and running for the stairs.

Maybe it was the freedom to be themselves without pretense. Or perhaps it was the lurking threat, but there was a wild playfulness to their antics. An unspoken agreement to lock the world outside and deal with their problems tomorrow. And as they approached Ronan's room, he stopped her with a hand on her arm and tilted her chin to meet his steady gaze.

"Hi. I'm Ronan Fucking O'Connor, and I'm mad about you, I am," he said as if being introduced to her for the first time.

She grinned, immediately understanding his intent to start fresh and leave all their previous woes behind them. "It's my pleasure to be meeting ya, Ronan Fucking O'Connor. Are you interested in sharing a drink with me, then?"

"Here, and I thought you'd never ask." With a chuckle and lightness in his heart, he opened the door and gestured for her to precede him.

Once inside, he strode to the cupboard, removed a bottle of

Armand de Brignac Ace of Spades Rose, and then held it up. "I've been saving this. For you. For us."

"For the day I would forgive you?" she asked softly, gentle understanding in her eyes.

"Do you? Completely?"

For the one long, heart-pounding moment she didn't reply, all of Ronan's fears came to the forefront, paralyzing him and numbing his mind. Only when she nodded and shot him a come-hither look did he breathe normally again.

"It took ya a feckin' lifetime to decide," he grumbled good-naturedly.

DUBHEASA LAUGHED AT RONAN'S LONG-SUFFERING EXPRESSION.

With capable hands, he uncorked the bottle and poured them both a glass. Just before giving her the champagne flute, he frowned and glanced around.

"What's wrong?" She didn't sense any disturbance around them, but she didn't have his capabilities.

"There's no romance to this place. It's a bit cold if I'm to be honest."

Her brows shot up, and she almost warned him to never speak that way in front of Bridget, but he was smart and had a healthy sense of self-preservation.

After passing off both drinks, he crossed to the bed, shooting a cursory look at the walls and ceiling. With an absent nod, he closed his eyes and waved his hands in a wide arch. Sheer white, billowy curtains appeared, adorning the corners of the four-poster bed. Pale, cream-colored pillar candles of every size sat haphazardly atop every available surface. The glow they cast caused the shadows to dance in the farthest reaches of the room.

With a nod of satisfaction, he returned to Dubheasa and, with a shite-eating grin, took one of the flutes from her hand.

"Sure, and I worry we'll need the fire brigade should we knock one of those grand candles into the curtains," she said, tongue in cheek.

The happy expression dropped from his face and was replaced with a worried frown.

Laughing, she tapped his glass with hers. "Relax, Ronan. It's after teasing you, I am."

"Look, and I'll not lie. Your feckin' sister scares the bejeezus out of me."

"You're not the first person to tell me that."

Dubheasa sipped her drink, and her eyes widened in delighted surprise. "This is delicious!"

The Armand de Brignac Rosé was a gorgeous salmon-hued wine. Hints of blackcurrant and other red berries tickled her palate. Elegant and refreshing, it was the perfect compliment to their upcoming evening.

"I've only had it once, but the flavor stuck with me, and I knew you'd appreciate the taste."

His thoughtfulness pleased her. Ronan was the type of man who would always strive to make their time together stellar. His brand of charm seemed effortless, yet Dubheasa suspected he wouldn't leave a single thing to chance when it came to seduction.

Her mind drifted to making love, and an appreciative shiver skated along her spine. It was easy to see how one memorable night had become the thing she obsessed about so frequently. How other encounters failed to measure up to their one passionate experience.

"What are you doing to me?"

After removing the glass from her hand and setting both drinks on the closest surface, he cocked his head to the side. "What do you mean, love?"

"You've got me twisted up inside, Ronan. All I can think

about is your lips on mine. Your bare chest pressed against my—"

Swooping in, he captured her mouth, and the taste of the rosé was enhanced by the rich flavor that was uniquely his. She inhaled the clean scent of his freshly washed skin. The faintest hint of laundry soap tickled her senses, and she mentally smiled at the idea of Ronan washing his clothes. Of a certainty, he'd conjure what he needed and hire out the service.

His mind must've gone straight to clothes as well, or rather the removal of said clothes, because his large, capable hands were already pushing aside the loose collar of her shirt to access the skin at the V of her throat. As he slid his sensuous fingers up to cradle the back of her head, his mouth rained scorching kisses along the column of her neck, and heat pooled between her legs.

Tipping her head slightly, she allowed him better access and sighed her pleasure when he found the sweet spot below her ear. His lips trailed along her jaw to her mouth, and when he kissed her again, there was a desperate urgency in the gesture. One she matched.

Dubheasa's knees were unsteady as Ronan pulled away to undo the buttons of her blouse. As soon as he parted the material, he sucked in a breath and released it with a low moan. "Jaysus! You're more beautiful than I remember, Dove."

Embarrassed by the reverence in his tone, she pressed against him and slid her arms around his neck to draw him close. "Shut the feck up and kiss me again," she ordered.

His delectable mouth kicked up at the corners. "Sure, and I can do that. But ya need to be knowing I'm driving his car, yeah?"

She released a low growl of frustration.

His responding chuckle sent heat to all the proper places.

"You'll do as I say, or I'll be knowing the why of it," she said.

But he didn't zero in on her lips, instead choosing to use

that magical tongue of his to lick and tease the sensitive skin between her breasts. Ronan made short work of her clothing, and within moments, she was laid bare before him. His hot quicksilver eyes ate her up, and she struggled to draw a breath under his searing gaze.

Her entire body clamored for his touch. And, as if reading her mind—and Goddess, she hoped he would—he teased the tip of her hardened nipple with his nose, lips, and tongue before drawing it into his mouth to suckle.

Jaysus!

The sensations he caused as his tongue swirled and his hands explored caused butterflies in her belly and goosebumps to form on her skin. The man was a master at passionate games, and she was the pawn, ready to do whatever he requested in any way he asked.

Ronan wasted no time lifting her and carrying her to the bed. Only releasing her long enough to strip his clothing, he joined her and pressed his body to hers. Dubheasa smiled as his rock-solid length came in contact with her belly. The rightness of his body against hers lightened her heart at the same time it fueled the fire in her veins.

Gripping her hand in his, he placed it on his cock.

"Touch me, Dove."

"Gladly," she murmured as she stroked the smooth flesh, delighting in the contrasting feel of this thick, hard dick and the silky skin encasing it.

As she pleasured him with her hand, his low moans emboldened her to spread her legs and guide him into her waiting passage. They both sucked in a breath as he seated himself fully inside her.

Closing her eyes in ecstasy, she arched up, pressing her hips to his.

"Jaysus, love! If ya don't slow down..."

She read his mind and understood completely, as she was

on the brink herself.

"It's been too long, Ronan. Let me have this."

"You can have all of me, Dubheasa O'Malley. Every last ounce."

His fervent promise aroused her further. She molded her body to his, spreading her legs wider even as she wrapped them around his firm arse to anchor herself for what was to come.

"And I'll gladly take it," she replied, ending with a gasp as he shifted and thrust into her. As his big body rocked forward and back again, like a rhythmic piston, she gripped his buttocks with one hand and wrapped an arm around his torso, digging her nails into his back with the other. With each deep thrust, she moaned, *"Yes!"*

As her pleasure built to a crescendo, she sank her teeth into his muscled shoulder, burying her scream against his heated skin.

With an impassioned curse, he thrust a handful of times and followed her over the edge to release.

He didn't immediately move off her, electing to stay connected as he buried his face against her throat and kissed the spot above her pounding pulse. "Somehow, that lasted much longer in my fantasies."

She giggled. "Mine, too, but I'll admit it was perfect, all the same."

And Dubheasa realized her comment was the absolute truth; it had been perfect. She swallowed hard, trying to find the proper words to express what was in her heart.

"I know, love," he murmured sleepily.

Stroking his thick hair, she marveled at the silky feel. "Never cut your hair, yeah? I want to fall asleep just like this every night."

She felt his grin against her skin and shivered.

"Aye. Every night," he agreed.

CHAPTER 22

"So the plan moving forward is this. We host the faux wedding, tempt Loman away from where we believe the island to be, then stage a rescue," Castor said. "The O'Malleys will be here, with Eoin glamoured into Dubheasa as Brenna stands in as a bridesmaid. Quentin will glamour into Ronan. That way, if Loman attacks, he'll face two formidable opponents in Brenna and Quentin."

"Draven has agreed to stay close and cloaked, as backup if things get bad," Alastair added.

"In the meantime, I'll take Ronan, Dubheasa, Trevor, Fintan, and half of Alastair's security team to where we believe the prison is located. There are a lot of outbuildings, so we'll need to split up." Castor tapped the rough sketch he'd drawn of Scotland and its outlying islands. "If we don't find what we're looking for, we'll head to the location Dubheasa initially suspected and search there."

"Our window is limited to the length of the wedding. My father will get suspicious quickly." Ronan couldn't stress the danger to this group enough. "He looks for traps in the most innocent of circumstances."

Alastair nodded. "It should also be known he's fond of explosives. If you see anything, don't be stupid. Get out of there as soon as possible." He gave Castor a pointed look. "Especially you, Alex. You have a terrible tendency to play hero to get all the attention and praise."

Castor smoothed back his hair and twirled a pretend mustache. "How else am I to impress the ladies?"

Quentin rolled his eyes and put a hand to his stomach. "Ohdeargod, I think I threw up in my mouth."

Normally Ronan would've laughed, but the seriousness of the situation weighed heavily on him. "If the wedding is tomorrow, how will we spread the word in time for my da to hear of it?"

"That's the Aether's part," Alastair replied. "He's appealing to the Authority to cast a suggestive spell to implant the knowledge of it into the collective magical community's brain with a nice boost encouraging them to discuss it at every opportunity."

Dubheasa nodded her approval. "Clever."

"The man's over two hundred years old, *cher*," Draven reminded her with a coolly amused expression. "He's seen and done it all." Pushing away from where he rested his shoulder against the wall, he reached across the table and picked up a petit tart. His mouth quirked on one side, but the partial smile was without humor. "Sounds like your Loman is as vicious as a copperhead and ten times as deadly. I have a few things to wrap up... just in case. I'll be back in the mornin'."

Once again, Ronan wondered about the man's past. Draven seemed to be void of caring, but Ronan could empathize. Prior to Dubheasa, he was much the same. Sabrina and his cousin Ruairí had proved to be the one soft spot in his hardened heart. However, the events of the last months had caused a monumental shift inside him. Opened him up to change and even the elusive feeling of hope. Hope that perhaps he and Dubheasa could have something real and that a "happily ever after" was within his grasp.

And this new knowledge scared the bejeezus out of him. It made him vulnerable in a way he never had been when he was a cold, unfeeling bastard like his da. To his father, everyone and everything Ronan cared about was a target at which to take aim. It was a miracle Loman hadn't discovered Ronan's relationship with Bec. For sure, he'd have exploited it to the utmost degree, using it to strike a blow to the Thorne family.

Dubheasa left to put on the kettle, and Ronan couldn't help following her, touching her at every opportunity in an effort to assure himself that what he was experiencing was real.

"You're scaring me, Ronan," she said softly, worry creasing her brow. "What aren't you telling me?"

"Nothing, but my skin feels prickly and my nerves are raw."

"You're worried about the plan?"

"In large part, yeah." He cast an uneasy glance over his shoulder at the others, who were huddled about the table. "I can't help feeling this isn't the right way to go."

"Do you have a better idea?"

Dubheasa's question was genuine and held no hint of sarcasm, so Ronan answered in kind. "No, but the thought of you comin' face-to-face with my da shrivels my bollocks. If the Devil had a face, it would be Loman O'Connor's. Please don't forget it, love."

"I won't."

When she wrapped her arms around his neck and drew his head into the crook of her neck, Ronan sighed his pleasure and kissed the skin exposed by the V of her jumper. Breathing in the subtle scent of her exotic perfume, he allowed himself a brief fantasy about what he'd do to her should he get her alone again anytime soon.

"Your thoughts have turned to shagging," she accused, using their personal connection.

"*Aye.*" Why bother denying it? She could sense his amorous leanings through their ever-developing bond. "*They always do when you're within five feet of me.*"

Her giggle was the balm his soul needed.

"*If we're to die tomorrow, we should definitely take advantage and shag again tonight.*"

His blood turned to ice at her ill-timed joke.

She placed her palm over his heart. "Ronan?"

"I'm sorry for checking out like that. But maybe you don't joke about dying, yeah?"

"I didn't mean to be insensitive."

"You weren't, Dove. The situation could use some levity, but a spirit walked across my grave when you mentioned dying tomorrow. I've a right powerful aversion to your death."

"But not Loman's?" she teased.

"Never his." Cupping the nape of her neck, Ronan hauled her against him. "Thinking about my da is the other thing that shrivels me bollocks. How about we discuss other more pleasant topics?"

"What did you have in mind?"

"How about you kiss me and we'll talk about the first thing that comes up?" he suggested with a low growl.

Her peal of laughter turned the others' heads. "Ronan O'Connor, you've got a naughty streak a mile wide, ya do."

"Only with you, Dove." He lowered his head and kissed her breathless. "Only with you."

"Walk with me, love," Ronan said.

Dubheasa took the hand he offered and rose to her feet, eager to be away from the gloom and doom of the upcoming battle with Loman. Castor and Alastair had drilled the rules into everyone for hours, and she was sick of the repetitiveness of the plan.

"Don't go far," Castor warned.

"Feck off. I'm after doin' what I want," Ronan replied, but he winked to take the sting from his words.

"Kids these days." Alastair shook his head, but a smile teased his mouth.

"Truth," Castor said with a hearty sigh. "They're never willing to listen or learn from those with experience, are they?"

With a chuckle, Ronan led Dubheasa to the back garden, where members of Alastair's security team were busy arranging flowers and chairs for the ceremony.

"Is this what you would want for our wedding if you could choose for yourself, Dove?"

"Is this your way of asking me to marry you, Ronan O'Connor?"

"Nah. You'll be the one to propose to me because you're a modern-day woman."

She laughed at his jest. Pausing to consider his question, she viewed the venue as a whole. A white runner ran the aisle between five rows of six white folding chairs. Wide-mouth planters overflowed with violet-blue hydrangeas at the beginning and end of every row. A low-rise wooden platform served as the main stage for the couple and was as wide across as the area for the guests. Pillar candles rested in the holders of five-foot-tall candelabras on all four sides of the platform. A six-foot-wide arbor with English ivy was centered per Ronan's odd request.

Dubheasa had no problem imagining him standing up there in a smart blue suit as he straightened his cuffs and fiddled with the buttons of his starched white shirt. He'd be nervous she might not show, but hopeful all the same. The moment she set foot on the runner, he would focus on her with the right amount of fervor to steal her breath away, and a beatific smile would transform his face from severe to blissful and loving.

"Yes. This is exactly what I would want," she said with a soft smile. "And you? Is it what you would want for your wedding?"

"The vision you just had? Aye." His voice was rough with emotion, and his eyes were full of a love so great that it was impossible to deny.

"You saw that?" Their link had grown stronger over the last twenty-four hours, and she shouldn't have been surprised he'd bore witness to her fantasy, but she was.

"It was a beautiful sight." He lifted his arm and, in a brilliant flash of light, created a perfect blood-red rose. With the velvety edge of the petals, he brushed her jaw, then presented it to her. "One I'll hold next to my heart until the day we can make it a reality."

"Me, too."

Ronan kissed their joined hands. "Are you worried about the binding of your abilities?"

"Not really. I didn't have any until recently, and I doubt I'll miss them either way. What about you?"

"Very."

His confession surprised her, and she shot him a questioning look. "Why's that?"

"I've never been without power prior to saving Aeden." His troubled silver gaze traveled the horizon, never stopping on any one spot. Ronan recounted the story for her from his viewpoint. How he found Moira and Seamus standing over Dubheasa's young nephew as he bled out from the wound to his throat. "I've never been so horrified by anything in my fecking life, Dove. And all I could think to do was right their wrong. To save him." Slowly, as if reliving the moment, he shook his head, and his eyes grew dark at the memory. "My cousins didn't know by doing what they did, another line of the prophesy would be fulfilled. It was as if my battery was drained when I used my fading magic to save the boy."

"And you hated the feeling?"

"I hated being weak." His expression was stark as he turned to her. "My da despised weakness and beat it out of us every chance he could."

Unable to bear the pain in his eyes, Dubheasa wrapped her arms around him and buried her face against his shoulder. "I'm sorry you had to live like that, Ronan. That you didn't have parents to honor and cherish you like you deserved."

"He can't be allowed to win, Dove. Can't be allowed to steal what we have."

"It will never be enough for him, will it?"

"No. And whatever he gains, he'll use to crush those who crossed him in the process. But not just them." Ronan gripped her forearms and held her away from him. Bending slightly, he made his face level with hers. "Do you understand what I'm saying, love?"

"Yeah. He'll go after anyone his enemies care about," she answered.

"Aye. And it terrifies me to think he'll hurt you or yours."

It occurred to her that Ronan believed Loman thought he was one of his father's greatest threats, which put him firmly in the enemy camp. Her heart began to thud painfully in her chest.

"What do you want me to do, Ronan? Flee? Fight? What would be better for you?"

His unsettling gaze touched on every aspect of her face, as if he couldn't get enough. Eventually, he hauled her against him in an embrace so tight she feared for his emotional health should she not survive their attack against Loman's compound.

"I don't know what to do," he confessed hoarsely. "If you go into hiding, will it be enough? Will I be distracted if you aren't with me, wondering if he'll find you?" His hold eased, and

Ronan tilted her head back to touch his nose to hers. "But you're a fierce distraction when you're around me, love. If he captured you, I'd give him whatever he asked for to free you, of a certainty."

"Don't you do that, Ronan O'Connor! Promise me."

"I can't, Dove."

"You can! What is one life against many?"

"To me? It's *everything*."

The sweetness of his answer melted the last of any resistance she might've had against claiming the title of his mate. In front of her was a man who would treasure her forever. One who would hold her heart close and see to her needs before his own. Who would never let her regret choosing him.

"I love you," she said softly. "And whether it's a single minute or a billion, I'll be grateful for any time we have together."

"In my entire life, I never thought I'd be lucky enough to find a love like this"—he touched the place above her heart and then his own—"and to have it returned. I'm not certain I deserve it, Dove. I've not been the best of men."

"Sure, and there you're wrong. You are the best of men, Ronan Fucking O'Connor. You are because I say you are."

His lips twitched, and his eyes lightened with humor. "Well then, if you say I am, I must be."

"Aye. And don't you be forgetting it."

CHAPTER 23

Ronan's heart was full as he gazed down into Dubheasa's glowing face. After they left the garden, they snuck away to his room to explore each other's bodies and to celebrate their love with a right proper shag.

But time was short, and he had a few things to see to before the morning. His strongest instinct was to find a place where Loman would never think to look for him and steal away with Dubheasa to live there forever. But that was the coward's way. The O'Malleys, along with Castor and the Thornes, were relying on him to take part in their carefully crafted plan.

"I'm after returnin' ya to your family now, Dove."

"Mmm." She stretched her arms over her head, exposing her breasts to his eager gaze. "And I'm after receiving more attention from you."

"You're a scheming witch," he accused as he lowered his head to toy with an erect nipple. "If we continue this course of action, I'll be as weak as a newborn *wean*, unable to stand on me own two feet when tomorrow comes."

Her fingers curled in his hair, and she moaned as he suckled her. "Sure, and that's a fine idea, I'm thinking."

With a gentle bite and a resigned sigh, he drew away and sat up. "We'll stay abed for a month—*after*. But I've work to do."

With a heartfelt groan, she rolled onto her stomach and buried her head into the pillow. "Why do you have to be so fecking responsible?"

"Get your lovely arse up, woman," he ordered with a light slap on her backside. Following it with a rub, he mentally calculated how long his errands would take and how quickly he could bring Dubheasa to orgasm again.

With the regretful conclusion that he couldn't delay, he stood. "I have to go, love. For real this time."

She rolled onto her side, propped her head on her hand, and smiled. "So serious."

"If I had Eoin's talent, I'd paint ya just that way, Dubheasa." He allowed himself the pleasure of studying her naked form, wondering if he should beg the Goddess to grant him an artist's skill as a gift.

"Even if you didn't, I'd let you paint me, Ronan. Long hours in bed with your grand eyes on me? Yeah, it would be a real hardship," she teased.

"Then that's the thing I'll look forward to after tomorrow."

The laughter left her, and she sat up, covering herself with the sheet as she hugged her legs tightly. "Will you lose respect for me if I admit I'm scared?"

He perched sideways on the edge of the bed and hooked his ankle behind his knee. "No, Dove. I'd be worried and caution you if you weren't."

"Your da has ended too many lives and ruined a shite ton more. I don't want us to be casualties of his evil war."

"If I don't—"

She surged forward and, kneeling, covered his mouth with her palm. "Don't you dare say it, Ronan. Don't voice what-ifs. You're going to come out of this just fine. I'm not going to entertain any other notions."

"We have to be realistic, Dove."

"No. It's pessimism you're spreading, and I won't have it. Tomorrow, Loman O'Connor dies. That's it. That's the end of his reign of terror. Tell me you agree."

Arguing with her would be fruitless, and Ronan didn't want to spend their treasured moments together contradicting her. Instead, he'd buy into her optimism and pray the Fates would, too.

"Aye, love. I agree. Tomorrow, Loman O'Connor dies."

The tension eased from her body as she hugged him around the neck. "Thank you."

"Yeah, and I'm the one who should be thanking you." He ran his hands down the length of her sleek back and cupped her arse. "I'm getting the better end of this deal, to be sure."

His comment did what he'd intended and caused her to laugh.

"You're a rogue." Shifting to straddle him, she bit his chin. "*My* rogue."

"Aye. Only yours."

Ronan captured her mouth and tasted heaven as her tongue made love to his. And as he fell under the enchantment that was Dubheasa O'Malley, he quickly decided his errands could wait a little while longer.

AFTER SECURING DUBHEASA'S PROMISE NOT TO LEAVE THE O'Malley property and to remain securely within shouting distance of Fintan or Castor, Ronan sent out a feeler for his destination to check for tourists. Once he had the all clear, he teleported to the Hill of Tara, the fabled meeting place of kings and Fae. But he knew it to be the one spot where Anu would always answer his call.

After creating a repelling enchantment to keep others away,

he cloaked the hill and lightly scored his palm to squeeze out exactly three droplets of blood onto a worn stone marker stained with the blood of others before him.

"Beloved Anu," he called out. "I'm after requesting an audience with ya!"

Nothing happened immediately, so he sat and waited. The deities had their own timetable, and being a fickle lot, they wouldn't be rushed. As the late morning melded into early afternoon, he laid back, tucked his arms behind his head, and closed his eyes. He could give her thirty minutes longer, but then he'd have to consult with Ruairí and his attorney. Over the last twenty years, Ronan had amassed a sizable fortune, and on the off chance he didn't survive the confrontation with his father, he intended to secure Dubheasa's future and that of his cousins.

A flare of emerald light split the sky as the ground beneath Ronan rumbled.

The Goddess had arrived.

Shifting positions, Ronan knelt at her feet and bowed his head. Only when she bade him to rise did he look up. No more than an inch or two over five feet, she possessed enough curves to make a man take note. Her hair was a waterfall of thick red, corkscrew curls that brushed her tiny waist. Alabaster skin was set off by the rich jewel-toned dress she wore. A gold chain woven with Celtic knots looped over her hips and dangled down to one knee. Other than a gold bracelet with ogham etchings, it was the only ornamentation.

But it was her bare, polished toes that made Ronan smile.

"Exalted One."

"Beloved." She lifted a brow and stared down at him. "What amuses you so?"

He gestured to her feet. "Your love of human cosmetics is fecking adorable."

"Does your mate not wear polish?" she asked curiously.

"Aye, she does, but in purple or red, not pale pink."

"Ronan O'Connor, you didn't summon me to discuss toes, I'll wager. Again, I bid you to rise."

Having no desire to waste her time, he did as commanded and kissed the knuckles of the hand she offered.

"What is it you wish to know, Beloved?"

"Fintan Sullivan proposes to bind my abilities along with those of Dubheasa. I need to know the why of it."

"And why haven't you asked him?"

"Because I suspect he'll not tell me what he's about. Can the Seer be trusted?"

"Yes. Though not as strong as the Aether's daughter, Fintan can see the true path. If he has suggested your powers be bound, it's to protect the future outcome of your skirmish with Loman."

Ronan wanted to tell her he was useless without his magic, but she probably already knew that. "I don't know how to beat him. I never have," he confessed.

Her expression softened. "You have friends for that, Ronan. Trust them to do the right thing."

"You and Isis encouraged me to take on the role of Guardian to find my mate. Now I've found her, I fear losing her just as fast."

"Life holds no guarantees. And I'll not promise what's not mine to give, but if there is a way to secure your happiness, I'll work to make it happen."

"Is there no advice you can offer, then?" he asked in desperation.

For a long moment, she remained silent, as if she were working through a problem. Finally, she touched a hand to his chest, just above his heart, and his skin tingled through his shirt. "Trust your friends to do the right thing, Ronan O'Connor. And should you decide to attack Loman, you must wait until the Death Dealer is present, or all will be for naught."

"That's it, then? Nothing more you can offer?"

Irritation drew her brows together into a deep scowl.

He sighed and offered her his most disarming smile. "Then I'll thank you now, Exalted One. Any blessing you wish to bestow will be welcomed, all the same." Ronan dropped to one knee and bowed his head. "And thank you for answering my call today, my queen."

She laid her palm atop his head, and the warmth of her unimaginable might passed through him. "Blessed be, Ronan O'Connor. Don't forget what I said. Trust your friends to do the right thing."

"Aye."

As quickly as she'd arrived, she disappeared, and Ronan's feelings gave way to the frustration that had been brewing inside him. Other than some cryptic response, he was still clueless as to how to defeat Loman. And that scared the bejeezus out of him.

CHAPTER 24

"Where did you need to go in such a rush?" Castor asked Ronan when they had a private moment alone at the pub.

"To see Anu."

"And what tidbit of information did you obtain from her?"

"Not much," Ronan replied grimly. "I'm no closer to learning the outcome of our invasion than I was going in, to be sure." An undefined, fleeting emotion flashed across his uncle's face, and Ronan's building sense of unease grew stronger. "You know," he said flatly. "You learned the truth from Sabrina and Damian last night."

"I guessed a few of the possible results, but nothing concrete. Damian refused to reveal anything that might alter the future. You know he's like that."

"But the plan you relayed is exactly as Damian believes it needs to be enacted, yeah?"

"Yes."

"Jaysus! I hate this uncertainty." Weary of the entire situation, Ronan scrubbed his face with his hands. "Then I suppose it'll have to be enough. We've nothin' else to go on."

They drank in silence as they watched Cian entertain the crowd with his music. The man had the type of voice that could charm the wings off angels, and he used it to seduce locals and foreign travelers alike. Primarily, he played lively Irish songs with a care for tradition, but Cian was always happy to sing a ballad designed to make all the pretty colleens swoon. Yet, if one looked closely, they would see his eyes were always for his new wife, Piper, as they were at that moment.

Whenever Ronan saw her, he was reminded of her mother, Rebecca. Like Bec, Piper was full of salty comebacks and saucy smiles. And the ghosts of the past sometimes rose up when she forgot herself to grin at him. In her amused expression, Ronan was transported back to when Bec was his lover and thought something he'd said was the craic. Piper had been a mere kid then, but now, she was bursting at the seams, ready to have her own child. She'd be present for hers and Cian's baby, and she'd likely be a better mother than Bec had been.

Bec's negligence had likely been his fault. He'd shown up at a time when her marriage was all but over, and after one look, he'd fallen madly in love. The kindness she'd shown him was the first he'd truly known in his life, and she became more than his standard dalliance. She'd become his everything. Until she wasn't. Until the day she confessed she didn't love him as he loved her and that she intended to return to her husband, Hoyt Thorne.

Crushed, Ronan hadn't cared whether he lived or died, and he hadn't bothered to fight his father for supremacy or question Loman's rule when he had the chance. He'd merely gone through life on autopilot. The only exception had been his desire to mitigate the damage his da tried to inflict on women or children, due to the strict rule that Ronan didn't make war on the innocent. After years of working at cross-purposes with Loman, he'd found a way to deliver his father to the Witches' Council.

Loman had never forgiven him.

Now, when Ronan had a reason to live again, when he possessed a love a thousand times greater than what he'd experienced with Bec, he had a mind for caution.

"The Death Dealer,"—he faced Castor as he spoke—"he's prepared to do what he must, regarding my da?"

"He is."

With a nod, Ronan turned his attention to Dubheasa.

Her movements were like an exotic dance as she wove her way between the tables and the serving station to pick up and place orders. For the second night in a row, one of the waitstaff had failed to show, and she'd stepped up to help. A few new plonkers attempted to work their wiles on her throughout her shift, but she laughingly pointed in Ronan's direction as she quipped a quick answer to whatever inquiry they put to her.

As the evening progressed, the patrons grew rowdier, and one or two thought to pinch Dubheasa's shapely bottom. But an ingrained sixth sense always gave her the advantage and allowed her to dodge a hand when needed. It didn't upset Ronan in the least as she dumped a pint over one particularly aggressive scut's head.

As Ronan stood to teach the fecking sod a lesson, she told him to calm himself, using their mental connection. *"He's a harmless eejit, love,"* she said. *"And he spends half his paycheck here each week, he does."*

When she glanced his way, Ronan shot her an evil grin. *"If ya let me kill him, I promise to double what he drops here each week."*

He chuckled as she buried her head in a bar towel to hide her laughter.

"What has you so amused?" Castor asked. "Or should I guess?"

"How did I get so lucky to win her? What did I do that was so fecking grand?" He didn't add the question plaguing him —*How do I keep her safe?*

"It's said the O'Malley clan was cursed with ill luck when the Sword of Goibhniu was stolen by our ancestors." Castor downed the last of his pint and used the table to steady himself as he climbed to his feet. His pale eyes were despondent as he stared down at Ronan. "But I think it was the O'Connors who were cursed. Never a one has experienced anything other than a fleeting happiness, and it's doubtful any will."

"Why does that sound like a miserable fecking prediction?"

"Perhaps it is," his uncle replied softly.

Skin clammy, Ronan fought the urge to vomit up the beer he'd consumed. The thought of losing what he was building with Dubheasa made him violently ill. "Tell me—"

A commotion by the bar caught their notice, and Ronan turned in time to see Bridget charge around the end of the counter toward a woman with whom Dubheasa stood nose to nose.

The word "Mam" drifted to him, and he looked closer at the black-haired beauty who had caused such animosity from the sisters. Shorter than Dubheasa and wider of hip, she resembled Bridget in stature, but her looks were pure Dubheasa. Perfectly arched brows, wide challenge-filled eyes, a mouth made for smiling, kissing, and scolding. Yet there was a quality about her that was different. A little more cunning, perhaps.

As he arrived beside Dubheasa, the woman turned chocolaty eyes his way, and he realized the O'Malleys' remarkable emerald shade must've come from their father's side. Her gaze was assessing, and though they'd never met before, recognition flashed across her face. Seconds later, she adopted an innocent air.

"Sure, and this must be your future groom," the woman purred as she looked her fill. "You're a big ride, yeah? I can see why Dubheasa is so smitten with ya."

When she would've touched him, he stepped out of her reach and pinned her in place with a blazing hands-off stare.

"I'll not have ya acting maggot at my wedding, Mam," Dubheasa snapped.

Bridget wedged herself between them. "Go back to whatever hole ya crawled out of and keep out of our lives. You're not wanted here, ya horrid wagon."

"Aye, and it hurts that me own daughters are so unwelcomin'." With a sniff, she delicately dabbed at her eyes with her sleeve.

Ronan suspected the action was as fake as the rest of her.

"Mam." Cian wrapped an arm around his mother's shoulders and directed her away from the O'Malley sisters. What words he spoke to soothe her were swallowed by the noise of the pub patrons, but Bridget's few choice statements were enough to make Ronan's ears scarlet from embarrassment.

"Don't tell me he's that gullible," Castor said from behind him.

"Aye," Bridget snapped. "He's got a soft spot for her, and he's taken in by her lies time and again. For so clever a brain, he's a feckin' fool when it comes to our mam. Just like our da was." She shook her head. "Da called her his 'Wild Red Rose' and doted on her—until the day he didn't."

"You think she learned about the wedding via the Authority's community-wide enchantment?" Castor murmured.

Ronan shrugged, not caring one way or the other. He shifted to face Dubheasa and rested a hand on her hip as he stroked the tension from the back of her neck. "Are you all right, Dove?"

"After all these years, you'd think I'd be numb to her presence, but she still makes my blood boil. It feels like ants crawling under my skin." She shook out her arms with a shudder. "And I know she's a chancer, but I don't know why I hate her as I do."

Trevor arrived to hear Dubheasa's comment. "She's soulless

and selfish," he stated flatly. "Her kind lives for the trouble they can cause."

"Can you sense it, then?" Bridget asked.

"To a degree, but it's more about her microexpressions." He shot Ronan a sharp glance. "You witnessed them, too, if I'm not mistaken."

"Aye." And like Dubheasa, it felt as if ants were crawling under his skin.

"The wedding is a ploy to lure you away from here," Rose Doyle-O'Malley told Loman as he poured her a generous glass of red wine. She glanced at the label and smiled. Only the highest quality was stored in his cellar. As she savored the fruity notes of her first sip, she met his calculating gaze. "You're not surprised."

"My son isn't as clever as he likes to think he is." He picked up a book of poetry and dropped it with a resounding thud. "And I was after lurin' him here first, I was."

"By reciting poetry?" she asked with a disbelieving laugh. The immediate backhanded slap he gave her knocked her into the wall, and she cringed as he lifted his arm a second time. "I didn't mean anythin' by it, Loman. I was just havin' the craic."

"Well have it somewhere else, woman. I'll not tolerate your insolence in me bed or out of it," he warned.

Rose suppressed a shiver to hide her building terror. Loman O'Connor was not a man to be crossed, and she'd do well to remember it.

"How is it ya tricked Ronan?" she asked, infusing curiosity and deference into her question and hoping to distract him.

For a painful heart-pounding minute, he watched her through narrowed eyes, as if he were trying to decide whether to give his temper free rein or to believe she'd been suitably punished. She prayed it was the latter. With a sneer, he lifted his glass tumbler and guzzled half his drink, and Rose decided she was going to find a way to escape for the night before he turned meaner than usual under the influence of the hard liquor he preferred.

"There are cameras in the cells. All cloaked, yeah, and I've paid special attention to Reginald's actions. He was too keen on the contents of that bleedin' book, to be sure." Finishing off his whiskey, Loman slammed the glass on the bar next to him, then poured himself another. "He found a way to talk to the outside world through his magic book. Clever boy."

She could almost believe Loman held a special place in his heart for his nephew—except he didn't possess one. Only an empty black hole existed in its place, and it sought to drag everything and everyone into its orbit to consume and destroy.

After downing the contents of his glass, he poured yet another. It wouldn't be long before his fists did the talking for him. One day, if she wasn't careful, he'd kill her.

"Yeah, and I slowly fed Reggie what I wanted the Seer to know, I did," he eventually revealed.

A trap.

"Who do you plan to catch in that snare of yours, then?" she asked with an attempt at eagerness. Yet her stomach tightened at the thought it might be any or all of her children. Sure, she was a wee bit self-serving, but she wasn't completely heartless when it came to her kin.

Loman's grin was pure evil intent as he locked gazes with her.

He didn't need to say a fecking word. Rose knew exactly who he was after.

The woman his son loved.

Dubheasa.

CHAPTER 25

Sleep eluded Dubheasa. Ever since she'd seen her mother, a pervading doom destroyed her sense of well-being. As the evening progressed, that feeling had swelled, growing stronger and nearly suffocating her.

Ronan shifted and curled around her, draping an arm across her waist. "Can't sleep?"

"No. Worry has dug its claws into me, and I can't seem to shake it off."

"Yeah. Me, too." His arm tightened, and he kissed her shoulder.

"What do ya think it could be?"

"Damned if I know." He sighed and rolled into a sitting position. "But mine started before your mam appeared. Though she didn't do anything to ease my feckin' nerves, mind ya."

"Should we delay the mission?" Dubheasa sat up and curled her arms around her knees. "Wait for a time when we don't feel the ghosts of our ancestors waiting to take our souls to the other side?"

Ronan's sharp, searching look was off-putting.

"What?" she asked.

"Why did you phrase it like that?"

Why had she? No answer seemed to come, and she shrugged. "I'm not quite sure. But this entire fecking thing feels off to me. Like disaster is waiting just around the corner."

"Fuck if I don't feel it, too." He ran a shaking hand through his mussed hair. "It's been eating at my insides for days now."

Placing her hand along his jaw, she turned his face to her. "Why didn't you insist we find another way, then?"

"I didn't want to put doubt in your mind if it was only fear of my da showing its ugly teeth," he confessed with a rueful grin.

Yet his eyes were haunted, and Dubheasa hated the trepidation she saw there. Ronan O'Connor wasn't afraid of much, and Loman had to be the Devil himself if he provoked that type of response in his son.

"What do we do?"

"Nothing for it. We've others relying on us to act," Ronan said grimly. "If we don't stop Da soon, he'll grow too strong, and then we might not be able to."

"And we can't leave it to the others? To Damian and Trevor? Don't they—"

The fierce denial in Ronan's expression cut her off. No, he wouldn't leave the dirty work to another. And if he was going to dive into the fray, Dubheasa intended to be by his side. They'd do it together.

"I fear for Bridget and my brothers." She toyed with the corner of the sheet, folding the edge over on itself. "If we leave them here for the fake wedding and Loman strikes, I could lose one, or all, of them."

"We've discussed this, Dove. The strongest Sentinels from the Authority will be here, prepared to protect them and any attending' guests. Damian and Castor have covered all the contingencies with a Traveler, another Death Dealer, and another Guardian." Ronan eased the sheet from her tight grip and tipped her chin up. "It'll be all right, love. And didn't I promise Loman O'Connor would die tomorrow?"

She forced a smile. "You did."

"Then it will be done. Consider it an early wedding present, yeah?"

"Who says I agreed to marry you? That's a bit presumptive." With an arrogant sniff and a mock glare, she said, "You still haven't proposed to me proper-like."

In a move that shocked her speechless, Ronan grabbed her around the waist and stood her in the center of the bed as he knelt on the mattress, in front of her. "Dubheasa O'Malley, you are my sun on the most overcast of days, my stars in the inky night sky, my... Well, look, I'm no poet, but I love you, all the same. Will you do me the honor of becoming my wife and making me the happiest man to ever live?"

Laughing, she crashed down on top of him and rained kisses all over his beloved face. "Yes, ya eejit. I'll marry you."

"Jaysus! I'll take back my proposal if you're going to insist on calling me names."

She grabbed his ears in her fists and locked him in position as she ravished his mouth. Drawing back, she lifted a brow.

Ronan grinned and cupped the back of her neck, pulling her back down. "I don't see the harm in you calling me an eejit. I don't care, especially if you're always going to be snogging me like that." As he lifted his head the remaining distance to touch her lips, he met her amused gaze. "I'll love you forever. I think I always have."

All humor dropped away, and her heart melted into a puddle of goo. "You're my forever love, Ronan Fucking O'Connor. Don't muck it up."

A brilliant smile transformed his face, and Dubheasa's breath stalled in her lungs.

"I'll never muck it up, Dove. Not in this life nor any after."

"Are you ready?"

"To have my magic bound? No." Ronan turned away from the window to see Dubheasa patiently waiting by the door with a look of quiet sympathy on her exquisite visage.

"I've only had mine for a few months, but I'm not thrilled to lose it either," she commiserated.

He lifted his arms and stared at his open palms. "All my life, I've been the strongest of the O'Connors, with the exception of my da. I made my cousins fear me, like they did him, because it was the only way I could keep them in check. That changed when Damian removed my abilities to save me. And I fucking hated every bleedin' minute of it."

Dubheasa crossed to him and gripped his hands. "It's only temporary, Ronan. Try to remember that."

"If the fecking Seer hadn't—"

She pressed her fingertips to his lips. "There's no point in what-ifs. We have to do this."

"Aye."

They joined hands, and static snapped and popped as their palms met.

"When this is over, Damian will give back what you surrendered, and I'll be supercharged. It'll be grand," she promised.

And Ronan wanted to believe her, but his unease had grown worse that morning, nearly crippling him. "I wish I had your optimism, Dove."

"I have enough for both of us."

As they descended the stairs, he couldn't help feeling as if he were heading to the gallows, and he had a difficult time believing he'd come out of this rescue mission intact.

The other members of their team, with the exception of Draven, were all present. Some appeared as worried as Ronan was, while others had their game face on and seemed hyper focused on what needed to be done.

"Damian is waiting for you in the rose garden between his estate and Baz's place," Alastair said without preamble. "I'm to take you both there and bring you back when he's done."

Dubheasa spent a few precious minutes hugging her siblings and extracting their solemn vow to have a care. After she returned to Ronan's side and laced her fingers with his, she nodded to Alastair. "We're ready, Mr. Thorne."

Rarely since they'd become better acquainted had Alastair been as solemn as he was at that moment, and Ronan was convinced the older man was privy to Damian's knowledge of the future.

And he fucking hated it.

"If there's something I should know, Thorne, come out with it already. This stiff upper lip shite everyone's got going on has me on edge."

The surprise on both Alastair's and Dubheasa's faces brought with it the realization Ronan had come across a bit too harsh.

"Feck. I'll apologize now and be done with it."

"You're forgiven, son. I understand tough choices, and you're wedged tightly between a rock and a hard place." Alastair met his gaze with a direct look. "All I know is what Alex has told me. I didn't ask, because I'd have been tempted to alter the situation to suit myself, and I'm trying to trust the process for once."

"You—"

He held up a hand to silence Ronan. "I'm an empath, and the emotions in this room are overwhelming, to put it mildly. On top of that, I'm worried about the safety of everyone present. My son-in-law's included."

Once Alastair made it clear he didn't have a hidden agenda,

Ronan felt like a fool for his rare bout of temper. But the other man's understanding smile said he was willing to forgive.

"Let's not keep the Aether waiting," Alastair suggested as he placed a hand on both his and Dubheasa's shoulders.

They arrived in the rose garden seconds later.

With infinite patience, Damian gestured to a stone-slab bench. "Dubheasa, if you will."

Casting one last glance toward Ronan, she smiled softly and complied.

"Don't be alarmed by the next step. I need to raise the standing stones for this process," the Aether explained.

Within seconds of him lifting his arms, palms up, the ground around them shook violently. One by one, pillars split the earth and rose until they encircled the altar, towering over their small group. Fourteen standing stones in all.

Walking to the closest, Damian traced the ancient symbols as he spoke the words to illuminate the etching. Latin, if Ronan had to guess, but unintelligible from this distance.

Joining Dubheasa in the center of the circle, he clasped her hand and gave it a squeeze. "Impressive, yeah?"

"I've never seen anything like it."

The awe in her tone made him smile. "Prepare yourself, love. Our future holds a lot more of this type of excitement."

As she soaked it all in, she laughed her delight, and Ronan logged another beautiful moment. "I have to admit it's fascinating in a way computer science can never be," she said.

"There's a science to magic," Alastair told her from the other side of her stone perch. "When all this is over, Damian can teach you, as he's been teaching Ronan."

"I'd like that, to be sure."

The Aether joined them, and his expression was as severe as Ronan had ever witnessed.

"Is this too dangerous for her?" The question popped out

before he could stop it, and the panicked quality in his tone caught Dubheasa's attention.

She hadn't let go of his hand, so she gave a little tug. "It's going to be all right, Ronan. No matter the outcome, it'll be okay."

"I can't lose you." His voice was as rough and raw as his battered soul. "I'll not survive it, Dove. I won't want to."

Her soft smile was full of love and understanding, and it was the most beautiful thing he'd ever seen.

"You won't get rid of me that easily, Ronan Fucking O'Connor." Her dark brows shot up in challenge.

Her stubbornness alone almost made him believe, but the little voice in his head was screaming a warning on repeat. Some instinct had him turning to look at Damian. Guilt, or something similar, came and went so swiftly in his friend's expression that Ronan wasn't positive he'd witnessed it.

"Promise me, if this fucking mission goes sideways, you'll get her out," he ground out.

"I promise to get you both out," Damian replied, and the sincerity in his voice struck a chord in Ronan. "We're out of time. The stones are supercharged and ready to go. Decide now if you want to do this."

Dubheasa spoke for them. "Do it."

CHAPTER 26

She hadn't expected the pain.

It felt as if her skin was being peeled back and her insides were being removed excruciatingly slow with a pair of tweezers. Agonizing and time-consuming was the magic-removal process, and if she never experienced it again, it wouldn't hurt her damned feelings.

From the corner of her eye, she saw Ronan struggle with acceptance. Her terrible discomfort was mild in comparison to the torture he was going through as he watched her writhe on the altar. Alastair had physically restrained him a time or ten.

Just as she thought she couldn't endure another second, relief came in a wash of cool breeze. Almost too cool, and she shivered from the chilly morning air. From nowhere, Damian produced a heavy wool blanket and wrapped it around her shoulders.

"You'll feel incredibly cold for a while, and perhaps a little desolate," he explained kindly. "It will be as if you're missing a piece of yourself. In another hour, you'll come to terms with the oddness of the sensation, and you'll be as you were prior to receiving the O'Malley magic after the prophesy was fulfilled."

"I'll be grand," she promised. "Thank you."

His perturbed gaze darted toward Ronan and returned to her. "Be careful, Dubheasa. Ronan believes I know what's to come, and to a degree, I do. The future, however, is fluid, and any small misstep can alter a timeline. It might be difficult to repair that gaffe."

She nodded her understanding and thanked him when he assisted her off the stone altar.

Ronan rushed to her and swept her into a tight hug. "How are you feeling, love? Are you all right?"

"Other than being suffocated by a giant oaf of a man?"

Cupping her face, he kissed her hard and fast. "You're a right gas."

"You're next, lover boy," Damian informed him. "Get comfortable."

"I've been through this with you before, and it wouldn't hurt you to be gentle this time," Ronan muttered.

"Where's the fun in that?" Alastair quipped.

"There are times I hate you both." Glaring, Ronan lay back on the slab and wiggled to get comfortable as the others laughed.

"Do you need me to hold your hand?" Dubheasa asked with a wicked grin as she leaned in and stroked his brow.

"You're after vexing me, woman, and I'll not have it," he growled as he wrapped an arm around her waist and tugged her closer. "It's time you learn who's to be the boss of this relationship."

With a disbelieving snort, she cradled his face, dropping her blanket in the process. "I already know who the boss is, and so do you. But I'll be sure to remind you whenever you're after forgetting."

Her sassy comeback made him laugh, and as he pushed the sweat-soaked hair back from her chilled face, he gave her the gift of warmth with his touch. "Aye. I'll need reminding from time to time." Gaze locked on hers, he brushed his knuckles along her cheekbone. "I love you," he told her in a low voice.

The kiss she bestowed on him was the sweetest they'd shared yet, and her heart felt full to overflowing.

"Try not to scream like a baby," she said tartly.

He groaned and shooed her away. "Go on with you, shrew."

After bending to retrieve the blanket, she backed to the spot where he and Alastair had stood during her binding, never breaking eye contact with Ronan.

Two minutes after the Aether began the process for Ronan, his body arched upward as his mouth opened in a silent scream, and Dubheasa struggled against the urge to run to him and ease his suffering.

Having gone through such a painful process, it was difficult to stand by and not do something.

"I understand your desire to go to him, but don't," Alastair said from beside her. "If he flails out, you could be injured."

"It's awful to watch."

"It is, indeed."

"Why is there no numbing spell to ease the discomfort?" she asked desperately.

"Actually, Damian has experimented with them in the past, but it delays the extraction, and the removal of magic takes twice as long."

Somewhat appeased, she gave in to her curiosity. "Why is there pain to begin with?"

"Our magic is woven into our DNA. Essentially, we're born with it."

"But I wasn't."

His brows drew together in a deep frown of concentration, as if he searched for a way to explain. Finally, he said, "Technically, you were. When you descend from a magical family, the potential is always there. Yours was suppressed due to a curse, but when it was lifted, you likely experienced an infusion of power." He smiled down at her. "If I had to guess, it was eye-opening. The world became brighter, and the auras of those around you were no longer muted and muddy. Your senses became sharper, no?"

Thinking back, she nodded slowly. "Yes. It happened just like that. A surge of heat throughout my body, as if my very cells had caught fire."

"Precisely. And they did. It's why the removal left you chilled."

"So it's not the damp air, but the fire gone out?"

"A combination of both, I imagine," he said. Opening his mouth, he was cut off by Ronan's muffled scream.

When she would've rushed forward, Alastair stopped her with a hand on her arm.

She released a savage curse under her breath and brushed him off. "I'll do better."

"Why don't you take a walk around the perimeter of the stones? It might help."

"I don't want to leave him."

"Your young man's abilities are hundreds of times stronger than yours and their removal, a thousand times worse. He isn't aware of your presence, my dear."

His encouraging look and another agonized cry from Ronan convinced her Alastair's suggestion was a good one.

"Ms. O'Malley?"

She cast a questioning glance over her shoulder.

"Please stay within the garden walls," Alastair said. "Damian has warded this area against attack, but you can never be too careful."

Nodding, she drew the wool blanket tighter around her and strolled away. Not usually one for prayers, she sent a silent one up to Anu, asking for her to watch over Ronan.

TOMBSTONES DOTTED THE GARDEN, EACH WITH ITS OWN separate climbing rosebush with blood-red blooms the size of both Dubheasa's hands put together. Cautiously, she brushed her fingertips across a velvety petal of the one closest to her.

Smiling at the sensation, she read the name on the headstone in front of a cracked and vine-covered tomb.

Isolde de Thorne.

Damian's mother.

"She's not there, you know," a young voice said from behind her.

Dubheasa half turned and met the dark eyes of Damian's daughter, Sabrina. "So I've been told." She cocked her head and smiled. "Would you care to tell me about her?"

With no further encouragement needed, the young girl regaled her with stories of the Enchantress and the epic battle when she'd returned to possess Baz's wife, Mackenzie Thorne-Drake.

"That sounds dreadful!" Dubheasa exclaimed. "And you say you were cast into the Otherworld when your da fought her?"

"Yes. Watch. I can conjure lightning, too." Holding out her small hand, Sabrina closed her eyes.

The atmosphere grew heavy, and blue light, like mini lightning bolts, crackled over the center of her palm. She made a fist and opened her eyes to stare at Dubheasa. A soft red glow was visible for an instant before it faded out, restoring her pupils to normal.

"That's called channeling electricity," Sabrina informed her proudly. "I've been practicing with Papa."

"Sure, and I admit to being suitably impressed."

"Ronan calls me 'wee wild beastie,' and you can, too, if you want."

Dubheasa laughed. "He might get salty if I borrowed your nickname to use, don't you think?"

"He never gets mad." With a sharp look toward the altar, Sabrina sighed. "Or he didn't."

Kneeling in front of her, she met the child's too-serious gaze. "Are you afraid he will in the future, sweetie?"

"Papa gets cross if I say." Withdrawing a necklace from the pocket of her coat, she gave it to Dubheasa. "This is for you, Ms. Dovie."

The pendant was lovely in its simplicity. A perfectly oval ruby gemstone, roughly the width of a small egg, was set in platinum metal and surrounded by a plethora of Pavé-style diamonds. The piece had an ageless quality to it, and an odd vibration flowed through to her hand.

"Yeah, and this looks too valuable for you to give to a stranger. I think you should ask your mam or da before giving away family heirlooms."

"It's not a hair-loom."

"Heirloom. It means it's old and meant to be treasured."

A slight frown marred her elfin-like face, but an instant later, she shrugged carelessly. "Isis said to give it to you, and when the time comes, you'll know what to do with it."

"But—" The question died on Dubheasa's lips as the child disappeared. With a sigh, she slipped it over her head. When Damian was finished with Ronan, she'd ask him what he knew.

CHAPTER 27

Back at the Black Cat Inn, Damian checked his watch for the third time in fifteen minutes.

Annoyed, aching, and thoroughly out of sorts, Ronan wanted to rip the damned thing from his friend's wrist and tell him to shove it up his arse.

"We're out of time, Ronan. The mission can't be delayed, and I need to get back to my family so Draven can return." Worry defined the reason for Damian's impatience. "I'm going to give you a boost to your system to help you recover."

The Aether's expression was no-nonsense, and Ronan reluctantly nodded.

Since his power was removed, he'd been unable to bounce back to normal, and none of them could figure out why. Initially, he'd been hesitant to accept help, worried the extra amp might give him a false sense of self and make him feel invincible when he clearly wasn't. But now, he'd accept whatever Damian was offering to get him on his feet again. No way was he facing off with his father when his legs were as shaky as a newborn lamb.

"Remove your shirt."

With an attempt at a grin, Ronan worked his shirt over his head. "Do you want to feel me up, then?"

Not bothering with a comment, Damian used his hands like defibrillators and sent a shock wave through him. Had Ronan not been sitting, he'd have surely fallen down from the explosion of energy.

"Jaysus!" His skin felt fried where it had come in contact with the Aether's palms. A wild glance down at his chest showed angry red burns. *"What the fuck?"*

Alarm was a foreign expression on the Aether's visage, and yet Damian looked as if someone had clubbed him on the side of the head and was about to go in for a second round. "That shouldn't have happened, Ronan. I don't know what the hell is going on with your system, but it seems to have had an adverse reaction to—ah! Of course!"

"Of course what? What the feck is happenin' here, man?"

"I honestly don't know why I didn't consider it earlier," Damian muttered to himself.

"Sure, and are you planning on the big reveal, or are you going to talk to yourself the rest of the bleedin' day?" Ronan snapped.

Cutting him a dry look, Damian conjured herbs along with a mortar and pestle. "You've been fighting the process, and it's manifesting into an allergic type of reaction."

"How is that possible?" Brenna asked from her seat beside Dubheasa. The O'Malleys were all gathered, waiting for the moment they were to kick off the wedding.

"Ronan was violently opposed to the binding to begin with. It's rare, but for those of the upper echelon—like Guardians or Sirens, such as yourself—the ability to manifest is tightly woven into the fabric of their power." The Aether shot Ronan a dirty look. "In other words, our friend here didn't trust me enough to let go. He was subconsciously holding back a part of himself, and it's developed into a nasty little monster with a mind of its own."

"Fuck." Furious with himself, Ronan shook his head in disgust.

"Precisely," Damian replied succinctly. "It's not a difficult fix, and lucky for us, we have a Siren on hand."

Brenna hopped up, an anticipatory smile lighting her face. "How exciting!"

With a snort, Ronan rolled his eyes. "For you, maybe. I'm feeling as if I've been hit by a high-speed train."

Ignoring him, she turned to Damian. "What can I do?"

"Sing."

"Excuse me?" She darted a nervous look toward Eoin.

"Brenna. When I tell you to, I need you to sing to remove what's left of Ronan's magic."

Her skin flushed such a bright red that Ronan was convinced she was about to spontaneously combust. With grim amusement, he waited, positive he knew what she would say. Dear Brenna, shy wallflower she was, didn't disappoint.

"But... but... I don't... I can't... I... we... *I can't have sex with him!*" she finally managed.

"Sex? What?" Dubheasa's indignation nearly rattled the rafters, rivaled only by Eoin's, *"Fuck. No!"*

The fierce effort it took Damian not to lose his composure was beautiful to watch. He opened and closed his mouth no less than seven times, and the struggle to contain his laughter caused his neck to flush fuchsia.

Alastair and Castor didn't bother to hold back. Those two eejits held onto each other, barely able to breathe as they howled like a pair of fecking hyenas.

"Brenna..." Ronan compressed his lips to hold back his own laughter. It wouldn't do to add to her embarrassment when she discovered she'd assumed incorrectly. "I believe what Damian intends is to have me drink whatever wicked concoction he's about to brew up, then have you sing to draw out the contained magic." He allowed a wicked grin. "And it's not that I'm not flattered, but no shaggin' is necessary, darlin'."

"Oh." She nodded. "Oh! Right. Okay. Sure. I—"

That she almost sounded disappointed as she rattled on wasn't lost on him.

Eoin, using his tried and true method, jumped to his feet and kissed her into silence. After a heated minute or two, he drew slightly away and touched his forehead to hers. "Are ya centered again, love?"

"Yes," she gushed, all starry-eyed and glowing. "Thank you."

"It's me greatest pleasure."

Ronan locked gazes with Dubheasa and lost his battle against the threatening laughter.

ONE HOUR LATER, RONAN WAS COMPLETELY DEVOID OF MAGIC, and he fucking hated it. After having nearly undefeatable power, he had become useless, with the exception of his brawn and brains for a physical fight. Certainly, he was no match against anyone with abilities.

"How long into the wedding do you think it will be for Loman to show?" Trevor asked him.

"If I had to guess, when it's time to repeat the vows and the officiant asks for objections to the marriage."

Castor snorted. "That sounds about right. Loman prefers a grand entrance, and what better one is there than objecting to your marriage to the woman he considers the enemy?"

"Exactly."

They were huddled in the O'Malleys' kitchen, waiting for everyone to take their places and start the fake ceremony so they could teleport to the island. Alfred, Alastair's butler, who Ronan had come to realize was better than the one employed by Batman, had dug up a rough map of the island and the layout of its buildings. No architectural plans existed of those structures, so they would be going in blind on that score.

"Damian will disrupt any signals to the outside world the instant we arrive, so even if Loman has alarms set, he won't get notified."

The nagging sense this entire plan would go wrong wouldn't leave Ronan alone. "Every building will be rigged with explosives. It's imperative you all realize that going in," he warned the others. Then, ignoring the guilt at excluding her, he said, "I think Dubheasa should stay behind and hide in the Black Cat's basement until we are done."

Her expected protest was immediate. "Fuck no! I didn't go through the binding of my power to be left behind as a sitting duck. I'll do my part and save those puir bastards Loman is holding prisoner."

"Love—"

"No, Ronan." She tapped the rudimentary map on the table. "There are too many buildings and not enough of us to stage this rescue. The time we have will be limited, at best." Swallowing hard, she shook her head and continued. "And none of you have said it, but we all know we may have to leave some behind to get out before Loman returns."

"I'm not getting out," Ronan retorted. When she gasped, he captured her hand and gently squeezed. "I didn't mean it the way it sounded, Dove. I meant I'm staying to see this ended with Trevor and Castor while the rest of you return home."

"I'm your chosen mate, as you are mine. We're to be Isis's and Anu's selected Guardians. You need to trust me, Ronan. Trust that I can help and be a worthy mate."

Her sincerity cut him to the core, and he wanted to strenuously object, but she had a point.

"I trust you to help," he replied gruffly.

The first strands of Cian's music drifted to them, and as one, they stood.

"Loman will have arrived just outside the wards." Castor checked his phone as it pinged. "Damian's removed the force field from the island. It's time to teleport." Addressing the hired security directly, he said, "You all have your assigned buildings and the location to meet up with any survivors. If they are too weak, leave them by the airfield. We have transports lined up."

Dubheasa's hand was clammy in his, and Ronan gave her a confident smile. "First one to find Reggie wins the prize, love."

"It better be grand, because I'm after winning it." She rose on her tiptoes and quickly kissed him. "Let's go."

Castor stepped up to them and clasped their hands. "I'll be your captain for today's flight. Buckle up. There may be turbulence during the ride."

Dubheasa's laughter was the balm Ronan needed to soothe his nerves.

"Fecking eejit," he muttered affectionately, surprising himself that he actually held his recently found uncle in such high esteem. "Just get us there already."

His cells warmed to almost burning, and without his own magic, the sensation was more uncomfortable than normal. It took him a precious minute or two on the other side of the teleport to recover and cool down. It appeared Dubheasa was similarly affected.

"You two okay?" Castor inquired.

"Aye. We will be. Go do what you need to."

"Make sure your ear com works."

First Ronan, then Dubheasa, tested their earpiece, sending and receiving a message to Castor after he'd walked twenty feet away. After giving them the thumbs-up, he ran toward his designated buildings.

Ronan grabbed Dubheasa's arm when she would've turned away. "Be careful, Dove. Please."

"I intend to." Her smile was beatific and punched him right in the heart. "I've a lot to live for."

"You've got your knife?"

"Aye."

Still, he was reluctant to let her go as he stared down into her excited emerald orbs. "This isn't some craic. It's serious, yeah?"

"I know." After a sweet pat to his chest, she turned and ran for the closest building.

The sense of wrongness was extreme, and Ronan almost ran after her. Holding his breath as she touched the door handle, he let out a hearty exhale when she went inside and nothing immediately happened.

"Fuck me, I'm getting paranoid," he muttered.

"But that paranoia has saved your life on more than one occasion, boyo," his inner voice reminded him.

"Fuck."

CHAPTER 28

Dubheasa was the first to find Reggie's cell, grinning when he stared at her in stunned disbelief. "I'm rescuing you, Reg. Tell me how to open your cage."

"You have to leave, Dubheasa. Loman knows you're coming, and he's planned for this."

His urgency spiked her already high adrenaline. "How?"

"Doesn't matter. You've got to go!" he ordered.

"But she's here now, Reginald, me boy," a voice purred from behind her. "I'm after thinking we should give her a room of her own, yeah?"

Heart hammering out of her chest, Dubheasa spun to see Castor's twin reclining against the bars of a cell diagonal to them. The difference was slighter than she'd imagined. Loman had more bulk, shorter hair, and soulless eyes.

"Run, Dubheasa," Reggie hissed in a low voice. "As if your fucking life depends on it, because it bloody well does."

"Sure, and it would be a feckin' shame if ya left without greetin' your host, girl. One would question your upbringin', yeah?"

Loman's taunts fueled a hereto-unknown anger within her

for his cruelty. Toward Reggie, toward Ronan, toward all the poor souls trapped within the walls of this dreary prison. "And would it have been better to be spawned and raised by *you*, ya fecking gobshite?" she snarled.

Reggie made a grab for her as she started forward, screaming in agony at the instantaneous second-degree burn he received from crossing the magical barrier that held him captive.

"Reggie!" Her helplessness to ease his pain fed the fire raging within her.

Loman's sadistic laughter rang out as Reggie cradled his arm to his chest. "Now, Reginald, ya had to know the consequences. You've seen it often enough, yeah?"

"Go bugger yourself, old man!"

"You'll never learn, boyo." Not bothering to straighten, Loman touched his bracelet.

The symbol above the cell lit, and a blue light traveled from the sigil, down along the walls, and illuminated the stones underneath Reggie's feet. Fear filled his light jade eyes an instant before a scream was wrenched from his throat and echoed down the corridor. His body convulsed for what seemed like forever before the supercharged floor shut off and he collapsed on the ground.

Dubheasa wanted to tear through the barrier to get to him, to see if he still lived, but doing so would cost her own life. As she faced Loman, her gaze locked onto the three-inch-wide steel bracelet around his wrist. The blue light slowly faded from the sigil matching the one above the cells. That damned band had to be how Loman was maintaining the enchantment to contain his prisoners.

"He'll live to mouth off another day, girl. Don't waste your tears on the likes of him," Loman sneered.

Unaware she'd been crying, Dubheasa swiped her fingers beneath her eyes. Sure enough, they came back wet. "At least someone cares enough about him to shed a tear. You'll go to your grave with no one to mourn you," she taunted.

"I've been to me grave twice already. Ya think it breaks me heart to have no mourners?" His bark of laughter was harsh and caused her skin to prickle. "I've no fear of death."

"You should, because it's coming for you soon enough."

Contempt curled his lip. "Not from the likes of you. You're a weak fool, ya are."

From the shadows of the cell behind him, Dubheasa detected movement, but she was quick to ignore it. Whoever, whatever, was in that cell was not her primary concern. Somehow, she had to get away from Loman, and her chances appeared slim at that moment. The island was massive, and the compound housed at least ten prisons with hundreds of cellblocks. Some of which, like the one she was in, weren't connected to the central building at all. The rescue team she'd arrived with was spread thinly, her earpiece was no longer transmitting, and her telepathic connection to Ronan had gone by way of her abilities, so rescue wasn't likely to be imminent.

"Weak?" She snorted. "I'm imagining everyone is weak to your limited way of thinking, yeah?"

"Aye."

He straightened from the bars, and it startled Dubheasa to realize he was as big and intimidating as Ronan. He might be Castor's identical twin, but this guy wore his bulk in the most threatening of manners. Neither Ronan's nor Castor's size had caused her a moment of fear, but Loman made her feel diminutive in comparison. Added to the fact that she was powerless, where he had magic on his side, and her predicament became more perilous.

Again, the shadows behind him shifted, and again, she ignored the movement.

"You have plenty of abilities, O'Connor." The smile she gave him was one she'd used on recalcitrant clients during her days at Lamda. Designed to cajole and charm, it had worked about ninety percent of the time. "You could afford to let Reggie and me go."

Distaste curled his mouth downward, and he shook his head. "You O'Malleys! Cowards, the lot of ya! And when I'm done with these pitiful eejits, I'll be retrieving what ya owe me, to be sure."

Righteous anger gripped her, and she dropped the pretense. "Owe you?" She scoffed. "We owe you nothing, Loman O'Connor. Nothing but a poisoned bullet to that dead black heart of yours. What you had from us, your family stole, and it was never yours to begin with!"

"Hold your *whist*, or I'll spell ya to silence, ya bleedin' she-devil!" Hands curled into fists, he looked ready to pummel her under those meaty weapons of his. "I—ugh—"

Thick, muscular arms plunged through the bars and wrapped around Loman's neck in a stranglehold. Blisters broke along the rapidly darkening skin, and the man's agony was made obvious by his guttural yell.

"Get the bracelet, Dubheasa!" the prisoner ordered. "Hurry, girl!"

Diving into action, she bolted across the aisle and grabbed hold of Loman's right wrist. He fought like a demon possessed, even as his face turned purple from lack of air. Between clawing at his captor's face and swinging at her, Loman made it difficult to remove the band. The clasp was tricky, and the precious seconds it took to unclip it caused Dubheasa to sweat. Just as she believed success was within her grasp, Loman's hammer of a fist grazed her jaw and knocked her down. Hitting the floor, she lost her grip on the bracelet, and it skittered through the bars of Reggie's cell.

She had only one choice—thrust her arm through the opening to retrieve it before Loman could get free. And by the looks of her rescuer's seared limbs, it wouldn't be long. Her current predicament would require her to burn her own skin to retrieve the controller.

Chancing one last glance at the prisoner, she met his agonized moss-green eyes.

Her heart stuttered.

She knew those eyes.

"Da?"

"I can't hold him for long, love. Get the bracelet, yeah?"

Her mind raced with the why and how of his presence here, but she was out of time. Her father's skin had begun to smoke, and the sheer torment on his face tore at her soul. Just as she would've reached through the bars for the band, Reggie's hand closed around it, and his gaze locked with hers.

"Go," he mouthed.

With a barely discernible nod, she scrambled to her feet. But she only made it the distance of one cell when a hand fisted in her hair and threw her to the floor. The force of the attack sent her across the expanse of aisle, and she collided with the bars containing her father.

The smell of his charred flesh triggered her gag reflex, and she valiantly fought to hold back the vomit. If he could endure, so could she.

"I'm sorry, Da," she whispered achingly.

The left side of his mouth twitched as if he intended to give her the standard half smile he always graced her with when she was a small child. After he disappeared from her life, she'd come to remember that small gesture as his silent way of telling her everything was going to be all right, although it never was.

The resonant clank of disengaging locks reverberated throughout the building, and to her shock, the cell in front of her opened. Wasting no time, she dove toward her father and cradled his head in her lap. Yes, she should've gotten the hell out of Loman's reach, but the man was in full-rage mode and any attempt to escape would likely see her dead at his hands.

"You're a pathetic mouse of a girl, ya are. Not fit to be the mate of my son," Loman said with a look of hatred. "He'll be well rid of ya, to be sure."

"He loves her, Uncle." Directly behind Loman, standing in the center of the corridor, was Reggie. Cradled within his arms was a crossbow, loaded and ready for bear. "And if you want him to kill you for good this time, then go ahead and hurt her. But I know Ronan—far better than you ever could hope to—and I can promise you he'll tear you limb from limb."

"Bah! Stop plaguing me with your blatherin', boy!" Loman snapped without turning. To Dubheasa, he said, "He makes me feckin' brain ache with all his dire predictions, he does."

Reggie's truth might've hurt her chances of survival, adding the nail to her coffin, so to speak. As much as Loman hated all O'Malleys, he seemed to despise her more than most. Perhaps the reason was that she held Ronan's affections, where his father never could.

Ronan didn't love lightly, and with good reason. Using fists and ugly insults, Loman had tried to mold his son into an unfeeling machine. A clone of himself. Ronan's abusive childhood had made him reticent and suspicious of everyone's motives, and yet, he'd offered Dubheasa unconditional love. Trusting her to keep his heart whole as she had put her trust in him.

She looked down into her father's tortured eyes.

He, too, knew the truth of it. One way or another, Dubheasa would be Loman O'Connor's next victim.

Holding her gaze, her father opened his mouth as if to speak, but no sound left him. Again and again, he repeated a single word, but she had no idea what he was trying to say. His body began to shudder as if he were freezing, which was at direct odds with the burning hot skin of his arms and the side of his face he'd pressed to the bars. Dubheasa only prayed he could hold out long enough for a healer to arrive, but her stomach clenched as she noted the rapid graying of his features.

"It's going to be all right, Da. I promise ya it will."

"You're a fool, girl. He's a dead man." The small hairs on her arms rose at the vehemence in Loman's tone.

Rising to a standing position, she faced him. Although her magic was bound, she hadn't come empty-handed, and she eased her hand close to her waistband, hoping to reach the knife there before Loman struck.

Reggie must've been warned by Loman's tone, and he raised the crossbow to his shoulder to take aim. "Back away from her, old man. I'll not tell you twice."

Loman did turn then. Hands raised to his shoulders as if he intended to surrender, he faced his nephew. "Are ya man enough to pull the trigger again, boyo? When I return, I won't be as kind to ya as I was this time, I won't."

There was no doubt or hesitation in Reggie's expression, and the thwack of the arrow hitting its target was overly loud to Dubheasa's ears.

As was Ronan's disbelieving bellow as it filled the cellblock.

It seemed to take a lifetime for her to glance down at her chest, possibly because of the dread of what she'd find. There was no real pain, just what felt like a forceful punch to her breast, clear through to her back. The clatter of the crossbow caught her attention as she dropped to her knees, barely registering the sharp pain of contacting with the stone.

Lifting her head, she met Reggie's dismayed gaze. In the depths of his eyes, she witnessed his remorse and the resignation that his life was over along with hers. His fear that Ronan wouldn't question why he had shot her, and the conviction that his cousin would kill him regardless.

As she collapsed and her shoulder bounced against the

ground, Loman flashed her a gloating smile, so evil in his pleasure. The fucker had anticipated Reggie's shot and teleported out of the arrow's path.

Not wanting his to be the last face she saw, she turned her head toward the rush of running feet.

Ronan's frantic eyes turned a deep gunmetal gray with his looming grief.

"I'm sorry," she said. A death rattle choked off the last of her apology as metallic-tasting liquid pooled in her mouth. She tried again. "I'm so—" Once again, coughs caused her body to spasm, and her blood splattered against his charcoal-gray shirt, adding to the dark stains of his enemies' blood already there.

"Don't talk, Dove," he cried urgently. "Don't try to talk. We'll get ya to the healer. Just hold on, love."

His words ran together the more panicked he became, and she tried to smile. To assure him he'd be just fine without her. Because he was Ronan Fucking O'Connor, the best man she knew.

Freezing and exhausted, with no more energy remaining, she closed her eyes and turned her face toward the warmth of his large palm. She lifted her lids to view—and perhaps memorize for the afterlife—his beautiful face one last time. "Love you," she murmured as she exhaled her last breath.

CHAPTER 29

When Dubheasa's ear com had stopped transmitting, Ronan's inner voice refused to give him peace until he returned to find her. But he wasn't prepared for the scene he'd stumbled across, and now he knelt, frozen in shock at the sight of her still form. With no magic to heal her, none to keep her on this plane with him, he was desolate.

"Save her," he cried hoarsely. "Please, Da. You're the only one with the power."

"Sure, and tell me, boyo, why would I be after revivin' her when I already have what I want?"

Ronan had momentarily forgotten the lessons of his childhood. Begging would gain him naught. Because he wanted Dubheasa more than his own life, Loman would deny him. Needing a new tactic, Ronan attempted to rack his traumatized brain.

"She was to be a Guardian," Reggie stated clearly and coolly as if he were simply imparting facts, with no care one way or another. "If you bring her back, you can take her power along with Ronan's."

Gratitude filled Ronan, but he kept his visage blank as his gaze lowered to Dubheasa's lifeless eyes. Raw panic tried to wrap its ugly, insidious fists around his mind. It crept forward, ready to turn him into a reactive Neanderthal. But he needed to keep a level head. Though she wasn't lost to him completely, the longer Dubheasa was in the Otherworld, the higher the chance parts of her soul would fracture off, leaving her dispassionate and distant when she returned to this plane. And Ronan needed her whole. Needed her fiery nature to keep his own soul warm and alive. Currently, the only person capable of bringing her back with any expediency was his heartless father.

"You have enough magic from all these poor bastards to revive her. If you save her, I'll give you more of what you want," Ronan found himself saying. Steeling himself, he glanced up and locked gazes with Loman. "I'll give you the power of a Guardian."

Greed lit his father's eyes even as a disgusted sneer curled his lips. "And hers. I want hers if it's true she was to be a Guardian."

"It's true."

A moan sounded a small distance beyond Dubheasa's body, but Ronan didn't look to see who had made the sound. Likely another unfortunate soul his kindhearted Dove had tried to save.

As Loman's head turned toward the person in the shadows, his smile became gloating. "See O'Malley? Ya came after me, thinking you could best me, didn't ya? I told ya before that I always win, I did."

Whipping his head in the direction of the prisoner he'd intentionally ignored, Ronan registered an elderly male with pain-filled green eyes locked on Dubheasa. The man's arms had suffered major burns, and angry blisters rose on the darkened skin, but still, he stretched them in an attempt to touch her.

"O'Malley?" The name fell involuntarily from Ronan's lips.

As their gazes collided, he saw what he'd missed. Dubheasa's father. It could be no other. The guy bore a remarkable resemblance to Cian, but bearing auburn hair laced with silver highlights.

Ronan's chest ached.

There lay the true reason Dubheasa hadn't tried to escape when Loman came upon her. The father she thought had left her and her siblings behind was, in truth, a prisoner of Ronan's own father. And Dubheasa, with her forgiving nature, was too loyal by far. Doubtless, she'd have tried to save him or remain to offer comfort in his existing state of injury.

Dismissing the wounded man, Loman lifted his hand toward Reggie. "The controller, boyo. I'll have it back now, I will. Sure, and the others are eager to go back into their cages."

The shuffling of feet throughout the cellblock finally penetrated Ronan's consciousness, and down the aisle, the captives who were capable of walking inched their way toward the main exit, trying desperately to go unnoticed.

"Let them go, Da." Ronan stood and blocked Loman's view of the hallway. "You've got me."

His father turned feral in a mere blink. "But you're powerless, ya useless fuck! Ya think I don't know that you bound your magic to come here? There's no light radiatin' off ya, like a true Guardian would have. Just as your *hor* had none," he spat.

Right when Ronan would've charged and pummeled his father to death, Reggie stepped between them and placed a hand on Ronan's chest, attempting to restrain him.

"It will take but one phone call to restore what's been bound, Uncle," Reggie said smoothly, presumably stalling for time for the remaining prisoners to escape. "Ronan can call the Aether and have his abilities returned in an instant."

"Aye, and I'm not sure if you're friend or foe, Reg, but ya can quit being helpful now," Ronan said tightly. He'd been secretly hoping Loman, with his mad desire to amass more power, would've failed to catch that the Guardian aura was gone. But he should've remembered Loman never missed a trick.

"The controller, boyo," Loman repeated, his tone bordering on lethal. "Toss it to me now."

After sharing a grim look with Reggie, Ronan nodded. "Aye. Give it to him."

"I'm not going back in that cage," his cousin said, inching away from Ronan and adding more distance between Loman and himself.

When they were children, their parents' favorite pastime was torturing them for imagined slights. The objective: teach the next generation to be as ruthless and unfeeling as they were. Whenever the adults felt a lesson needed to be taught, one unfortunate O'Connor child was beaten and locked in the damp, window-less tower for days on end. Similar to the dank prison where they now stood, the rooms had been spelled against escape.

Their cousin Moira had gone half mad and returned from her punishment crueler than when she'd started it, much to the delight of Loman and his siblings. So it was understandable that Reggie would balk. And for as much as he'd tried to play it off, to remain careless and seemingly unfeeling, he'd become highly claustrophobic, the same as Ronan. Neither could stand to be confined.

"For Dubheasa," Ronan said in a low voice for Reggie alone. "Please, cousin."

Reggie forgot himself, and his British accent slipped. "Jaysus! You're askin' a lot of me."

"The longer we delay..." Swallowing hard, Ronan shook his head.

With a savage curse, Reggie chucked the bracelet at Loman's feet.

"Yeah, and it's time ya return to your cage, Reginald," Loman crowed. *"Where you belong!"*

The taunt was one too many, and the rabid animal buried deep within Reggie tore loose of its restraints. With a chilling, outraged cry, he launched himself at Loman and played right into the man's hands.

Already expecting the reaction, Loman snapped his fingers, and the forgotten crossbow was propped against his shoulder, locked and loaded. With a sweep of one arm, he used his magic to throw Reggie into his former cell.

"*Clostra!*"

The bars slammed into place with a reverberating clank.

Reggie paled as Loman aimed the crossbow.

"No!" Ronan shouted and charged forward, directing the weapon upward with the heel of his hand. "If you want me to cooperate, you'll kill no one else."

The back of Loman's elbow crashed into Ronan's nose, and the crunch of bone on bone, followed by a riot of pain exploding in his face, was another reminder of his father's teachings. The most ruthless family member made the rules and expected those rules to be obeyed.

"Ya dare tell me no, boy? You? The eejit snivelin' over a worthless dead girl?"

A side kick to his gut sent Ronan flying backward, and his head slammed into the cement wall between the cells, causing an explosion of stars behind his lids. Using every ounce of restraint, he didn't so much as grunt. Any sign of weakness brought with it a harsher beating. For Reggie and Dubheasa, he'd take the punishment without complaint.

Wiping the dripping blood from his nose with the back of his wrist, he met his father's contemptuous gaze. "I'm after begging your pardon, Da. It was an instinctive reaction." Cautiously straightening, he gestured toward Reggie with his head and immediately regretted it when the room spun around him. He tried to appear casual as he leaned against the wall for support. "If you kill him, you can't convert him back to your side. Reggie's always been useful in the past, hasn't he?"

With a considering expression, Loman studied Ronan for a long moment. A crafty smile curled his lips, and before anyone could react, he pointed the crossbow and pulled the trigger.

Dubheasa's father grunted once, then breathed no more.

"If ya see her again, be sure to tell your *hor* that your insolence was what caused her da to die, yeah?" Loman told Ronan. "See how she feels about ya when she learns you're to blame."

Never had Ronan's desire to tear Loman's smug head from his body been as strong and necessary as it was at that exact moment. His muscles fired and shook in an effort to break his tight control.

"Yeah, and it's time for you to enter your own cage, Ronan, me boy." Loman eased down to pick up the controller, careful to keep his son within his sight. "Now."

Feeling decidedly insolent, Ronan swept his arms wide. "Sure, and I don't see any with my name on them."

"I'd have thought it obvious. It's the one with your dead lover and her da."

His stomach rolled and vomit threatened. If Loman closed him in with two dead bodies, one being Dubheasa, Ronan would lose what was left of his rapidly declining sanity.

His father, however, didn't give him a choice. "Get in the cell, boyo, or I kill your precious cousin here and now."

FINTAN RELEASED THE CRYSTAL GLOBE RESTING ON THE ALTAR and faced Damian. "Ronan's magic cannot be restored yet. But know this, if you deny him his request, he'll hate ya for it, and an O'Connor's hate is a powerful thing."

Damian watched the real-time vision of Ronan stepping into the cell, and wondered if their decision to send him in without his power had been a wise one. "He'll go insane, locked up with her without a way to escape." Just as Damian himself would've, had it been Vivian in Dubheasa's place. "We can't leave him there."

"Now's not the time to rescue him, all the same. We have to prepare."

"Dammit, Fintan! He's my friend!"

The Seer winced from the lashing pain Damian's anger caused but remained silent.

"Forgive me," he said after regaining control of his temper. Hurting others was the last thing he intended. "What do you suggest we do?"

"Castor's the only person to have escaped that island, and he's the only one wily enough to fight his twin and win."

"He's already there, with no idea of what is happening."

"Aye, but I'm going back to tell him."

"I'm going with you."

Fintan shook his head. "There's nothing you can do, Damian. The Authority wants the girl dead for reasons they'll not reveal, and your presence will fuel Ronan's anger, making him a mindless animal."

"Then I'll go have a discussion with those in charge," he replied grimly. Already suspecting what the Authority was after, he gave Fintan a tight smile. "Get Castor, Simon, and Trevor to that building. Now."

The instant the Seer teleported, Damian went in search of Sabrina and Vivian.

He found them in the kitchen, preparing lunch.

"I have to go. If I don't return by nightfall, find the panic room and seal yourselves in until either Isis or I return for you."

"Damian!" Vivian's alarm was expected, and he brushed his knuckles along her silky cheek.

"Please, Viv. We've discussed this, and I've got to help in any way I can. If it means bargaining with the devil we know…" He shrugged, trying to make light of a heavy decision.

"But the Authority? They'll demand too much."

"They will." Meeting the wary eyes of his daughter, he winked. "But I've a few tricks up these old sleeves of mine."

"We'll be safe, Papa," she assured him. "I'll protect Mama and Nate."

His heart caught in his throat at her wording. "Will you need to?"

"I don't think so."

"I'll be back as soon as I can."

CHAPTER 30

Castor had been studying the sigils above the cells when the doors for the entire cellblock buzzed and swung open.

"Go!" he shouted. "Get out now!"

Moving as swiftly as he could, he checked each room for stragglers or those who couldn't walk on their own. Only three were too weak, but a few kinder witches stepped up to offer their support. One or two he recognized from encounters years past.

"I thought he was you at first," a woman behind him said.

Turning, he tried to place the face. Utter shock struck him when he recognized her. "Sylvie?"

She smiled tiredly. "Hello, Alex."

"*Christ!* Everyone thinks…" He shook his head. "How?"

"Victor Salinger caught me years ago, probably as another strike against Alastair, via his brother-in-law, Jace. Victor burned my home down in the process, killing my family." Her expression haunted, she shook her head.

"But that was decades ago," Alex protested.

"The Désorcelers created a roster of prisoners once upon a

time." Her dull gaze absently swept the cellblock. "It put me on Loman O'Connor's radar. I was one of the first people he sought to lock up again."

Unable to calculate the trauma a second capture must've caused her, he did the only thing he could and hugged her tightly. "I'm sorry, Sylvie. So fucking sorry."

For a second, she embraced him back, then drew away. "Save the rest of them if you can. They've been through the same as me. We can talk when it's done."

"Always practical and sweet," he said softly and kissed her forehead. "If you can teleport, go to Thorne Manor and tell them who you are. If not, head north to the clearing. A chopper is making runs."

She nodded and shuffled for the door, the faded blue scrubs she wore hanging off her slight frame.

Rage detonated in his brain.

Loman had a lot to answer for, and Alex intended to extract it out of his ass in as painful a process as possible.

"Castor!"

Fintan and Trevor appeared in the doorway in front of Sylvie, edging sideways to let her pass.

He met them halfway. "What?"

"Dubheasa..." Trevor gulped and gestured to Fintan.

"Dubheasa's dead," Fintan said flatly. "Loman never left the island, and he's captured Ronan."

"Jesus Fucking Christ!" Castor wanted to throw up. In as much as he knew something would go wrong, he'd hoped it wouldn't be his nephew. Ronan's life until meeting Dubheasa had been a goddamned nightmare, and it looked like it would continue to be. "Where?"

"The building where you teleported in."

"Let's go," he snapped.

Fintan put a hand on his arm. "You need a plan, ya do. Charging in unprepared will get us all killed."

"Then fucking explain it to me, Seer. I don't have all fucking day!"

"Sure, and you'll be calming the feck down, or I'll not be tellin' ya a feckin' thing."

"I swear to—" Closing his eyes, Castor inhaled and exhaled a few deep breaths, hoping to chill the hell out and get rid of the curtain of red blocking his vision.

"Blane will go with you, cloaked, and you'll enter from the south door as I enter with another Death Dealer from the north."

Trevor shot Fintan a sharp glance. "What other—"

"Me." From behind his brother, Simon Blane approached. "Rumor has it you don't have enough juice on your own to kill the bastard, Trev. I thought I'd add my new abilities to yours."

"No! You have no experience with this shit, Simon. There's no way in hell I'm letting you do this."

"It's the only way this feckin' thing will be workin'." Fintan, in a fit of temper, shoved Trevor. "And it's tired I am of the lot of you questioning the process."

Both Trevor and Castor froze in their surprise.

"Any more feckin' questions, or are ya done wastin' me time?"

Simon grinned when they remained silent. "I think that means we're ready to go."

As they ran toward the fray, Castor's fury grew and he made a concerted effort to shove it away. Anger had no place in battle. He needed to be levelheaded and calculating. As he got to the south entrance, he shot Trevor a sharp look. "Remind me when this is over and we're home again, to punch Damian in his perfect fucking face—about five or six times."

"Done."

"Do you have a cloaking sp—Okay, then," he said as Trevor vanished before his eyes. Fintan counted down through the earpiece, and Castor didn't wait for ONE.

"*Fuck!*" Fintan's curse rang in his ear, but Alex didn't give a shit. He had a brother to kill.

Loman greeted him with a sneer. "Sure, and I was wondering when you'd show up. Shouldn't your keeper be with ya?"

Knowing damned well he meant the Aether, Castor pasted on a bored expression. "He didn't think you were important enough to bother."

"You'll not bait me this time, ya feckin' gobshite!" Loman snapped.

"Hmm, sounds like I already have."

The door behind his brother slammed shut, and Loman lobbed a lightning bolt in the direction of the newcomer. Already anticipating the move, the Seer stepped out of the path and lifted his middle fingers in salute.

Alex didn't think he had any humor left at that point, but the gesture was so Fintan Sullivan that he laughed. "Looks like we're all quaking in our boots with fear of you, Loman."

"You're a proper fool if you aren't."

"Meh."

"Let me ask ya, then, are ya prepared to sacrifice your beloved nephew to the fight this time?" Standing in the center of the aisle, Loman lifted his arms and gestured to the cells on either side of him. "Sure, and ya might save one, but which one would ya be after savin'?"

Castor refused to look, refused to have his concentration broken by anything he might see.

A cunning light entered Loman's eyes as he grinned. "It always comes back to this, doesn't it, Antoine?"

"Alex," Castor snapped, not really caring if his brother used his given name or not. His goal was to keep Loman preoccupied until everyone was in place. "And what is it that it always comes to?"

"You tryin' to outsmart me and failin'."

"Pfft. You're a delusional motherfucker, Loman." Risking a glance at Fintan, he said, "Correct me if I'm wrong, Fin, but didn't we kill him twice already?"

Reggie shifted toward the entrance of his cell and raised his hand like a star pupil. "I can answer that one. Yep, and I'll gladly claim credit for the arrow to the chunk of coal he calls a heart."

With a snarl, Loman threw a ball of fire in his direction, only to have it bounce back. He dove for the floor with a vicious curse.

"Weren't expecting that, Uncle?" Reggie said with a harsh laugh. "Is it senility creeping in? I mean, you *were* the bloody bastard who cast the boomerang spell on my cell to begin with."

"Shut the fuck up! You're as thick as manure but half as useful, ya are!" Loman snapped.

Castor clapped his hands. "Good one, Lo."

Behind him, Fintan gave the signal Alex had been waiting for.

"Okay, I'm tired of this game now."

With a simple swipe of his hand, he froze time.

Only Loman wasn't the statue Castor had expected him to be.

"Ya think I don't learn from past mistakes, brother?" He threw back his head and laughed as Alex tried twice more to lock the room down. "You'll wear yourself out tryin', ya will. Reginald, would ya like to explain to me thickheaded brother just why his parlor tricks won't be workin' here?"

"I'll leave the honor to you."

"You're a humorless dryshite, boyo." Loman shrugged and crossed his arms over his chest. "Those Désorceler feckers built these compounds to keep people like you contained, Antoine. I'm shocked you're not after rememberin' since I found your name on their roster, I did."

"Yeah, I'm afraid my stay was short-lived. I didn't quite care for the accommodations."

Loman lifted his wrist and continued as if Castor had never spoken. "See this bit of jewelry here? Yeah, and it's a useful tool, to be sure. I can control this entire cellblock and everyone in it with a touch of a button, I can." With a dramatic flair, he swirled his finger in the air, then dropped it to press one of the symbols.

He never made contact before his arm was halted midair. "Wha—!"

The cloaking spells fell from the Blane brothers. Each held one of Loman's wrists in theirs, keeping him firmly secure as Castor approached. Without warning, Alex kicked out and connected with Loman's balls, feeling no remorse for the gray hue of his skin as he fought not to throw up his guts.

"That's because I hate you." Ripping the bracelet from his brother's wrist, Castor hit the sigil he knew would open the doors and powered down the entire corridor to halt the theft of abilities from those present. When he was satisfied, he turned to Ronan. "Stand down, son. We have a plan, and you'll only screw it up in your rage."

RONAN CHARGED THE OPENING, UNCARING OF ANYTHING BUT crushing his father's skull. Blind rage consumed him, and the need to take action overwhelmed in its intensity.

But Castor had anticipated his action and threw up an invisible barrier, locking Ronan in his cell.

"Let me go," he growled.

"Can't do that, Ronan."

"I'll not tell you again, Castor. If you don't release me, I'll kill you instead."

Ignoring him, his uncle nodded at the Death Dealers. "Obliterate him."

Loman's eyes flew wide at the realization of what was to happen. Like a wild stallion trapped in a too-small stall, he bucked and kicked, attempting to throw off the Blane brothers. Although he fought like a man possessed, he was no match for those who held him. Still, he stretched and strained as he reached for the controller in Castor's hand. The Blanes, sweat streaming from their faces and ragged breaths sawing in and out of their lungs from the effort, dragged Loman into the closest cell and chained him to the wall.

Ronan banged up against the clear barrier again and again like an enraged bull. His only thought was to rip Loman's heart from his chest before it stopped beating, with the arrow used to murder Dubheasa. Even if it was only physical pain, and not emotional, his father needed to feel a fraction of what Ronan was going through.

"Let me out, Castor, you fucking *sonofabitch*!"

Reggie approached his cell, and the sympathy shining from his dull gaze robbed Ronan of breath. "Let me be your hands, cousin. Tell me what it is you'd have me do."

"I need to be the one to kill him, Reg." His voice was hoarse and barely above a whisper. "I need to be the one."

With a quick glance over his shoulder, Reggie leaned forward. "I'll release you to do what you must, but let the Death Dealers do their job first, Ronan. Promise me, or he'll be back to terrorize the world again." His cousin placed his palm flat against the barrier, level with Ronan's. "Promise me."

Closing his eyes, Ronan rested his head against the invisible shield, then drew back and banged it. Again and again, he smacked his forehead on the wall, screaming from his soul. When he would've done it a sixth time, the barrier dissolved, and he fell forward into Reggie's waiting arms.

As they crashed to the floor, he heard his cousin's sob. "I'm so sorry, Ronan. Please don't hate me."

"I'm reserving all my hate for Loman." Rough and overused,

his voice sounded as if it belonged to another. Shoving off the ground like an Olympic athlete, he ran for the cell containing his father, arrow shaft in hand.

Loman's soul was barely hanging on by the time Ronan plunged the tip of the arrow into his cold, ruthless heart. In a fit of grief and rage, he repeated the gesture until his arm gave out and his father's chest resembled Swiss cheese.

The others wore looks of pity or shock and, in Fintan's case, resignation as if everything had turned out the way he expected but had hoped it wouldn't. Unable to bear the weight of their judgment, he glanced down at his blood-soaked hands. Somehow, Ronan had thought his father's blood would ooze black.

"He's gone? No coming back?"

"No coming back," Trevor assured him quietly.

"How does it work, the disintegration of his soul?"

"The way it was explained to me is that we snuff out his energy and he simply ceases to exist," Simon replied.

Gaze locked on the trail of blood running from his arms to his elbows, Ronan nodded. "Is there ever a time you simply kill people and their souls move on?"

"Don't even think about it, son." Castor placed his palm flat against his back, but Ronan shrugged him off. "You'll see her again. This isn't the end for the two of you."

"Get Damian."

CHAPTER 31

As Castor left to make the call, Ronan crossed to Dubheasa's cell and sat down beside her. He'd have lifted her head into his lap, but he didn't want to taint her with his father's evilness. And by that yardstick, he should probably leave her in peace when Damian restored her soul.

As he contemplated life and death, it occurred to him that the Blane brothers should be able to revive as well as dispatch souls. Death Dealers had the ultimate power when it came to manipulating the living.

"Can you bring her back, Trevor?"

"No." The gruffness in Blane's voice spoke of finality.

"Sure, and why not? You're a bleeding Death Dealer," Ronan spat. "You hold sway over the living and the dying. Why the fuck not?"

Trevor's look was one of helplessness. "I'm sorry, O'Connor. It's not within my ability to do."

"Not within your ability, or you're after being the Authority's fuckin' puppet?" Ronan challenged with a glare that promised retribution. *"She was your fucking friend!"*

The air within the cellblock contracted and expanded as the

Aether stepped through a rift in the fabric of space. Behind him, Ronan glimpsed the high table of the Authority just before the opening sealed shut.

"I can't reach..." Castor trailed off as he returned and saw the Aether had already joined them.

"I was unreachable." Damian didn't approach Ronan right away, instead strolling the length of the prison, silently absorbing the empty cells and the intricate symbols above the openings. "So much death," he murmured, trancelike. "And pain."

Ronan attempted to recall his attention to the immediate issue. "Damian, you need to bring Dove back."

Ignoring him, the Aether paused to stare dispassionately at Loman. "He's not presently here, but are you sure you decimated his soul, Blane?"

"It's done."

"Thank you." He nodded to the others. "I'd like you all to leave now. I need to speak with Ronan."

A warning bell clanked in Ronan's brain. Damian refused to look at him, and Castor shifted uneasily as he glanced between them. Whatever was about to come out of his friend's mouth would sever Damian's and his relationship forever.

Feeling as if he were hundreds of years old, Ronan climbed to his feet and shuffled toward him. "Damian."

"This conversation needs privacy."

His heart stopped in his chest at Damian's severe tone, and he shot a panicked look in Castor's direction. The rising unhappiness darkened his uncle's irises to a wintery blue.

"Don't," Ronan cried in desperation. "Don't tell me you won't bring her back, man. I know ya can."

Damian's expression remained aloof, his gaze unfeeling.

Ronan snapped, and in a red haze, he curled his sticky hands in the Pima cotton fabric of Damian's shirt. *"You have the ability!* You can pull her back from the Otherworld if you choose."

"I don't choose."

Staggering back, Ronan stared at the man he'd once believed to be his friend. The frosty tone, the finality, the flinty stare... No, it wasn't Damian, the man. The Aether, the unfeeling judge, jury, and executioner of the witch community, stood in his place.

With jerky movements, his disbelieving gaze still locked on Damian, Ronan turned his head toward Castor. "Reset time, Uncle. I'll never ask another favor of you, but I'll be forever in your debt. You've only to ask me, and I'll be there without question."

"He won't go against me," the Aether stated with an arrogant assurance Ronan could never duplicate in a million years. Expression easing marginally, Damian infused compassion into his voice. "Come with me, Ronan. I'll take you home. The O'Malleys—"

"No!" The denial was torn from the very fiber of his soul. Backing into the cell, he sat on his arse beside Dubheasa's hip. His wild stare locked with Reggie's where he stood observing the entire exchange with an astonished expression.

"Jaysus! Tell me I'm havin' a nightmare here. Tell me the lot of them aren't after betraying me." He clenched and unclenched his fists as he stared at the drying blood. "Please. Tell me this is a mind game of Loman's and not reality you're trying to shove on me," he whispered brokenly as he sent them all a pleading look.

With a hand on Trevor's shoulder, Simon spoke to his brother in a low tone for his ears alone, and Trevor's apologetic gaze dropped to Dubheasa before meeting Ronan's.

"I'm sorry, Ronan," he said gruffly and turned on his heel to stalk away, shaking his head the entire length of the corridor.

Simon followed in his wake and shoved the swinging door in what might've been anger at the situation.

Unable to bear looking at his betrayers, Ronan stared at the empty doorway and blinked. The sky outside was bright and bold with not one bleedin' cloud in sight. He frowned, confused that the day should be so lovely when it was colorless and dark inside.

"Restore his Guardian abilities, Dethridge. Do it now. Let him save her himself," Reggie demanded.

"No."

"No?" Disbelief rocked his cousin, and Reggie shook his head as if he couldn't believe what he was hearing. Ronan couldn't either, and the finality in the single-syllable word punched him low in the gut.

"I didn't stutter, Mr. White," Damian bit out. "And I suggest you rethink the plan you're concocting in that clever brain of yours. You'll never get close enough to kill me and acquire my abilities."

Color leeched from Reggie's countenance, and he gulped.

"The *only* reason I'm allowing you to live is because I sense your impulse to help Ronan." Obsidian eyes flashed red as the air around them took on a distinctive chill. "Never again entertain the notion of ending my life. Understood?"

"Yes."

"Excellent. If you insist on remaining, do so outside the exit door."

It spoke well of Reggie that he was reluctant to leave him, but Ronan didn't want him fighting a battle he couldn't win. "Look, and it's all right for you to go, Reg. I'm not leaving her."

"It's my fault. If I hadn't conjured the crossbow… It's all my fault."

The crushing guilt weighing on his cousin was too much for Ronan at the moment. "Aye. You're a fool if you thought my da wouldn't anticipate your reaction. But I'll right your wrong like I always do." He dropped his head as he listened to Reggie's retreating footsteps.

"Ronan. Let me take you home, and we can discuss this at length." Damian's compassionate tone grated, and Ronan shied away from what he knew to be false to seek the truth.

Dubheasa. Eyes still open. Still lifeless. And she wasn't waking up.

"Go away."

"I'm not leaving you here," his uncle declared. If he was inclined to believe it, Ronan could almost imagine he heard caring in Castor's voice when he shouted, "Goddammit, Damian, this isn't right!"

"It's the way it has to be, Alex."

"I know, but—"

"Go the fuck away already." Sick and tired of the back and forth, Ronan pressed the heels of his hands into his eye sockets.

In a rush, Castor entered the cell and squatted next to him. "Ronan, son—"

Ronan struck.

His punch contained all the anguish and fury building inside him. A lifetime of hurt and abuse. Grief of a lost love. And that driving blow sent Castor into the cinder-block wall behind him. The sound of his head impacting the stone would've normally sickened Ronan, but not this time. One had to care, and he didn't. Not anymore.

"Go!" he yelled, and in a burst of inspiration, he crawled over to tear the arrow from Patrick O'Malley's chest and held it up. "And never come back, or I'll carve your fucking heart out with this, yeah?"

"Leave us, Alex," Damian ordered softly.

"I can't—"

"Please, do as I say. And have someone see to your injuries. It sounded like you cracked your skull along with the bones of your nose."

Pushing himself upright, Castor swayed on his feet. After stabilizing himself with a hand against the wall, he swiped his arm across his face and grimaced at the quantity of blood his shirt had soaked up.

Not breaking eye contact with Ronan, Damian turned his head to address Castor. "I'll take care of this. Get yourself checked out by Draven."

From his peripheral, Ronan saw the flash of light. "Now it's your fecking turn to leave, ya bastard. I'll clean up my own bleedin' messes. I've been doing it my entire life."

"I'd like to explain."

The salty sting of tears burned behind Ronan's lids as he closed them and shook his head. "I'm not willing to hear anything you have to say unless it's that you intend to revive Dove."

"I can't."

"Then go by way of the others. You're not wanted here."

"For fuck's sake, Ronan! *Listen to me!*"

The sting of the Aether's frustration could be felt along Ronan's skin all the way from the crown of his head to the tips of his toes. But he was no stranger to physical pain, or that of the heart, for that matter.

"Jaysus! I don't fucking care what your excuses are, Aether." Standing, he stalked toward him. "You bleedin' well knew the outcome! You *knew*!" He threw the useless arrow to the ground and stared in disgust at his newest enemy. "You fucking knew, and ya didn't say a goddamned thing. Just let her walk into a trap like a lamb to slaughter, yeah?"

Guilt. The lone expression on Damian Dethridge's perfectly constructed visage.

"Yeah, ya fucking knew. And you should kill me, ya bastard, because you can be sure I'll kill you if I ever get the chance."

CHAPTER 32

The weather was almost as miserable as Ronan. Bitterly cold rain lashed sideways, obscuring vision and causing those with an ounce of self-preservation to seek shelter. Still, he stayed staring down at Dubheasa's headstone, and he was empty of anything but an unbearable, unending ache. A desperate need for her light to warm his dark soul.

The service was long over, the mourners scattered to the wind. Yet, he couldn't bring himself to leave. Imagining her body laid to rest in that lonely grave, with no one to keep watch over her, was slowly killing him, so he remained. He didn't have magic to keep himself warm—he had his hatred for that. Deep, abiding hatred. For Loman. For himself. For his uncle. For the Aether. Mostly for the Aether, who had denied him what he needed more than his next breath of air —Dubheasa.

And though Ronan had sworn his revenge, Damian's only response was a pitying look.

Remembered rage bubbled inside him, and the only outlet was to strike out. Ronan's knuckles crunched as they impacted the marble stone, and he felt the bones of his hand splinter.

The hurt was welcomed. A mild distraction from the one in his heart.

"Jaysus, Dove," he whispered raggedly. "I'll not survive this without you, ya know. And I don't fucking want to. Why couldn't you have taken me with you? Why did you leave me here to suffer alone?"

Fatigue swept through him, and Ronan fell to his knees. Mud saturated his dress pants, but he didn't care. Sleep had been elusive over the last week since the raid on the island. Her unseeing eyes and cold-to-the-touch form haunted him whenever he tried to rest. There were times in the hours he'd been stuck in the cell when he thought he heard her voice, but ghosts weren't real. She'd never linger when the peace of the Otherworld awaited.

"From the second we met, I felt the spark. The one only you could bring to life," he said hoarsely. "I'm destined never to see you again, and I can't bear it, Dove." He closed his eyes and swallowed hard. "If I can do what I want to, I'm going to kill Dethridge, but I'll also be consigning myself to hell."

What Ronan found he couldn't tell Dubheasa was that Damian's death would be too easy. His ex-friend needed to suffer first, live in torment like Ronan himself. He should learn what it was like to lose the only good thing in his world. To lose all he loved, before dying by his enemy's hand.

Curling his legs up to his chest, Ronan rested his head against the headstone and slowly traced the letters of her name. "My dream was to hold you each and every night, Dove. To lay there with your fingers laced with mine as I listened to you tell me all about your day. Maybe one you spent at Lamda, doing your computer thing, or maybe a mission for the Goddess." He swallowed down a sob. "And the last thing I would see before I closed my eyes to sleep would be your beautiful smile as I declared my love for you. And I do love you. More than life itself."

His tears tracked down his cheeks and blended with the sheeting rain.

Still, he sat, the rock-hard tombstone his pillow, and the cold permeating his bones.

"We d-didn't have enough t-time to create mem-mories," he said through chattering teeth. "I'd have w-welcomed a *wean* who l-looked just l-like ya, with your eyes, the c-color of *Éire* in spring."

The rain stopped with a suddenness that jarred him, and the sun parted the clouds, burning hot and causing steam to swirl up from the drenched headstones in the O'Malleys' private graveyard. Heat infused Ronan's body, and it instantly angered him. He didn't want to be warm when his heart was frozen solid. Didn't want the day to be anything but a dark and dreary wasteland like he suspected the rest of his life would be.

He felt the child's presence before she spoke.

"Ronan."

He turned his head from the carved letters and looked at Sabrina.

The perfect tool for his revenge.

In her arms was a puppy too large to hold comfortably, and Ronan had the fleeting thought the thing should be squirming within her grasp. But it stayed eerily still, legs dangling as it watched him with the same curious expression as the girl who held it.

"I brought you a present, Ronan. To keep you company."

Unable to respond, he watched her and tried to calculate the most expedient means to take her life. He didn't want *her* to suffer, only her father. Murdering her would gain him unimaginable power—greater than that of a Guardian—and the ability to be steps ahead of Damian when the time came. But her death would need to be as clean and painless to her as possible.

For a child who could access his thoughts if she wanted to, she seemed uncaring of her own safety as she moved forward and knelt next to him to place the pup in his lap. The exact one she'd helped Ronan pick out to give Dubheasa.

His heart hiccuped as he stared down into the wide, trusting eyes of the dog. Lifting his gaze to meet Sabrina's, he saw the same damned expression, and he wanted to howl his pain. It seemed she already knew what he was just realizing; he could never harm her. The capricious girl who reminded him of Dubheasa whenever she cocked her head and graced him with a mischievous grin. Dubheasa, who would despise him for making war on a child after he'd sworn he never would.

"Go home, ya wee wild beastie. Your da will be worried about you," he ordered dully. "And take the pup back to Baz. He'll find her a better home than I could ever give her."

"No take backs. Mack said so. She said you need Buttercup to make you smile again."

He snorted at the ridiculousness of naming a Rottweiler *Buttercup*. "Sure, and if Mack was truly psychic, she'd know I'll not give so regal a girl the name Buttercup."

"Mack said it's from the Princess Bride." Sabrina shrugged and rubbed the dog behind the ear. "She said that 'Death cannot stop true love. All it can do is delay it for a while.' That's from the Princess Bride, too. Wesley said it."

Ronan closed his lids against the stabbing torment her cheerful conversation brought. He opened his mouth to speak, but shut it again, as the words remained locked behind the lump of emotion clogging his throat.

When Sabrina patted his cheek, he looked at her, meeting her clear-eyed gaze.

"I miss her," he croaked, only able to confess the truth to *her*, the child with the ability to see beneath the outer layers, all the way down to his soul.

"Don't worry, Ronan. You'll see her again. As soon as you're done here."

Knowing he could be stuck on the earthly plane for a

century or two if he accepted the return of his Guardian powers, he nodded tiredly. Ronan looked down at the black-and-tan puppy as she burrowed against his belly and gazed up at him with adoration he wasn't deserving of. "She'd have loved you, Buttercup," he said softly.

Buttercup barked, giving him the equivalent of a canine grin, mouth open and tongue lolling.

Sabrina's giggle made him smile, bittersweet though it felt.

"Are you still cross with Papa?" she asked, and she sounded as if the idea of Ronan being upset with Damian was the worst thing she could think of. To her, it probably was.

"Yeah."

They sat in silence for a while as Buttercup gnawed on the fingers of Ronan's uninjured hand.

"You shouldn't be mad at him, you know."

Her tone was so matter-of-fact Ronan almost smiled again. "Why shouldn't I?"

"Papa wanted to save Dubheasa, but Fintan said he couldn't. He said the Authority wanted her dead."

Fury exploded in Ronan's brain, and he swore viciously, blind to the fact a child was present. Fintan Sullivan had earned himself a place on Ronan's hit list.

Buttercup whined and leapt to the ground to hide next to Sabrina. Unperturbed, she gathered the puppy to her chest and placed a tender kiss on her head. "He's hurting, Buttercup. Mama says when people are hurting, we have to forgive a swear word or two."

Awash with shame, Ronan bowed his head and squeezed his eyes closed. "I'm sorry I used such language in front of you both."

"I don't mind, but Buttercup was scared. Papa says we can't show anger in front of innocent animals. They don't know why we're mad."

"I don't care to hear what your da has to say, and if you're trying to tell me you *can't* talk to animals, I'll call ya a liar, wee beastie," Ronan said dryly. "I was there when you asked the pups which ones wouldn't be sad to leave their mam and go home with you."

She grinned. "Okay, Buttercup knows why you were mad, but she doesn't like it."

"If I promise not to curse your puir ears bloody, will you tell me the why of it?"

"Why the Authority wouldn't let Papa save Dubheasa?"

"Aye."

Sabrina's shoulders lifted as she widened her eyes and grimaced.

Again, Ronan almost smiled. If there was one thing that annoyed Sabrina Dethridge, it was not being privy to certain knowledge.

"That's a question for the Authority or Fintan," Damian said somberly from behind him.

"Leave me be, Dethridge," Ronan stated coldly. "You're not welcome here."

"I'm well aware." The Aether approached and waited as Sabrina placed Buttercup in Ronan's reluctant arms. Then he clasped Sabrina's hand to help her to her feet. "I merely came to fetch my disobedient daughter."

Concentrating on the puppy, Ronan scratched its chest. He wasn't ready to see the compassion in Damian's eyes. He needed to hold onto his rage a little longer to get through this endless day.

"For what it's worth, I'm sorry, Ronan. You and Dubh—"

"Don't!" His lungs felt as if they were collapsing every single time someone spoke her name, and to hear it fall from Damian's lips would send Ronan spiraling out of control.

"The panic attacks will go away."

His head came up, and he exhaled a harsh breath. "Panic attacks?"

With a sympathetic glance his way, Damian squatted and turned Sabrina to face him. "I need to talk to Ronan, Beastie. Please teleport to your mother and help her with Nate and the hellhounds."

Unable to help himself, Ronan barked a laugh. "Hellhounds?"

With a wry grimace, Damian nodded. "I'm positive Beastie picked the worst of the litter." To his daughter, he said, "Go now, my love."

She pulled away to run to Ronan and wrapped her arms around his neck. Pressing her mouth to his ear, she whispered, "Don't forget. You'll see Dubheasa again when you're done here." She left with a quick peck to his cheek.

Once she was gone, Ronan placed Buttercup on the ground and rose to his feet. "It's hard to hate a man who loves his child as you do."

"I'm not your enemy, Ronan. I'd have brought her back if I could've."

"You're the fucking Aether! You can do anything."

Damian shook his head and expelled a frustrated breath. "I can't go against the laws of magic and man."

"Fuck you! And *fuck* the Authority!" Hands balled into fists, Ronan charged forward. "You could've ignored their dictate. For me. For what I've done for you and your family. Sure, and you've done it when it's convenient for *you*."

The Aether's black eyes lit with an unholy light. "Your Guardianship of Sabrina? Are you trying to say that's all been an act to call in favors?"

It wasn't. And they both knew it.

Deflated and defeated, Ronan turned away to stare at the headstone. "Dubheasa was my saving grace," he said in a low voice.

"No, my friend. You were your own saving grace." Damian picked up the puppy and joined Ronan at the head of the grave.

"You broke the cycle of abuse and became your own man. You helped the O'Malleys restore what was lost to them for centuries."

Damian buried his nose against Buttercup's ear, and the affectionate gesture dissolved the last of Ronan's resentment toward him.

"And you became the savior of so many others. All those prisoners, whose lives would've ended had you not gotten them off the island, are singing your praise right now."

"I don't give a shite about any of them," Ronan growled.

"Perhaps not, but there are many loved ones not suffering what you are now, all due to your heroism." Damian handed him the puppy. "You *are* a hero, Ronan O'Connor. Whether you want to be or not. And sometimes, heroes pay the steepest penalties in life."

Ronan's throat tightened around the scream trying to work its way up from his soul. Squeezing his eyes closed, he hugged Buttercup to him. "I'm no one's hero."

"There you're wrong, my friend." Damian cupped a hand over Ronan's shoulder in comfort. "The panic attacks will eventually lessen. And though they are few, embrace the memories of Dubheasa. She wouldn't want you to suffer as you are."

CHAPTER 33

After Damian left, Ronan gave way to his pent-up emotion, and as the sobs wracked his body, he dropped to his knees. Buttercup released a barely audible whine and tried valiantly to lick the waterfall of tears as they flowed down his face.

He didn't know how long he'd sat there, giving in to his grief, but eventually, the darkening shadows woke him to the fact he was neglecting the puppy in his arms. At the very least, she needed to be fed and walked. Not necessarily in that order.

Cradling her in one arm, he used the other to dry his face.

"Are you done here, then?" a cheerful female voice asked.

His heart skipped a beat, and he looked down at the dog in shock.

An amused chuckle sounded from behind him. "Tell me you don't think a puppy is having a conversation with you."

Fearing he'd lost his mind completely, Ronan shifted his weight to his hip, falling back on his arse when he registered what his brain refused to comprehend and what his heart daren't hope.

Dubheasa.

Perched on a waist-high headstone, ankles crossed and swinging front to back, she rested her weight on her hands as she leaned slightly forward. Her soft smile held amusement, but the glow in her brilliant green eyes was pure love.

"Have I died and joined you in the Otherworld?" he asked, scarcely able to believe anything else.

She frowned and easily launched herself off her stone seat. "Not that I'm aware of." Dropping to her knees in front of him, she caressed his face. Her sharp gaze missed nothing as it skimmed his ravaged visage. With a tug, she pulled a chain from beneath her jumper and showed him a ruby pendant. "Apparently I had a charm that allowed me to see all portals to Earth, and no one thought to seal the one Loman used to return, time and time again." She grinned. "Or maybe the Goddess feared your fierce temper would eventually get the best of you if you didn't have a mate to keep you in check, and she let me go."

"You're really here?"

Her mouth curled up as she brushed a lock of his hair back. "I'm really here." Her kiss was fast and firm, unsatisfying in its quickness. "Didn't Sabrina tell you I'd return as soon as you were done?"

Dropping his head back against Dubheasa's tombstone, he gave a short, disbelieving laugh. "I thought she was talking about my time here on Earth." After setting a sleepy Buttercup on the grass beside him, Ronan reached for Dubheasa, drawing her down into his lap. "Ya'd think I would know better than to assume when it comes to the wee wild beastie's predictions."

"The child tends to be literal."

"That, she does."

Ronan cradled Dubheasa's head in his palms as he drank in her lovely face. "What took you so long, love? I almost made terrible choices in the meantime."

Her smile was luminescent. "I had faith you wouldn't. You

wouldn't be Ronan Fucking O'Connor, the man I fecking adore, if you had."

Wrapping his arms around her, he crushed her to his chest. "I'm still not certain you're not a figment of my tormented mind, but I'll never let you go, either way."

"And I never want to be let go." She wound her arms around his middle and rested her ear over his heart, and Ronan was positive she could hear the rapid, unsteady rhythm. "All I could think about as I faced down Loman was that I'd missed my chance to tell you how much you truly meant to me. I worried you'd never know the true extent of my feelings."

"I knew," he said gruffly.

"I had a lot of time to reflect in the holding room of the Otherworld, and I realized I loved you from that first sip of wine," she confessed with a soft laugh. "Looking back, it was why I felt so disappointed when you disappeared the next day."

"And the betrayal was made worse when you were sacked by Nick Lamda, no doubt." Ronan's guilt reared its miserable head.

"Yeah. I felt like a woman scorned. I wanted your bollocks mounted and hung on my wall." She drew back and met his regretful gaze. "But it brought us to this moment, Ronan. Loman is dead, for good this time. The surviving victims are back with their families. And I'm here with you, where I was always meant to be."

But one of the victims who didn't make it through Loman's house of horrors was Dubheasa's father, and Ronan's heart ached that she'd never get that relationship back.

"I'm sorry about your da, Dove," he said gently.

One side of her mouth curled upward in a sad half smile. "It wasn't your fault. You understand that, right?"

"I wish I'd had the courage to end Loman twenty years ago, before he concocted his plan."

"If my father had never tried to go after yours alone, he'd have never walked into Loman's trap. That's not on you."

"Did you see him in the Otherworld?" Ronan hoped she'd had a small measure of closure.

"I did, and he was better than I remembered. Happier, somehow."

A tear escaped down her cheek, and he tenderly brushed it away with his thumb. His guilt was eating a hole in his stomach, and the discomfort was great. "I'm glad you got to talk to him. His last actions were to save you. But his death was my fault, Dove."

Frowning, Dubheasa shifted and straddled his lap to look him more fully in the face. "I don't see how it could've been."

Although he dreaded her response, he manned up. "My father said it was due to my insolence and to make sure I told you that if I ever saw you again."

She laughed.

"Not the reaction I was expecting," Ronan muttered.

"The idea of a forty-plus man paying for his insolence, like a child, is what's ridiculous, to be sure." Pressing her forehead to his, she slowly rolled her head from side to side. "You weren't to blame for that scaldy bastard's actions, Ronan. Loman's evilness was his own, and murdering my da was one more way he could think of to sabotage your happiness." With a butterfly-soft kiss, she said, "Anyone with two eyes could see he couldn't bear it that you were your own man. That you didn't subscribe to his brand of hatred. Loman wanted you to be the image of him, and he despised you when you weren't. Of course he was going to do whatever it took to make you miserable, to pay for your 'insolence.'"

"How is it you're so wise, love?"

"Well, this *is* my second lifetime," she replied with a saucy smile.

"Aye, and it's happy I am for it. I've never been so lost and alone as I was this week without you."

"We'll make a pact to share a long and healthy life together. Guardians ready to fight the good fight as soon as the Aether supercharges us." When he nodded his agreement, she scrunched her nose. "And there's likely no coming back. I may have sealed the portal on my way out."

He grinned and did what he had wanted to since she first appeared on the headstone. Tangling his fingers in her thick, silky hair, he lowered his lips to hers.

As Ronan savaged her mouth, Dubheasa moaned her pleasure and returned his kiss, tongue thrust for tongue thrust, tasting the last of his fading grief and desperation. Wishing she could erase his suffering, she clung to him and pressed her body to his.

What she didn't tell him was that she'd been present in the cell the entire time. His tortured thoughts, however brief before his rescue, were hers, and although their connection had been suspended when she was on the earthly plane, it had been restored the instant she received the arrow to her chest. He'd just been too distraught to hear her. If she'd ever doubted his feelings for her, they became clear in those moments, and yet again as she listened to his confession by the grave when he believed no one was around to hear.

Buttercup's pitiful whine caused them to part.

"No shagging in front of our child," Dubheasa scolded with a mock frown.

"The pup needs to learn the art of timing."

"Or you do. I'm guessing my family's graveyard isn't the best place to get down and dirty."

Ronan barked a laugh and rolled her onto her back on the muddy mound as he grinned down at her. "You've much more living to do, Dove, if you've never shagged in a graveyard."

A giggle bubbled up, and she shook her head. "I'm not after getting soil in places it doesn't belong, Ronan O'Connor."

"But that's half the fun of bathing after." He leered, flaring his eyes wide.

Laughing, she pushed at his chest. "Get off me, ya fecking giant. I want to meet my baby."

Ronan rolled onto his back and flung his arms wide with an overly loud sigh. "I can see I'm to be replaced in your affections by Buttercup. Look, I had a small window of time, but I lost it."

"Hold your *whist*, ya eejit." Dubheasa tapped his stomach with the back of her hand, then held out her arms and made kissing noises to tempt the puppy closer. "Come, Buttercup. Your new mam wants to spoil you."

The impact of the large pup knocked Dubheasa backward, but Ronan was there to break her fall with an arm around her shoulders.

Two wide pools of chocolate, the color of Cadbury Milk Bars, stared up at her as Buttercup's tail swished back and forth so hard, it rocked her entire body. No match for the soft, pleading light in the dog's eyes, Dubheasa kissed Buttercup's nose. "I already love you."

"You say that now, but what about the wee hours of the night when she needs to go outside?" Ronan warned good-naturedly.

"That's what I'm keeping you around for."

He snorted. "Is that all?"

Dubheasa laughed at the suggestive quality of his question. "Among other things."

After a few minutes spent playing with Buttercup under Ronan's indulgent eye, Dubheasa sighed and looked toward the Black Cat Inn in the distance. "I suppose it's time to tell the others I've come back."

"Can't we be selfish a while longer?"

"No." Dubheasa gestured to a lone figure in the distance, heading toward them. "Unless I miss my guess, Bridget's on her way here with a basket of food and a stern lecture for you."

"Feck."

"You should be prepared to catch her if she faints. It's not every day your sister and da return from the dead."

Ronan whipped his head back around to stare at her. "Da?"

Scrunching her brow, she tried not to giggle when she said, "Yeah, and didn't I tell you that my da stepped through the portal with me?"

Wildly, he looked around, as if he were a callow youth, worried he was about to be caught in a compromising situation and expecting her father to step from behind the trees at any moment.

"He is waiting at his flat in Galway," she explained. "I wanted to tell Bridg and my brothers first."

Ronan scooped up Buttercup in one arm, then clasped Dubheasa's hand in his. After bussing her knuckles, he winked. "You'll have to be the one to catch Bridget if she falls. My arms are as full as my heart."

EPILOGUE

Full of bitter rage but bearing an aloof expression, Damian stood center stage in front of the U-shaped table of the Authority. From the raised platform, the thirteen council members watched him with varying degrees of curiosity. He resented them all for forcing his hand.

But now that they'd allowed Dubheasa's resurrection, he had a promise to keep.

"Are you prepared to stand by your word and do your duty, Aether?"

Damian met the gaze of the smug-faced leader. "I am."

"You'll be contracted for life," another council member warned.

If he didn't know better, he'd almost believe the stately woman held compassion for his plight. But those belonging to the Authority were ruthless and controlling, without an ounce of empathy for others.

"I'm well aware of the conditions, Ms. Otherman," he replied coolly.

What he didn't say was that he intended to end his employment at his earliest opportunity. He'd grant them twenty years, and when his children were old enough to survive without him, he'd find a loophole. The Goddess Isis would assist him, he had no doubt. She'd been against the Authority's blackmailing scheme from the start. But if he couldn't trick his way out of his contract, he'd accept the penalty of death that went with breaking trust with the Authority.

"And you'll lead a team of Sentinels on missions of our choosing," the lead council added.

"You act as if I've forgotten the terms, Butthanger," Damian said, tone as dry as dirt.

"It's *Buttagier*," the man snapped.

"My bad."

Someone along the sweeping panel snickered, earning a dark look from Buttagier.

A buzzer sounded, and a glass panel on the floor in front of Damian slid to the side. From beneath the ground level, a desk-sized altar rose, and the stone it rested on locked in place of the previous panel.

"Step forward," Buttagier ordered.

Teeth gritted, Damian moved to take position behind the ceremonial table.

A female dressed in the long black robes of the Authority rose from her seat and crossed to him.

"This will require not only your signature, but your blood to seal the deal, Aether." She lowered her voice for his hearing alone. "Do you understand what you are giving up, Damian?"

"Yes, Mattie." Had it not made her a target of Buttagier's ire, Damian would've smiled at her. Mathilda Price had been in his corner during negotiations. She'd tried to be the voice of reason and had gone toe-to-toe with the lead council to cut the terms of Damian's employment down. All she'd earned for her troubles was their displeasure.

"Ronan deserves to be happy, and if I have to give up a few years of my life to do it, I will," he said quietly.

"But it's more than a few years. It's forever if you're not careful," she argued. "You'll be under *Butthanger*'s thumb."

Lips twitching, he remained silent and nodded. Mattie hated the man as much as Damian did, and her slip almost sent him over the edge into laughter.

"Fine. When you read the contract, pay special attention to page seven. The loophole you need is written there." With her back to the council, she winked.

Not many people surprised him, and it took an effort to keep his jaw from sagging open. How she'd guessed what he intended was a mystery. One he'd solve in due time.

Mattie turned slightly and, raising her voice to include the others, said, "Very well, Aether. We shall proceed."

With great pomp, she withdrew a white quill and handed it to him. The tip wasn't a hardened shaft carved into a nib, as was the norm, but instead, it was metal with a razor-sharp point. Damian was expected to pierce his skin and sign his name in blood.

"Is this sanitary?" he quipped.

Biting her lip to keep a laugh at bay, Mattie darted a quick look toward the lead council. "Probably not, but you'll survive."

"True, but I'd like to keep all my fingers intact. I can't have them falling off from rot."

She did laugh then.

"Sign the bloody contract, Aether, and let's be done with it," Buttagier snapped from his perch.

To taunt him further, Damian slowly and continuously caressed the barbs of the feather, following the vane. "I'm going to want assurances that my blood cannot be removed from the parchment and that this lovely quill will be destroyed." He locked eyes with Buttagier and, in an arctic tone, said, "We can't have anyone attempt to manipulate me through dark blood magic, can we?"

Nothing had been proven, but there were rumors aplenty

about the Authority and dark magic. Damian didn't intend that he should fall victim to another's foul play.

For the first time, the lead councilman lost his arrogance and sweat beaded along his brow. He shot a glance to his left, down the length of the table. Councilwoman Otherman met Buttagier's gaze, and something unspoken passed between them.

Seemed a few others were in favor of Damian's request. Lifting his brows in challenge, he smiled. "That's not too much to ask, is it, Butt"—he paused deliberately—"agier?"

Resentment flared in the other man's eyes, but he gave an abrupt nod. "You may take or destroy the quill, as is your right to protect yourself. The contract will be secured in our vault system. None have access but those on this panel."

"Not good enough. I ask the contract be given to the Goddess Isis for safekeeping."

It didn't take a genius to recognize Buttagier wasn't thrilled with his demand, but Damian had his family to protect.

Councilwoman Otherman rose to her feet and slapped the wooden table in front of her. "Done."

After pausing to take a long look at her, Damian smiled at what he saw. "Exalted One, I almost didn't recognize you."

Isis shed her glamour in an instant. Her long black hair was loosely braided and fell down her back. A gold circlet set atop her glossy head. Eyes the color of amber topaz glowed with a goddess's knowledge and power. She had discarded the black robe of the council in favor of a sky-blue gossamer gown that enhanced her shapely body and was caught at the shoulder with a gold clip in the shape of the sun.

Isis sauntered down the steps of the dais and approached him. "Beloved."

Dropping to one knee, he lightly kissed the back of the hand she extended toward him.

"You may rise." She took the quill from him, casually examining the nib.

"Have you always been on the Authority's panel, or am I simply lucky?" he asked her.

"I have a vested interest in today's outcome." With a frown, she set the quill alight, then pinned Buttagier with a stare. "Did you know the nib contained a toxin, Councilman Butthanger?"

If the seriousness of her question hadn't struck Damian at the same time as her use of Buttagier's hated nickname, he'd have laughed. But as it was, he had to work not to freak the hell out. He'd been minutes, at most, away from pricking his finger to sign the contract.

Buttagier paled. "N-no! I..." He rose and met Damian's angry glare with a sincerity that was difficult to ignore. "You have to believe that I would not condone anyone coming to harm under my reign as lead council."

Picking up the contract, Isis snapped her fingers, and the paper caught fire. When it would've reached her fingers, she dropped it on the marble floor to finish burning. "The Aether is free of his promise to us," she proclaimed.

And immediately Damian understood what she'd done. For him. For his family. By claiming there was a traitor in their midst who would seek to harm him, she'd set him free. Dubheasa would live, the Authority wouldn't hold him to his promise, and they wouldn't send anyone else to threaten his children.

Relief swept through him, and the gratitude he felt at Isis's protective gesture nearly overwhelmed him.

"But we need him!" Buttagier protested.

Because he was a man of principle, Damian proposed a new deal. One that was readily accepted.

For the next five years, he would consult on an as-needed basis. If required, he'd step in without objection. No contract. No blood oath. Merely a statement of intent to lead a team of Sentinels of his choosing, and they took him at his word.

LEGS OUTSTRETCHED, DAMIAN RESTED HIS BACK AGAINST THE large oak in his garden to watch Dubheasa as she laughed and fended off three ginormous puppies. Sabrina's high-pitched giggles blended with her mother's deeper ones. Not far from the trio of females, Ronan stood guard, a happy grin eating up half his handsome face.

"Sure, and ya did the right thing," Fintan said as he rounded the tree to stand at Damian's side.

"He shouldn't have had to suffer as long as he did."

Fintan shrugged. "Maybe he needed to learn to appreciate the deities' gifts."

"Anu's or Isis's?"

"Both. They worked together to bring the O'Malleys their happiness."

"And what about the O'Connors? There are a few good ones left."

"Aye. Castor will find a mate soon enough. Reggie, too."

Damian nodded toward Ronan and Dubheasa. "They likely have years of chaos ahead of them as Guardians. Will they always be as happy as they are at this moment?"

Fintan grinned. "Yeah, and I don't think ya need to be worryin' about those two. They've been soulmates in the past, they have. When connected on a cosmic level like Ronan and Dubheasa are, two souls will always find a way to make it work."

The comment caused Damian to reflect inward, and his gaze locked on Vivian as she laughingly gripped Sabrina's hands and danced in a circle around Nate's bassinet. In his entire life, he couldn't recall such a beautiful sight.

"You'll find your way back to each other again, Aether. Never fear on that score, yeah?"

Lifting his head, he met Fintan's compassionate stare.

"Sometimes, there are moments when I feel she'd be better off having never met me." Damian swallowed past the sudden lump in his throat. "And what do I do when she's gone? We won't age at the same speed."

"Are you wantin' a prediction?"

"No. I've seen my future, and it terrified the fuck out of me. I don't need you to cement what I already know."

"The future isn't concrete, Damian Dethridge. Say you'll be rememberin' that, yeah?"

"I'll remember."

"Good."

As Fintan's form faded away, another appeared through a golden rift a few yards away.

Isis.

Damian climbed to his feet and met her halfway. "Exalted One."

"Beloved."

"I believe I owe you a debt of gratitude."

She waved a careless hand and smiled at the puppies tumbling about. "You allowed Sabrina two? Are you a glutton for punishment?"

"Perhaps. But mainly, I'm a sucker for Beastie's pleading eyes."

"Mm, yes. Children have that unique ability to manipulate an adoring parent."

He couldn't argue the fact.

"Not that I don't enjoy conversing with you, but you rarely visit without an agenda," he said with a smile to show he meant no offense. "Why have you come?"

"To speak to the Oracle."

No sooner had the words left her mouth than Sabrina came running over. After dipping into a curtsy, she grinned up at the Goddess, expression saucy.

"Walk with me, child," Isis commanded, extending her hand

for Sabrina to take.

They didn't wander far, but Damian was careful to remain within reach as Ronan positioned himself on the opposite side of the garden. The two men acknowledged each other with a wry grin. Their friendship was not as solid as it once was, but they had found a new normal these last weeks.

Hopefully, Ronan would never discover the sacrifice Damian had been prepared to make on his friend's behalf. The Guardian should be here of his own free will, ready to protect Sabrina because he wanted to, not as repayment. It would mean the difference between truly caring for her and simple duty.

Having been lost in thought, Damian failed to hear Dubheasa's approach.

"We'll never let anything happen to your children," she said gently. "Ronan loves them as if they were his own."

Turning to face her, Damian smiled his welcome. "I know."

"Do you ever plan to tell him about your deal, then?"

Nonplussed, he shook his head. "You weren't supposed to know, either."

"Yeah, I may have figured it out while I was still in the Otherworld's waiting room," She looked across at Ronan and grinned. "He will, too. Eventually."

"You won't tell him?"

"It's acceptable to keep a secret now and again, don't ya think?"

With a light laugh, he wrapped an arm around her shoulders and drew her to his side.

In return, she gave him a sweet smile and rested her head on his shoulder. "Thank you for giving us a second chance, Damian."

"You're welcome."

"What do you think they're discussing so intently?" she asked with a gesture toward the Goddess and Sabrina.

"One never knows with Isis. But she seems to have a soft spot for my daughter."

"Hmm." Shifting, Dubheasa kissed his cheek. "I'm going to steal your son from his mother for a few hours. With Ronan on watch, it's the perfect time for you to hustle your wife away for alone time. Start rebuilding your relationship."

"Remind me to do the same for you and Ronan when *your* son is born—" Damian jerked and whipped his head around to look at Isis. Across the short distance, she met his shocked gaze and winked. Bending, she said something to Sabrina, then sent her off with a light swat to her bottom.

When she launched herself into his arms, he caught her midair, acting on instinct since he was still numb with surprise from the new development.

"The Goddess said you're not supposed to tell the future, Papa." Her grin was cheeky as she parroted the words he repeatedly said to her.

"I guess this means my ability has been restored," he said dryly.

"Yep!" Sabrina patted his shoulder. "Isis said you're going to need it."

He shook his head and cast the Goddess a wry smile as she gave him a small salute and stepped through the rift she'd created to return to the Otherworld.

"Are you telling me I'm pregnant?" Dubheasa demanded with a disconcerted expression.

Damian shared a look with his daughter. "What do you think, Beastie? Do we tell her what we know?"

"Maybe just this once," she replied primly.

Thank you for reading Dubheasa & Ronan's story. I hope you fell in love with them just as I did.

If you want more of the O'Malley family, you aren't alone. More ideas are popping up daily, so I won't end the series quite yet. I think Dubheasa's father, Patrick O'Malley, needs a HEA, don't you?

In the meantime, if you would like to get your Damian and Beastie fix, be sure to preorder **THE AETHER**. The expected release date is October 17, 2023. Fingers crossed all goes well!

Also, if you never want to miss a release or sale, be sure to sign up for my text alerts. Currently for North American residents only, but the UK and Ireland will be coming soon.

Text **JOIN** to **1-877-795-1526** to subscribe.

Also, if you haven't already subscribed to my *newsletter* (http://www.tmcromer.com/newsletter) or joined my *Facebook reader group* (http://bit.ly/tmc-readers), I encourage you to do so. It's the best way for you to stay current on upcoming stories and receive bonus content for available books.

Keep reading for a list of available T.M. Cromer books.

Books in The Thorne Witches Series:
SUMMER MAGIC
AUTUMN MAGIC
WINTER MAGIC
SPRING MAGIC
REKINDLED MAGIC
LONG LOST MAGIC
FOREVER MAGIC
ESSENTIAL MAGIC
MOONLIT MAGIC
ENCHANTED MAGIC
CELESTIAL MAGIC
EVERLASTING MAGIC
ENDURING MAGIC

Books in The Unlucky Charms Series:
PINTS & POTIONS
WHISKEY & WITCHES
BEER & BROOMSTICKS
COCKTAILS & CAULDRONS
WINE & WARLOCKS

Books in The Holt Family Series:
FINDING YOU
THIS TIME YOU
INCLUDING YOU
AFTER YOU (Aug 2023)

Books in The Sentinels of Magic Series:
THE AETHER (Oct 2023)

Ingram Content Group UK Ltd.
Milton Keynes UK
UKHW031418270423
420877UK00016B/975